P9-CBR-526

THE MAGDALENE DECEPTION

THE MAGDALENE DECEPTION

A Novel

GARY McAVOY

LITERATI EDITIONS

Printed in the United States of America
Hardcover ISBN: 978-0-9908376-4-0
Paperback ISBN: 978-0-9908376-5-7
eBook ISBN: 978-0-9908376-6-4

Library of Congress Control Number: 2020908575

Published by:
Literati Editions
PO Box 5987
Bremerton, Washington 98312 USA
Email: info@LiteratiEditions.com
Visit the author's website: www.garymcavoy.com
v1.3

1

Southern France – March 1244

The relentless siege of the last surviving Cathar fortress, perched strategically on the majestic peak of Montségur in the French Pyrenees, entered its tenth month.

The massive army of crusaders dispatched from Rome, thirty thousand strong, were garbed in distinctive white tunics, their mantles emblazoned with the scarlet Latin cross. Knight commanders led hordes of common foot soldiers, some seeking personal salvation, others simply out for adventure and the promise of plunder. They had already devastated most of the Languedoc region of southern France in the years preceding. Tens of thousands of men, women, and children had been slain, regardless of age, sex, or religious belief. Entire villages were burned, rich crops destroyed, and the fertile land which yielded them was poisoned, in a cruel, single-minded quest to root out and extinguish a small and peaceful, yet influential mystic order known as the Cathars.

The defeat of the impregnable Montségur remained the ultimate prize for the Church's troops. Rumors of a vast treasure had reached the ears of every soldier, stirring up the passion with which these feared European mercenaries carried out their holy mission. As was the customary practice during a crusade, whatever pillage remained after the plundering—*spolia opima,* the richest spoils for supreme achievement—could be claimed by the victor. That temptation, bonded by the personal assurance of the pope that all sins would be forgiven and their paths to heaven assured, was enough to seduce anyone, nobleman or peasant, to take up cudgel, pike, or arrow in the name of God.

In 1209 Pope Innocent III had ordered a Holy Crusade to crush the spirit, and if necessary, the life of each and every dissident in the Languedoc region bordering France and Spain.

This independent principality had distinguished itself by fostering an artistic and intellectual populace well beyond that of most northern European societies at the time. The people of the Languedoc practiced a religious tolerance that encouraged spiritual and secular diversity. Schools teaching Greek, Hebrew, and

Arabic languages and the customs which accompanied them flourished, as did those espousing the Cabala, an occult form of Judaism that dated from the second century.

Most settlers in the Languedoc viewed Christianity with the utmost repugnance; at the very least its practices were perceived as being more materialistic than godly in nature. The irreligious of the region passed over Christianity in large part due to the scandalous corruption exhibited by its local priests and bishops who, unable to influence the heathens within their provinces, came to prefer the rewards of commerce and land ownership over the tending of a meager flock.

Consequently, the authorities in Rome felt compelled to deal with this unforgivable heresy once and for all, in towns such as Toulouse and Albi within the Languedoc area.

Consigning his troops to their commanders, Pope Innocent III invoked a special benediction to all, lauding the divinity of their mission. Asked how they might distinguish their Christian brethren from the heretics, the crusaders were simply told, "Kill them all. God will spare His own."

And so the Albigensian Crusade began.

The new moon cast no light over Montségur as night fell on the first day of March 1244, obscuring not only the hastened activities of its occupants, but the lingering threat conspiring outside its walls. A dense alpine fog had settled over the mountain, and the castle that straddled its inaccessible peak had withstood nearly a year of unceasing battle.

Weakened by the tenacity of their predators and yielding to the hopelessness of their situation, Raymond de Péreille, Lord of Château du Montségur and leader of the remaining four hundred defenders, commanded his troops to lay down their arms, and descended the mountain to negotiate terms of their capitulation.

Though offered lenient conditions in return for their surrender, de Péreille requested a fourteen-day truce, ostensibly to consider the terms, and handed over hostages as an assurance of good faith. Knowing there was no alternative for their captives—nearly half of whom were priest-knights, or *parfaits,* sworn to do God's work—the commanders of the pope's regiment agreed to the truce.

Over the next two weeks, reprieved from the constant threat of attack they had been enduring for months, the inhabitants of Montségur resolved to fulfill their own destiny before relinquishing their fortress—and their lives—to the Inquisition.

On the last day of the truce, as if guided collectively by a single will on a predestined course, the surviving members of the last Cathar settlement made special preparations for their departure.

Four of the strongest and most loyal of the *parfaits* were led by Bishop Bertrand Marty, the senior abbé of the fortress, as they descended deep within the mountain down a long, stepped passageway carved into alternating layers of earth and limestone. The end of the passage appeared to be just that, as if the original tunnelers had simply stopped work and retreated without finishing the job. But, while the others held torches, Abbé Marty withdrew a large rusted key-like wedge from beneath his cassock, thrusting it into a hidden cavity near the low ceiling.

The abbé manipulated the key for a few moments. A muffled sound of grating metal from beyond the stone wall echoed through the tunnel, and the seemingly impenetrable granite slid inward slightly, revealing a door.

Aided by the *parfaits*, the door swung open into a small dank chamber filled with an enormous cache of riches—gold and silver in varied forms, gilded chalices and bejeweled crosses, an abundance of gems and precious stones, sagging bags of coins from many lands.

And, in a far corner removed from the bulk of

the treasure itself, stood a wide granite pedestal on which rested an ornately carved wooden reliquary, crafted to hold the most holy of relics, next to which sat a large book wrapped in brown sackcloth.

Standing before the legendary treasure of the Cathars—glittering and hypnotic in the dim torchlight—would prove seductive for most men. But the Albigensians held little regard for earthly goods, other than as a useful political means to achieve their spiritual destiny. Ignoring the abundant wealth spread before them, the abbé fetched the sackcloth while the other four *parfaits* hoisted the ancient reliquary to their shoulders, then they left the room and solemnly proceeded back up the granite stairway. In the thousand-year history of the Cathars, these would be the last of the order ever to see the treasure.

But the most sacred relic of the Christian world would never, they vowed, fall into the unholy hands of the Inquisition.

Emerging from the stone passage, Abbé Marty led the *parfaits* and their venerable cargo through the hundreds of waiting Cathars who had assembled outside, forming a candlelit gauntlet leading to the sanctuary. All were dressed in traditional black tunics, all wearing shoulder length hair covered by round *taqiyah* caps as was the custom of the sect.

Once inside, the *parfaits* lowered the reliquary onto the stone altar. The abbé removed the ancient book from the sackcloth and began the sacred Consolamentum, a ritual of consecration, while the four appointed guardians prepared themselves for their special mission.

Armed with short blades and truncheons, the *parfaits* carefully secured the reliquary in the safety of a rope sling, then fastened taut harnesses around themselves.

"Go with God, my sons," Abbé Marty intoned as he gave them his blessing, "and in His name ensure this sacred reliquary be protected for generations to come."

The four men climbed over the precipice and, assisted by their brothers gripping the ropes tied to their harnesses, gently and silently rappelled hundreds of meters down the escarpment. Sympathizers waiting at the base of the mountain assisted the *parfaits* in liberating their holy treasure, guiding them away from the danger of other troops and hiding them and the reliquary deep in one of many nearby caves.

Throughout the night, those remaining at Montségur celebrated their brotherhood, their holy calling, and their last hours alive. Descending the mountain the next morning, in a state of pure spiritual release from the material world, Abbé Marty led the last of the Cathars as they willingly marched into the blazing pyres awaiting them, martyrs to their cause.

The holy reliquary of the Cathars has never since been found.

2

Present Day

Rounding the northern wall of the Colosseum with a measured stride, a tall young man with longish black hair glanced at the Tag Heuer chronometer strapped to his left wrist. Noting the elapsed time of his eighth mile, he wiped away the sweat that was now stinging his eyes.

Damn this Roman heat. Not even sunrise, and it's already a scorcher.

Approaching the wide crosswalks flanking the west side of the immense Colosseum, he wondered if this was the morning he would meet God. Dodging the murderous, unrestrained traffic circling the stadium became a daily act of supreme faith, as the blur of steel sub-compacts, one after another, careened around the massive structure on their way, no doubt, to some less hostile place. Since his arrival here he had discovered that this was the way with Italian motorists in general, though Roman drivers excelled at the sport. Veteran observers could always tell the difference between natives and visitors: a local would cross the road seemingly ambivalent to the rush of oncoming traffic. Non-Romans, who could as likely be from Milan as from Boston or Paris, approached the threat of each curb-to-curb confrontation with a trepidation bordering on mortal terror.

Crossing the broad Via dei Fori Imperiali, his route took him through the Suburra, the most ancient inhabited area of Rome and off the beaten path of most tourists. As a newcomer to a city whose normal pulse was barely evident beneath the confusing ambiguities of new and old, the runner felt most comfortable here in the Suburra, a semi-industrial working-class neighborhood, much like the one he only recently left in New York. In the summer, people got up early to tend their gardens before the real heat forced them indoors. The early morning air was thick with alternating scents of Chilean jasmine, honeysuckle, and petrol fumes.

He ran another five miles, long blooms of sweat accentuating a lean, muscular frame beneath a gauzy white t-shirt as he burst into a sprint up the final few blocks, past the empty trattorias and shuttered shops whose merchants were just beginning their morning rituals.

Slowing to a cool down pace as he crossed the Sant'Angelo bridge spanning the Tiber River, he turned left up Via della Conciliazione as the massive dome of Saint Peter's Basilica loomed suddenly ahead. Though it could be seen from almost anywhere in Rome, this approach always gave him the impression that the dome seemed to tip backwards, being swallowed up by the grand facade of the church the closer he got to it.

"*Buongiorno, padre.*" Several female voices, almost in unison, broke the cobblestone pattern of his reverie.

Father Michael Dominic looked up and smiled politely, lifting his hand in a slight wave as he swiftly passed a small cluster of nuns, some of whom he recognized as Vatican employees. The younger girls blushed, leaning their hooded heads toward each other in hushed gossip as their eyes followed the handsome priest; the older women simply bobbed a chilly nod to the young cleric, dutifully herding their novitiates into obedient silence on their way to morning Mass.

Though he had only been in Rome a couple of weeks, Michael Dominic's youthful exuberance and keen intellect had become known quickly throughout the cloistered population of Vatican City, setting him apart from the more monastic attitudes prevalent since the Middle Ages.

But despite the fusty parochialism and an atmosphere of suspended time he found within its walls, Dominic still felt the intoxication of privilege at having been assigned to Rome so early in his religious career. It had not been even two years since he lay prostrate at the altar of St. Patrick's Cathedral in New York City, ordained by his family friend and mentor Cardinal Enrico Petrini.

It was no secret to Vatican insiders that the eminent cardinal's influence was chiefly responsible for Dominic's swift rise to the marbled corridors of ecclesiastic power now surrounding him. The young priest's scholarly achievements as a classical medievalist were essential to the work being done in the Vatican Library. But the progressive cardinal was also grateful for the vitality Dominic brought to his vocation, not to mention the charismatic ways in which he could get things accomplished in an otherwise plodding bureaucracy. Though Dominic could not account for his mentor's vigorous inducement that he come to Rome—and knowing this particular prince of the Church so well, it was surely more than a familial gesture—he had trusted Enrico Petrini completely, and simply accepted the fact that this powerful man had believed in him strongly enough to give him an opportunity which he most certainly would not have had otherwise.

Pacing slower now, Dominic drew in rhythmic gulps of searing air as he neared the Vatican. A block or so before reaching the gate, he stepped inside the Pergamino Caffè on the Piazza del Risorgimento. Later in the day the cramped room would be filled with tourists seeking postcards and gelato, but mornings found it crowded with locals, most nibbling on small, sticky cakes washed down with a demitasse of thick, sweet coffee.

Across the room Dominic spotted Signora Palazzolo, the ample wife of the proprietor, whose wisps of white hair were already damp with perspiration. Seeing the priest approach, the older woman's face broke into a broad, gap-toothed smile as she reached beneath the counter and withdrew a neatly folded black cassock that Dominic had dropped off earlier, which she handed to him with deliberate satisfaction.

"Buongiorno, padre," she said. "And will you take *caffè* this morning?"

"Molto grazie, signora," Dominic said, accepting the cassock graciously. "Not today. I'm already late as it is."

"Okay this time," she said with a gently scolding tone, "but it is not healthy for a strong young man to skip his breakfast, especially after making his heart work so hard in this unforgiving heat." Her hand reached up to wipe away the dampness as she spoke, coifing what little hair she had left in a vain attempt to make herself more attractive.

Heading toward the back of the shop,

Dominic slipped into the restroom, quickly washed his face and raked his hair into some semblance of order, then drew the cassock over his head and buttoned it to the starched white collar now encircling his neck. Emerging from the restroom minutes later and making for the door, he glanced back to see the signora waving to him, now with a different look on her face—one beaming with respect for the clergyman he had suddenly become, as if she herself had had a role in the transformation.

Of the three official entrances to the Vatican, Porta Sant'Anna, or Saint Anne's Gate, is the one generally used by employees, visitors, and tradesmen, situated on the east side of the frontier just north of Saint Peter's Square. Although duties of security come first, guards at all gates are also responsible for monitoring the encroachment of dishabille into the city. Dominic learned from an earlier orientation that casual attire of any sort worn by employees or official visitors was not permitted past the border. Jeans and t-shirts were barely tolerated on tourists, but the careless informality of shorts, sweatpants, or other lounging attire on anyone was strictly forbidden. An atmosphere of respect and reverence was to be observed at all times.

Vatican City maintains an actual live-in population of less than a thousand souls, but each workday nearly five thousand people report for duty within the diminutive confines of its imposing walls—walls originally built to defend against the invading Saracens a thousand years before—and the Swiss Guards at each gate either recognize or authenticate every person coming or going by face and by name.

One of the Guards whom Dominic had recognized from previous occasions, dressed in the less formal blue and black doublet and beret of the corps, waved him through with a courteous smile as he reached for his ID card.

"It is no longer necessary to present your credentials now that you are recognized at this gate, Father Dominic," the solidly built young guard said in English. "But it is a good idea to keep it with you just in case."

"*Grazie,*" Dominic responded, continuing in Italian, "but it would be helpful to me if we could speak the local language. I haven't used it fluently since I was younger, and I am outnumbered here by those who have an obvious preference. You know, 'When in Rome….'"

The guard's smile faded instantly, replaced by a slight but obvious discomfort as he attempted to translate, then respond to Dominic's rapid Italian.

"Yes, it would be pleasure for me, padre," the

young soldier said in halting Italian, "but only if we speak slowly. German is native tongue of my own home, Zurich, and though I speak good English, my Italian learning have only just started; but I understand much more than I speak."

Dominic smiled at the younger man's well-intended phrasing. "It's a deal then. I'm Michael Dominic," he said formally, offering a sweaty palm.

"It is an honor meeting you, Father Michael. I am Corporal Dengler. Karl Dengler." Dengler's face brightened at the unusual respect he was accorded, extending his own white-gloved hand in a firm grip. Recently recruited into the prestigious *Pontificia Cohors Helvetica,* the elite corps of papal security forces more commonly known as the Swiss Guard, Dengler had found that most people in the Vatican—indeed, most Romans—were inclined to keep to themselves. It was never this difficult to make friends in Switzerland, and he welcomed the opportunity to meet new people. He also knew, as did everyone by now, that this particular priest had a powerful ally close to the Holy Father.

"An honor for me as well, Corporal," Dominic said a bit more slowly, yet not enough to cause the young man further embarrassment. "And my apologies for soiling your glove."

"No problem," Dengler said as he smiled.

"With this heat it will be dry in no time. And if you ever want a running partner, let me know."

"I'll take you up on that!" Michael said with a wave as he passed through the gate.

Already the Vatican grounds were bustling with activity. Throngs of workers, shopkeepers, and official visitors with global diversities of purpose made their way along the Via di Belvedere to the myriad offices, shops, and museums—any indoor or shaded haven, in fact, that might offer escape from the heat of the rising sun.

Another Swiss Guard stood commandingly in the center of the street—looking remarkably dry and cool, Dominic thought, despite the obvious burden of his red-plumed steel helmet and the traditional billowy gala uniform of orange, red, and blue stripes—directing foot and vehicular traffic while smartly saluting the occasional dignitaries passing by.

To any observer, Vatican City appears to be in a state of perpetual reconstruction. Comprising little more than a hundred acres, the ancient city state is in constant need of repair and maintenance. Architectural face-lifts, general structural reinforcement, and contained expansion take place at most any time and in various stages, manifested in the skeletal maze of scaffolding surrounding portions of the basilica and adjoining buildings. *Sampietrini,* the uniquely skilled maintenance workers responsible for the upkeep of Saint Peter's, are ever-present throughout the grottoes, corridors, and courtyards as they practice time-honored skills of the artisans who have gone before them, traditionally their fathers and their fathers' fathers. It was quite probable, in fact, that a given *sampietrino* working on, say, a crumbling cornerstone of the basilica itself, could very well be shoring up work that was originally performed by his great-great-grandfather more than a century before him.

Dominic walked to the end of the Belvedere, then turned right up the Stradone dei Giardini and alongside the buildings housing the Vatican Museums, until he reached the northern wall of the city.

A priest learns early that his life will suffer many rituals, and in at least one secular aspect, Michael Dominic's was no different. Every day he ended his morning run with a meditative walk along the inner walls surrounding the immaculately maintained papal gardens. The fact that many of the same trees which lined the paths have been rooted here for centuries—serving the contemplative needs of whichever pope might be ruling at the time—gave Dominic a more natural feeling of historical connectedness, in subtle contrast to other abundant yet more imposing reminders of where he now happened to be living and working.

"Ah! Good morning, Miguel." It was a gentle breeze of a voice, yet Dominic recognized it clearly in the early warm quiescence of the Vatican gardens.

"*Buongiorno*, Cal!" Dominic said brightly. Brother Calvino Mendoza, prefect of the Vatican Archives and Dominic's superior, was approaching the entrance to the building. Clad in the characteristic brown robe and leather sandals of his Franciscan order, Mendoza was a round, timorous man in his seventies—quite pleasant to work with, Dominic thought, if a little indiscreet in his obvious affection for men.

"You are up early today," Mendoza said in heavily-accented English, furtively appraising Dominic's form beneath the cassock. "But then, defying the wicked heat and traffic of Rome is best done before sunrise, no?"

"It is, yes," Dominic laughed easily, his damp hair glistening in the sun as he shook his head in amusement, "but in another hour or so I expect the pavement to start buckling."

Dominic had come to enjoy Mendoza's fey demeanor and playful flirting. Nearly everyone he had met here seemed overly stern and impassive to be really likable, and Dominic was naturally drawn to people he found more hospitable anyway. This gentle man had a quick mind for humor and was never, Dominic found, lacking for a proverb appropriate to the moment. It was also common for Mendoza to call many on his staff by the Portuguese equivalent of their name, maintaining an affectionate cultural touchstone to his native home of Brazil. As for the subtle intimations, Mendoza grasped early on that Dominic's vow of chastity was not likely to be compromised, and particularly not by another man.

"You'll get used to it," Mendoza nodded, smiling. "It is worse in the mornings, to be sure, but come late afternoon we are blessed by the *ponentino*, a cool wind off the Tyrrhenian Sea.

"And besides," he quipped, "'*To slip upon a pavement is better than to slip with the tongue—so the fall of the wicked shall come speedily.*'" He finished by glancing around the garden with mock suspicion, as if every word were prey to overcurious but unseen ears.

"'Ecclesiastes,'" Dominic responded. "And thanks for the admonition."

Pleased that the young priest indulged his occasional whimsy, Mendoza shuffled up the few steps of the entrance to the Archives.

"Now, come Miguel, your days of orientation are over. Let's get on with the real work," he said dramatically, his arms nearly flapping as his large body moved up the steps into the Archives. "Today is a very special day."

"I'll catch up with you shortly, Cal. I've got to take a quick shower first. But why is today so special?"

From the top of the steps, Mendoza turned around to face Dominic and, like a child with a tantalizing secret, whispered with barely contained excitement, "The treasures we are about to exhume have not been seen by any living soul for several hundred years."

Clearly a man who enjoyed his work, Calvino Mendoza's eyes gleamed with anticipation as he lifted one heavy eyebrow in an arch, then spun as quickly as his heavy frame would allow and disappeared through the heavy wooden door.

As Dominic walked back to his apartment at the Domus Santa Marta, the resident guesthouse just south of Saint Peter's Basilica, two men in a golf cart were heading in his direction, both dressed in the familiar black and red garb of cardinals. The cart stopped directly in his path, and one of the men stepped out, approaching him.

"Father Dominic, I presume?" The heavyset man had a thick Balkan accent, with an intelligent face bearing an inscrutable mask of expression.

"Yes, Eminence? How can I help you?" Dominic said.

"I am Cardinal Sokolov, prefect of the Congregation for the Doctrine of the Faith. I simply wanted to extend a hand of welcome on behalf of those of us who have been expecting you."

Dominic recognized the cardinal's department, better known as the infamous Office of the Holy Inquisition before someone came up with a less diabolical name.

"Good to meet you, Your Eminence," he said, surprised by the comment. "I didn't realize anyone was actually expecting me, though."

"Oh, yes," Sokolov said, holding Dominic's hand in an uncomfortably firm grip as they shook. "Having Cardinal Petrini's endorsement carries a great deal of influence here. But it also comes with certain expectations. First and foremost, keep to yourself. Do not expect to make many friends here. One is surrounded by vipers masquerading as pious souls.

"Secondly, know that you are being watched at all times. Conduct yourself appropriately and you may survive your time here. There are many who were vying for your job as *scrittore* in the Secret Archives, and they will seek any opportunity to displace you.

"Lastly," the cardinal said scowling, his eyebrows a black bar across his fleshy face, "come to me directly if you witness or suspect anyone of illicit or unbecoming activities. Such careful scrutiny will be viewed with admiration by His Holiness, for whom I speak in this regard."

Dominic was dumbfounded by the man's audacity, hardly the kind of welcome he would have imagined, one that shed a darker light on his exhilaration at now working and living in the Vatican.

"I will keep all that in mind, Eminence," he said, forcibly pulling back his hand from the cardinal's cloying grasp.

Sokolov stood a moment longer appraising Dominic's face, then turned and shuffled himself back into the golf cart, which pulled away with a mounting whine as it headed into the papal gardens.

Troubled by the encounter, Dominic returned to his apartment, the fresh burdens expected of him weighing on his mind. *What have I gotten myself into*? he thought, stepping into the shower.

3

For centuries, *L'Archivio Segreto Vaticano*, the Secret Archives of the Vatican, have enjoyed—some would even say have suffered from—a closely guarded anonymity. The fact is, the Archives are not really that secret at all.

But access to its legendary collection of historical documents and accumulated written treasures is, at best, difficult to obtain. Permission is granted in writing ultimately by the pope himself, and then only to about a thousand bona fide scholars each year. Moreover, because it was thought that potentially sensitive historical revelations might be publicly judged without regard for their larger context, journalists and photographers were generally banned from access altogether.

Consequently, the rest of the world knows so little about the Secret Archives that a tempting air of mystery and conspiracy has justifiably shrouded it from the public's understanding, and for hundreds of years wild rumors have circulated as to its true nature.

In contrast to the Vatican Library, which consists largely of individual artistic works, books, manuscripts, and other treasures comprising the broader studies of religion, art history, and philosophy, the Secret Archives serve as custodian to mountains of illuminated parchments and sealed manuscripts of immense historical value. The vast majority of these are packed up in sealed crates buried in the underground section of the Archives, and have never been seen in modern times, much less catalogued by earlier archivists.

During the recorded life of the Church as a bureaucracy—which is to say the last fifteen hundred years or so—documents of every nature and purpose have been accumulating with staggering abundance, scattered throughout Europe as the mercurial winds of war and resulting pillage influenced the shifting fortunes of the papacy.

Since its formal establishment by Pope Paul V Borghese in 1612 as the central store of knowledge for the Church, the Secret Archives have served as the working files for the Curia, the administrative body which daily governs the ecclesiastical business of a billion souls worldwide. But the Archives are not so much a Roman Catholic repository of things past as they are a living portrait of the entire human race—and the most exhaustive chronicle of original documents on Earth, addressing virtually every theological, political, scientific, and artistic pursuit through the ages.

The allure of such an exquisite collection bred the envy of many European rulers. Roman history abounds with both religious and secular plundering expeditions, resulting in the disappearance or outright confiscation of the Church's treasures at one time or another. But the most historically damaging episodes can be attributed to Napoleon Bonaparte in his quest for European domination. Italy was not the only nation pillaged by French forces, but its unwilling surrender of the Church's priceless treasures would prove most devastating for future custodians of history.

In 1809, shortly after annexing the Papal States as the property of France and arresting Pope Pius VII, Napoleon claimed title to the Vatican Archives and directed that they be shipped to Paris, where it seemed only natural that the world's greatest library and art collections should reside. Officials of the French National Archives were thus dispatched to Rome, where they packed up everything they could find into some three thousand cases, which were then escorted back to Paris in hundreds of fortified wagons drawn by teams of oxen and mules.

Following Napoleon's abdication in 1814, a decree was issued for the repatriation of all books, parchments, and other treasures taken from Rome.

But it soon became evident that, in the interim, much of the collection had been pilfered or was otherwise unaccounted for. Indeed, of the three thousand cases originally seized from the Vatican alone, no more than seven hundred found their way back to Italy. It was later learned that one of the obstacles in effecting restitution was the vast expense necessary to pack and transport the shipments. And in one of history's most lamentable decisions, papal commissioners—conveniently influenced heavily by the chief French archivist—judged that great masses of documents were of insufficient interest or value to warrant the expense of their return all the way back to Rome, and so they were either retained by the French Library, or sold off by weight for use in making cardboard and as wrapping paper for fish and meats in the butcher shops of Paris.

It was the seduction of this monumental legacy that had captured Michael Dominic's imagination, from the moment his mentor invited him to serve as a *scrittore,* or assistant archivist, in the Vatican itself. For any paleographer, this on its own would crown one's wishes. But realizing he would be involved in the Vatican Library's historic digital preservation project presented an opportunity Dominic seized upon without a second thought.

Cardinal Enrico Petrini—Uncle Rico for as long as Dominic could remember—had, since the younger man's birth, assumed the role of a father figure in Michael's life. Dominic's mother, Grace, had worked for nearly thirty years as cook and housekeeper for Petrini from the time he was a young parish priest in New York's Queens borough until she died two years ago, just before Dominic was ordained a priest.

Enrico Petrini had the good fortune to be, as was said of European nobility, "born to the purple." Since the Middle Ages, Italy had been a country of stark economic contrasts: the very rich governing the very poor. Elected governments came and went with hopeless instability, but for centuries two branches of aristocracy had generally held court in affairs of the nation while bequeathing an influential undercurrent to the papacy. Among these were the legendary families whose basis of power had stemmed from Italy's past military campaigns—the Orsini, Conti, Frangipani, and Colonna dynasties. Later came the illustrious papal families—the Medici, Borghese, and Barberini, among others. For generations such nobilities collectively and individually provided singular personal services to the popes—but the most elite of these were bestowed a special honor as intimates in the pope's *Consulta,* or Council of State. Members of the *Consulta* enjoyed the privilege of virtually unrestricted access to the pope, as their wisdom and counsel even to the present day furnish the pope with many valuable persuasions.

For generations the Petrini family had claimed a long ancestry of consultors to the papal throne; consequently, Enrico Petrini viewed his wealth with little relevance compared to the historical privilege and responsibilities accorded him. It was even presumed by many within the Vatican—privately, of course—that Petrini would likely be chosen as the next pontiff, when that time came. But much like his old friend, Albino Luciani, the late Pope John Paul I, Petrini neither desired nor sought the job of Christ's Vicar on Earth.

For Dominic, though, he would always be Uncle Rico. From the time the boy was strong enough to cast his own line, Petrini would take him fly-fishing on the Ausable River in the Adirondack Mountains of upstate New York. They stood knee-deep in the gentle currents and talked quietly for hours, about nothing in particular and yet about everything that mattered to a young boy. Uncle Rico was always there for him, Dominic knew, so he never really felt that he was without a father figure.

That his mother was uncomfortable talking about Dominic's real father was something she didn't hide well anyway. He was born out of wedlock and his father left his mother shortly before his birth—that much he had been told. He also knew now that abortion was simply not an option in those days, not as if his mother—a textbook example of a devout Catholic if there was one—would have even considered it.

Still, though he loved Enrico Petrini as much as he could the presence of a genuine father, from time to time he wondered what *he* would have been like. That Dominic would ever find resolution to the matter of his biological father had pretty much been settled in his own mind since childhood, where he allowed it to remain.

Concerned observers at the time might have admired the boy's seeming acceptance that his family could hardly be seen as traditional, but the simple fact that young Michael was branded a bastard was painfully brought back to him time and again by the cruel taunting of other boys at the various Catholic schools he attended. And over that time, Dominic had tempered a slow, cold resolve toward self-reliance, finding satisfaction in the solitude of his own company. Despite his amicable nature and an uncommon attractiveness, he was by design a social introvert, keeping and trusting few close friends, and generally preferring the companionship of books and Diogee, an old black Labrador retriever that had been adopted by his mother at the rectory.

Aside from his scholarly performance, Dominic's singular achievements in athletics pretty much formed the rest of all he cared to remember growing up. He often found a strangely comforting remoteness from everyone around him, as if he were observing every person and action from a distant vantage point—a place where he could nourish himself vicariously on the experiences of others.

Now, just a couple of years after his ordination, Dominic felt the priesthood had been his inherent destiny all along, despite the absence of any particular calling. Maybe that would come later, he thought; maybe not. His personal belief in God was more of an intellectual understanding than a religious one. Beyond that, the issue of a deeply abiding faith just didn't seem to be a major obstacle to living the more-or-less ascetic life of a Jesuit scholastic. If God came into the picture in a more meaningful way some time later, so be it.

It was at Petrini's urging that Michael considered the priesthood in the first place. Dominic sensed in his mentor a deep personal responsibility to help guide his foster son toward whatever safe harbor he might be attracted to, and he trusted the older man's wisdom and guidance without question.

So, after graduation from high school, Petrini made arrangements for his ward to take a week's retreat at the Jesuit's St. Ignatius House near New York City. During the retreat, Dominic observed firsthand the daily life of an intelligent and highly disciplined religious order. In that brief visit, and for the first time in his life, he finally felt he had found a place where he belonged.

With Petrini's accommodation, Dominic enrolled in the spring semester at Fordham University, undertaking not only a rigorous curriculum in spiritual, theological, and pastoral formation, but demonstrating marked proclivities in both computer science and natural languages.

Following his early stages of Jesuit formation, Dominic went on to the Pontifical Institute at the University of Toronto, again facilitated by the impeccable credentials of now Cardinal Petrini, where he earned a master's degree in Medieval Studies with an emphasis on paleography and codicology, the study and interpretation of ancient documents. It was in ancient history where Dominic felt most comfortable, unencumbered by the pressing social complications of the modern world. He was utterly fascinated with, and became quite expert on, the Middle Ages. To now claim the privilege of translating and interpreting archaic parchments written many hundreds of years earlier, not to mention bearing responsibility for their care and preparation for posterity, went well beyond the narrow threshold of his adolescent dreams.

Still, there were times Dominic felt like an impostor, struggling with the ethics of priesthood when all he really longed for was proximity to the historical treasures of the Church. Though he took pleasure in his current surroundings, he was constantly haunted by an unshakable shallowness. *Will I ever know the depths of faith others seem to have found?* he often pondered. *Am I really cut out for this life?* The apprehension was unremitting, and he knew the time would come when the challenges would be too great not to take a stand one way or another.

Having showered and quickly dressed in his apartment, Dominic savored a fresh late summer apple he had plucked from a tree in the papal gardens on his way back to the Archives. The clean black cassock he had changed into quickly absorbed the penetrating heat of the risen sun, and he eagerly anticipated the cool reprieve awaiting him inside the thick stone walls of the Archives and Library buildings adjoining the north wall of the Sistine Chapel.

Bounding up the steps, Dominic entered the Library's foyer and turned left up a long, dark corridor. At the end of the passage, he followed the hallway as it veered to the left, admiring the ornate curved walls supporting the Borgia Tower high above. Turning into what was once a small chapel but had since been conscripted for use as an administrative office for the archiving team, Dominic nearly collided head-on with Vatican Secretary of State Cardinal Fabrizio Dante.

"Pardon me, Your Eminence," Dominic said, retreating a pace and reflexively lowering his head in deference to the second most powerful man in Vatican City.

Dominic had seen Dante only once before, from a distance, shortly after settling into his rooms at the Domus Santa Marta, the Vatican's hotel adjacent to Saint Peter's Basilica. Cardinal Dante kept his own opulent apartment in the San Carlo Palace overlooking the gardens of Saint Martha's Square, but made it a point to personally greet every new Vatican resident and employee. On Dominic's arrival Mendoza had hinted to him that Dante's welcomes were more like the Inquisition—a paranoid litmus test to determine if any troublemakers had breached his domain. Curiously, Dante had never officially welcomed Dominic, and did not seem about to this morning. The tall, aristocratic prince of the Church—a seasoned diplomat recognized for the efficient governor that he was—had not been admired for his warmth of character.

"Good morning, Father Dominic." Dante

greeted him brusquely, his demeanor that of a nobleman speaking to a street urchin, with a haughty emphasis hovering over the pronunciation of certain words. "I trust you enjoyed your—what do you Americans call it, *'jog'*—this morning?"

Throughout his own life, Dominic rarely allowed himself to be intimidated, but the legacy of his Catholic upbringing conditioned him to respect authority—especially Church authority—without challenge. And though he did so by force of habit, Dominic found his reflexive submission unsettling in the face of Cardinal Dante's attempt to belittle Dominic's exercise routine. In the sudden shadow of this man's presence, however, there was no time for him to feel anything beyond the weight of the cardinal's penetrating gaze. And the void of his answer.

Dante's look perforated the space between the young priest's eyes, but he didn't bother waiting for a response. He raised his hand as if intending to dispense a blessing, but which Dominic took to mean *step aside*. Dante broke a slight smile, satisfied by the young priest's reaction, then turned and walked imperiously down the corridor in the direction of the Government Palace.

Reminiscent of the toughs he had faced down for years on the streets of Queens, Dominic realized that he had just been tested, and by his own estimation it was a draw. *This,* he thought sarcastically, *must be one of those epiphanic Jesuit moments that build character and humility.*

Calvino Mendoza was hovering inside the former chapel, a few feet back from where the cardinal had just stood, his face nearly transcendent with the reckoned giddiness of one having observed an electric moment which begged for assessment.

"Shades of Diogenes!" Mendoza whispered in a gush, after first craning his thick neck out into the hall to ensure the cardinal was not within earshot. "What do you suppose *that* was all about, Miguel?"

"I've no idea, Cal," Dominic said flatly, "but if he's trying to charm me with his winsome ways, he'll need a rematch."

"Well, Dante *is* a misanthrope of the first order," Mendoza said. "There's nothing anyone can do to win him over. Most people dismiss him as being arrogant—but he knows better than that." The monk's dewlap bobbed as he chuckled at his own wit.

"What was he doing here, anyway?" Dominic asked.

"He just asked me to locate some Curial documents from the Miscellanea section for him," Mendoza replied. "He's the one person here you must watch out for, Miguel. His Eminence has many eyes in this place, ones that observe not so much out of loyalty as for abject fear of the consequences. Don't forget the words of Saint John: '*And ye shall know the truth, and the truth shall make you free.*'"

Dominic's furrowed eyebrows questioned Mendoza's meaning, knowing a pithy response was moments away.

"As it happens," Mendoza provided, "those words are inscribed on the lobby wall of your own country's Central Intelligence Agency. Just don't forget, Dante has his spies here as well."

"Good advice, Cal. Thanks," Dominic said reflectively. "Now, you mentioned some excitement in our work today?"

Brother Mendoza briskly led the way to the freight elevator, the *slap-slap-slap* of his leather sandals on the marble floor echoing throughout the lofty arched hallways. They entered the waiting elevator and descended to the spacious, dimly lit underground section of the Secret Archives.

The cavernous depository, built deep beneath the sun-drenched expanse of the Pigna Courtyard, was completed in 1980 after years of painstaking excavation and considerable structural reinforcement, ever cautious to the discovery of artifacts from prior ages, a common archeological challenge when digging up ancient Rome. Sturdy shelves of gray galvanized steel extended in a maze that, row by row from beginning to end, measured well over fifty miles. The tall bookshelves, specially constructed for the Vatican in New Jersey, gave the illusion of supporting the low, wood-planked ceiling for as far as the eye could see in nearly every direction.

As they moved through the darkened aisles, sensors activated amber lighting overhead, which automatically extinguished after a few minutes with no movement. Passing through musty aisles lined with books bathed in soft, fluent pools of light gave Dominic the oddly comforting impression of being in a deep underground cave.

"It's still not enough space," Mendoza lamented. "I keep warning the Cardinal Librarian that one day we just may have to move everything into Saint Peter's. He's never amused, you know."

Surveying the subterranean realm, dubbed the Gallery of the Metallic Shelves, Dominic found himself reminded again of the stark comparison between the Holy See's global influence and the nearly claustrophobic confines of its seat of government. It was an odd dichotomy. Everything and everyone he had encountered in the past few days revealed a stifling anachronism, confounded by bureaucratic tedium. That the Vatican functioned at all, he thought, had to be one of heaven's minor miracles.

On the west side of the Gallery Mendoza led Dominic through a set of heavy, ornately carved wooden doors and into an astonishingly bright fluorescent room, air-conditioned and brimming with state-of-the-art computer equipment. Emerging from the vast dimness of shelved antiquities into this spacious modern lab left Dominic slightly disoriented, adding yet another layer to the contrasting nature of this strange new world he was absorbing.

A dozen or so technicians in white lab coats, some moving about the room, others seated at computer workstations, were all preoccupied with the privileged task of digitizing thousands of treasured books and manuscripts resting on the shelves outside the doors through which they had just passed.

A tall, scholarly man with wire-rimmed spectacles was standing over the shoulder of a technician seated at an imposing array of computers, scanners, monitors, and digital cameras. Both were gazing intently on the larger of two adjacent display monitors. As Mendoza and Dominic approached the men, they saw the object of their fascination: pictured on the screen was a beautiful manuscript—painstakingly illuminated on a pale caramel-hued parchment, two pages side by side, clearly bound together in a larger volume—and displayed in brilliant color.

The standing man looked up, a little startled but clearly pleased to receive visitors. By his reaction it appeared he didn't get many.

"Brother Mendoza!" he said, removing a white cotton glove from his right hand, which he extended to the monk. "What a pleasant surprise! Welcome to the lab."

"Good morning, Pedro," Mendoza said cheerfully. "I'd like you to meet Father Dominic, our new *scrittore*. He'll be working with you on our little project here. I'm hoping you can orient him today on your procedures. Miguel, this is Pedro—I mean, Peter—Townsend, chief scientist of the digitizing lab."

"Please, call me Michael," Dominic said, extending his hand. "Good to meet you, Peter."

"Peter, have you got a moment?" The technician seated at the computer console beckoned Townsend while closely inspecting the larger display.

Townsend turned back to the console, following the technician's focus of attention. He leaned over to resume studying the image, then he stood back up, startled and apologetic.

"Ah! Where are my manners? Forgive me, gentlemen," he said, "Brother Mendoza, Father Dominic, this is Toshi Kwan. Toshi is one of our brilliant steganographers. We're fortunate to have lured him away from Watson." IBM's Thomas J. Watson Research Center in New York was one of the more prestigious research facilities in the world. Much of the groundbreaking work in cryptography and digital watermarking had emerged from their labs, but some of their more provocative developments were currently in the area of steganography, the ingenious but little-known art of hiding information within information.

The three men alternately shook hands and exchanged brief greetings.

"Toshi was just showing me some of his work," Townsend continued, motioning to the manuscript displayed on the screen. "Toshi, why don't you describe to our guests what we're up to here, starting from the initial scan process."

"You bet," Kwan replied enthusiastically, clearly pleased to have a new audience. Toshi Kwan was typical of most young technophiles today, rabid about new developments in technology and eager to share his discoveries with anyone interested enough and capable of understanding his effusive discourses. But his work inside the Vatican, though satisfying his technical competencies, was largely done in isolation due to stringent security policies.

He led the group over to a cluster of equipment adjacent to his workstation. "The heart of the process begins with the IBM Pro/3000 Scanner here," Kwan gestured to a large floor-standing unit consisting of an integrated copy stand and digital camera. "Based on IBM-proprietary imaging sensor chips, the Pro/3000 provides a signal-to-noise ratio greater than 3000:1."

Unimpressed with technology more complicated than a telephone, Mendoza's eyelids inevitably drooped when confronted with arcane technical dissertations. "If you gentlemen will excuse me, this all sounds lovely but beyond my comprehension. Miguel, please meet me in the Miscellanea section at the north end of the Gallery when you're finished here—which will be soon, I hope." He tilted his head in hopes of meeting Michael's eyes, but the younger man was already absorbed in Kwan's discussion.

"Sure thing, Cal," Dominic said absently. "I'll find you. Please, Toshi, go on. I'll try to keep up."

Kwan continued. "Probably the most noteworthy feature of the system is a unique colorimetric filter set that captures remarkably accurate color nuances of non-photographic materials, like papyri, parchments, vellums, fabrics—pretty much anything that isn't made up of photographic dyes."

Peter Townsend stepped in to explain. "Because we're dealing with irreplaceable books and manuscripts that are, on average, five to six hundred years old, our primary responsibility is to ensure that no damage is done to the originals. These documents are extremely sensitive to temperature and humidity, which is why this is one of the few areas in the Vatican with air-conditioning, constantly monitored to stay within a restricted range."

"Now to the operation itself," said Kwan. "Most of the originals we process are bound manuscripts of varying size and thickness, and they must be supported in a way that doesn't stress the bindings or damage the pages. For example, a book is placed on the scanning bed here..." Kwan indicated a large glass surface approximately 18 inches wide and 24 inches long supported by a sturdy easel, "... and another pane of heavy glass is placed on top of the manuscript to help flatten the image while maintaining focus over the entire page, without flattening the pages so much that any wrinkles acquired through the centuries would vanish.

"Once the image has been captured," he continued, stepping back over to the workstation, "our process corrects for faithful color reproduction, associates the images with detailed descriptions for indexing and retrieval purposes, reduces the image to the desired size, sharpens and rotates the image for proper viewing orientation, applies a visible digital watermark, and compresses the image to JPEG format for transmission over the internet."

Kwan took a deep breath, clearly proud of both the efficiency of the system and his role in maintaining it.

"It's the watermarking process that Peter and I were discussing when you came in," Kwan said as he sat back down at the console. "You'll probably recognize the Rossos–San Vito translation of Homer's *Iliad* on the screen now."

Leaning in closer, Dominic did indeed see the object of their earlier attention: this extraordinarily beautiful codex was an original fifteenth-century translation summarizing Book I of Homer's *Iliad,* a companion version to the *Odyssey*. Opposing parchment pages featured exquisite illumination surrounding Greek text on the left and Latin on the right. The richly colored illustrations convincingly represented the Greek and Trojan heroes clad in their ancient costumes and battle armor. The priest Chryses, depicted as an ancient pagan in one panel, is shown spurned by King Agamemnon, leader of the Greeks during the Trojan War, while another panel showed Chryses avenged by the archer god Apollo, who shoots down the Greeks with a passel of arrows.

It was an outstanding piece, Dominic marveled, and one of the only images in that original series to have been completed. Owing to a lack of either time or money in 1477, later images were either merely sketched in or entirely omitted.

On the left page, subtly hidden within the Greek text yet visible to the naked eye, Dominic spotted a digital watermark embedded in the image. It featured the orbicular seal of the Vatican Library—the Keys to Heaven crossed beneath a bishop's miter, encircled by the Latin words *Bibliotheca Apostolica Vaticana.* A similar watermark appeared on the opposite page, though in a clear area so as not to obscure the fine hand lettering.

Grabbing the computer's mouse, Kwan positioned the cursor over the watermark image on the right-side page, clicked the left mouse button and, holding it down, drew a box around the image. Releasing the mouse button caused the displayed image on the bigger monitor to enlarge by 300% of its previous size—clearly illuminating not just every pixel in the seal's image but the blemishes and natural striations of the sheepskin parchment itself.

While Kwan worked with the computer, Peter Townsend elaborated on their mission.

"You see, Father Dominic, the Library itself can only accommodate a thousand or so scholars each year. And," he said, raising his hands and opening his eyes wide, "with perhaps a hundred thousand or more scholars as well as students requesting admission, this project could provide access to Vatican Library materials for the worldwide community of scholars. Now, any scholar with access to the internet from anywhere in the world—with proper authorization, of course—can instantly acquire and study important documents essential to their own research."

"Which is why," Kwan interrupted, taking his boss's lead, "digital watermarking is so important. With some eight million of the Library's most valuable images having been digitized, there's a valid concern that they might fall victim to unauthorized use—perhaps in ways that might diminish their historical value or misconstrue their original meaning or context.

"Of course, we could just distribute lower-resolution images, rendering them virtually useless for such purposes as lithographic printing. But that would also make them unsuitable for the level of detail needed for scholarly study. So, by adding a watermark, each image can be clearly identified as belonging to the Vatican Library. As you can see, we've tried to make the image as unobtrusive as possible, yet readily visible."

"But what prevents someone from simply removing the watermark?" Dominic asked.

"That's a good question, and one we've spent a lot of time figuring out." Kwan pointed to the monitor on the left that displayed the entire image.

"To defeat the watermark, one could just calculate pixel depth and use that estimate to enhance pixels already darkened by the program. Fortunately, we have several ways of countering that strategy." Kwan motioned to the enlarged watermark image on the right-hand monitor.

"We also make the watermark as difficult as possible to calculate. You'll note that marks have been applied at various locations on each page. The size and location of the watermarks are subject to random parameters under program control, and marks of varying sizes are applied at different locations."

"We feel confident that protection of the Vatican Library's treasures is fairly secure given today's technology," Townsend added. "But you can always count on someone, sometime, to come up with a nefarious scheme to undermine our efforts. They'll just have to work that much harder on this one," he chuckled.

It was clear to Dominic these men were gratified by their work, and justifiably so. He was impressed at the lengths to which the scientists had gone to create a nearly foolproof system.

But, as time would tell, little would protect the Church from the damage its own treasures could do to it.

4

Accompanied by the eerie pools of amber light forging his path, Dominic made his way to the Miscellanea section in search of Mendoza, which proved to be a brisk ten-minute walk from the digitizing lab through the Gallery. Along the way he marveled at the sheer abundance of crated materials on shelves high and low, stretching many linear miles.

He had inquired of Mendoza shortly after his arrival—during his first tour of the Secret Archives and on the monk's revelation that precious little of it was indexed at all—why there hadn't been a better way of organizing the vast quantity of material.

Mendoza's response revealed sobering statistics. The special area of the Archives known as the Miscellanea housed fifteen enormous *armadi*, or poplar cabinets, each bearing the Borghese coat of arms and filled with thousands of documents which have never been catalogued much less seen for centuries—and also known to be the most intriguing of all collections in the Vatican. The few catalogued treasures alone included such priceless artifacts as the extensive record of Galileo's trial for heresy during the Inquisition of 1633, and the vain petition of seventy-five English lords asking for the pope's annulment of the marriage between Henry VIII and Catherine of Aragon. This section also contained vast materials relating to various periods of religious and political history, including extensive collections on John Calvin and Martin Luther documenting the formation of their own Protestant theologies after breaking with the Catholic Church. Tantalizing fragments of trials for sorcery, summaries of unspeakable atrocities committed during the Inquisitions, secret letters from popes to their lovers, many of them in code—all this and more had been tucked away in the Miscellanea and only partly explored over time.

The Archives only had a full-time staff of some eighteen *scrittori* and assistants. To inventory just one package of materials—and of the fifteen enormous cabinets in the Miscellanea alone, each contained an average of ten thousand unexplored packages—would require the full-time effort of two experts over a week's time. Consequently, to record the contents of all ten thousand packages in one cabinet alone would require nearly two hundred years.

Dominic's mind reeled not only at the math, but at the exhilarating and nearly limitless possibilities of discovery he was about to undertake. What could possibly be lying in wait for his own excavation was anyone's guess, but it was a moment unlike any other in his life, and his imagination soared at the prospect.

Searching the aisles, he didn't see Mendoza anywhere in the general area, but he did spy a heavy wooden door hanging open against the back wall. Peering inside he found a small, square room fortified with thick concrete walls and secured behind the massive carved wooden door, which he now saw was lined with a steel plate. His eyes wide with amazement, Dominic realized this was the enigmatic Riserva, the closed section of the Archives where the Vatican's most sensitive documents were stored. Mendoza, as prefect, possessed one of two keys to the vault, and policy decreed that no one be permitted in the room outside the presence of the prefect.

"Cal?" Dominic asked in a low voice. "Are you in here?"

"Miguel!" Mendoza cried out, gasping. *"Come quickly!"*

As Dominic entered the room, he found the stout monk standing tiptoe on a footstool, attempting to retrieve an enormous volume from a high shelf deep inside one of the poplar cabinets.

"Madre mio!" he huffed, panting heavily. "You are just in time, Miguel! Be so kind as to relieve me

of this unforgiving burden." Mendoza's normally pink face had shifted to mauve, with thick veins pulsing at his temples and pearls of sweat forming on his forehead.

Dominic leapt across the room and grabbed the volume, leaning a shoulder into Mendoza to steady the heavy man against the cabinet.

"Careful, Cal!" Dominic said between clenched teeth. "Couldn't you have waited for me? You might have broken your neck, or worse, damaged this old book."

"Very funny," Mendoza wheezed, wiping his forehead with a lace handkerchief he pulled from his pocket as he stepped down from the stool with some effort, knees protesting as his sandals negotiated the floor. Reaching his hand out he gripped Dominic's shoulder to steady himself.

"I do suppose I am grateful to you on both counts. This *armadio* is one I have been meaning to explore for some time, but my own anticipation got the better of me." Mendoza was breathing heavily, and now began swaying a little. Still holding the heavy book, Dominic set it on a lower shelf in the cabinet.

"Cal, you better sit down for a few minutes." Looking around the bleakly furnished vault, Dominic found little to provide adequate support. A rickety wooden chair and reading table were the only furniture in sight, and that chair looked as if it would barely contain his own weight.

"Perhaps you're right," Mendoza said weakly, his face now an ashen hue. "I am feeling a bit nauseous, Miguel. I think I should go back to my room and rest for a bit." As he said this, Mendoza fell against the table, causing its legs to scrape against the floor.

Dominic quickly reached out to stop him from falling, then put his arm around the monk, steadying him with some difficulty as they both walked slowly back through the Gallery to the elevator. Mendoza's apartment was just inside the foyer of the Archive building. Once they arrived Dominic helped the monk inside. As Mendoza laid down on the bed, Dominic fetched a bottle of mineral water.

Accepting it, Mendoza drank eagerly. Suddenly his eyes opened wide and he nearly choked on the stream making its way down his throat.

"*Dios mio!*" he gasped. "Miguel, I left the Riserva unlocked! Dante will have my head if he finds it open."

Mendoza tried to get up off the bed, his fear of Dante propelling him upright.

"Relax, Cal." Dominic's hand pressed on the monk's shoulder. "I'll go back down and lock it for you."

His stomach cramped with fear, Mendoza

relented. He reached behind his head and grasped a black leather cord hanging around his neck. At the end was a solid brass Medeco security key, the kind that required special codes for restricted duplication. Withdrawing the cord from around his thick neck, he handed it to Dominic.

"Go, lock the door. Let no one see you, and please bring the key back to me when you've finished." Dominic took the key, folded the leather cord neatly and pocketed the bundle.

"I should have known better than to try to act your age," the monk mumbled. "Please hurry, Miguel."

He laid back down on the bed and his eyes fluttered shut. Dominic saw that he was breathing better now, his color returning to normal. He dismissed the notion of calling the Vatican dispensary. A doctor probably wouldn't arrive for hours anyway.

Dominic made his way back down the elevator, through the vast expanse of the Gallery, and to the open door of the Riserva. He looked inside, making sure the small room was empty before closing the door, then locked it and pocketed the key.

He began to turn away, then slowly came to a stop. Standing there in the dim light and quiet of the vast Gallery, he weighed the options of his temptation.

The sensation began in his chest. It was the same inner trembling he experienced at the Pontifical Institute whenever they brought out the Good Stuff for students to examine and interpret. It was an unspeakable thrill: a new archeological dig was about to begin—one perhaps revealing secret marginal ciphers in Aramaic or Ancient Greek, markings no one had ever noticed before, as he had done in graduate school to the amazement of his professors.

He could barely imagine the treasures waiting for him alone on the other side of the ornately carved wooden door. His eyes lingered over the bas relief designs fashioned by some long-ago artisan. Hundreds of years of use had blackened the wood around the bronze handle, its antiqued significance only adding to the intrigue now gripping his mind.

Simply *imagining* it, he finally reasoned, was not enough. Feigning nonchalance, Dominic walked back and forth to the ends of nearby aisles, making sure no one was in the vicinity, grateful there were no security cameras. Then he turned back, facing the door of the Riserva with determination along with conflicting measures of guilt. *Well,* he considered, *I've long ago abandoned the concept of Hell, so burning there for such a minor transgression is hardly a deterrent.*

Slipping the key back into the lock, he turned the bolt, swung open the heavy door and quickly stepped inside, quietly sealing the entrance behind him and securing the lock. Both his heart and his mind were racing.

He inspected the room more closely now. It was quite small compared to the vastness of other rooms in the Archives, maybe only six hundred square feet. The walls, floor, and ceiling were composed of cellular concrete. Two low-level incandescent lighting fixtures hung from the ceiling. A vent on one wall maintained a gentle but uniform flow of conditioned air. A gauge near the light switch indicated 35% relative humidity, ideal conditions for strict archival conservation.

Dominic picked up the volume Mendoza had struggled with earlier from inside the *armadio* and placed it on the old mahogany table on one side of the room. The table groaned under the added weight. The book was remarkably heavy; at least twenty pounds, he estimated. He pulled over the creaky wooden chair and sat down.

His eyes transfixed on the cover of the book, he withdrew two white cotton gloves from the pocket of his cassock, gloves all archivists carried while working with precious documents. His hands trembled slightly as his fingers slid into each glove. Carefully unfastening the leather closure, he drew back the thick dusty cover, gently letting it come to rest on the desk. With some astonishment, he found that it wasn't a book at all, but a sturdy wooden box adorned with intricate Gutta-percha ornamentation on its cover, giving the appearance of a bound book. Inside were dozens of loose parchments of varying size and toning, some formed into small packets entwined with colored hemp, others tenderly fastened beneath fraying ribbons, many affixed with wax seals.

"What have we here?" Dominic whispered to himself. He sorted through the fragile items one by one, briefly scanning those he could understand in Latin, French, or Italian. His mind drifted to what life must have been like in the Church of former centuries.

Most of the documents were indulgences, official pardons of punishment for sins forgiven, often in exchange for fasts, floggings, prayers, or—in many cases—money. Indeed, it was the sale of indulgences that compelled Martin Luther and other Reformation leaders to abandon that particular practice, and ultimately the Roman Church altogether.

There were scores of petition registers, requests for all manner of papal favors and sovereign influence—many from luminous names well known to history: Petrarch, Newton,

Boccaccio, Mary Queen of Scots…. It was a veritable Who's Who of legendary supplicants seeking the almighty grace and mercy of God's Vicar on Earth.

Dominic had been so transfixed in his sifting of history that he lost all track of time. Glancing absently at his watch, a gift from Cardinal Petrini on his ordination, Dominic was startled to find that two hours had passed since he had returned to the Riserva. *I'd better get out of here,* he thought. He hoped Mendoza was napping by now.

The hours of sitting motionless had taken its toll, and as he rose Dominic felt his right leg start to lose feeling—the prickling sensation of a thousand needles working its way up his leg. Standing up, he had to place both hands on the edge of the wooden desk, putting most of his weight there to support his rising. All at once the table leg supporting him gave out, sending Dominic, the old leather box and all of its contents scattered across the cold concrete floor.

Sitting upright in humiliation, he shook and massaged his dormant leg until feeling began to return. The real suffering he felt was for the manuscripts which lay spread about him on the floor; his chagrin would be complete were he to have caused damage to any one of them. He set about recovering the strewn treasures to return them to the leather conservation case.

Reaching over to seize the nearly empty box, Dominic noticed the remaining contents were askew. In a panic, he assumed one of the parchments had become balled up or folded over, creating a lump not only beneath the remaining papers but in his throat as well. On closer inspection, he found no damage to the contents, but that the box had a false bottom, cleverly designed to make it appear melded to the leather walls within, which had become dislodged.

With cautious excitement, he carefully emptied the leather case and gently pulled up the false bottom. The stiff leather insert made a soft croaking sound as it pulled away from the box's actual base. There, resting inside, was a small sheaf of aged papers bound together with a deep purple satin ribbon in the form of a triangle, bearing a brittle red wax seal at its apex.

Dominic simply stared at the packet, as if it exuded some mystical property, when suddenly he heard the unmistakable sound of steel-meeting-steel as a key found its way into the lock on the door of the Riserva.

In a spontaneous panic, Dominic quickly snatched the packet and tucked it into the breast pocket inside his cassock. He rolled onto his knees as he feigned the act of cleaning up. He felt a sudden rush of foolishness doing so—but then another feeling, one not so benign, rose in his chest and stayed there, as he looked up to meet the smoldering gaze of Cardinal Fabrizio Dante.

5

Hana Sinclair sat in a powder blue and gold cushioned Louis XIV chair set against a luxuriously upholstered wall facing an ornate fireplace, devoid of wood for the summer but adorned with a sumptuous flower arrangement. She visually mapped the room with a reporter's deftness, taking in the salon's classical Empire style replete with symbolic tributes to Napoleon's reign. Swarms of golden bees, representing prosperity, clustered high in each of the four corners of the room. Laurel wreaths and winged victory embellishments, symbols of triumph, met the eye at every turn. Before her, a marble slab table with winged lion supports connoted strength and courage. The only sound was the monotone ticking of a Louis XVI clock on the mantle of the enormous fireplace, the simple ornamentation of its later period an interesting contrast to the rest of the room.

Her appointment in Paris's Elysee Palace had been for ten o'clock, but it was already twenty minutes past. She removed a compact from her purse, checked her makeup, then briefly sighed and put the compact away. She disliked being kept waiting.

Reaching into her valise, Hana withdrew copies of several World War II-era photographs she had acquired from the public archives of the *Bibliothèque Nationale de France,* the French National Library. She was still smarting from the polite but firm refusal she received earlier in the week when she had demanded access to the Special Documents Area, a secured floor containing sensitive papers normally reserved for authorized government officials. The French were obsessive about preserving their history, and Hana was certain the documents she sought had to exist somewhere in the Bibliothèque. Vowing to deal with that issue later, she turned her attention to the faded black-and-white images before her.

By and large, the prints, though grainy and somewhat indistinct, depicted groups of men in various activities, taken, she presumed, by well-placed spies with hidden cameras. These particular photos had been declassified and thus were evidently found to have little value in terms of damage to national security, which explained their presence among other public documents.

Hana had been looking for one man in particular, and the absence of his name from any written records had stymied her for several weeks. All she had to go on was his wartime code name, "Achille," and the fact that he was a highly placed group leader in the Maquis, a shadowy arm of the French underground resistance movement. This captivating detail came to her in the form of a short personal note she discovered wedged inside a book in the public archives, folded in half lengthwise and tucked in close to the spine. It had undoubtedly been overlooked in the material declassification process, but, she assumed, it's value would be dubious to the reader anyway.

Hana reached for her notebook. As she began checking her notes an aide walked into the room.

"His Excellency will see you now, mademoiselle. Please observe that thirty minutes have been scheduled for your interview."

Hana gathered her notes and photos and tucked them inside the bag, smoothing the wrinkles out of her dark navy suit as she stood and followed the man out into the spacious marble hall and down toward the office of the president of France.

At twenty-nine, she was strikingly tall, with an imposing demeanor that often came in useful as an investigative reporter for *Le Monde*. Her shoulder-length chestnut brown hair swept naturally inward, framing a smooth, tanned face. A graceful confidence in her bearing suggested years of boarding and prep schools, and she owed her fit, stalwart build to a privileged Swiss heritage.

Reaching the end of the hallway, the aide swung open two towering doors leading into the president's suite. Hana stepped into a small anteroom, beyond which she took in the great formal office. Sunlight flooded in from lofty floor-to-ceiling windows that adorned the better part of two walls. The aide led her into the spacious room, then turned and silently closed the doors behind him.

Silhouetted against the bright center window, Pierre Valois sat writing behind a massive dark cherry desk. He looked up as Hana came into the room, then capped his fountain pen and rose to greet her, shooting the cuffs of his impeccable Givenchy suit coat as he stepped around the desk.

"*Mon petit* Hana," he said affectionately, a wide smile welcoming her into his outstretched arms.

"*Bonjour*, Excellency," Hana said, warmly embracing the man in kind. "You look to be in superb health, despite rumors to the contrary."

"Oh, pay no attention to the press," Valois chided her with a wink, leading her to a cozy settee near a window. "They would sooner see me buried than survive another term. But you! Thank goodness you are on the side of truth and honor." As Hana sat on the sofa, Valois settled into a gold-tufted armchair facing his guest.

"I'm not so sure taking sides would be a good

idea for a reporter, Excellency." Hana replied with a mock look of reprove. "But I do bring a message from one of your loyal supporters—Grand-père sends you his warmest regards and hopes you can join him for supper soon. He's in town, you know."

"Armand? In Paris? Well, he simply must pay me a visit. It has been…oh, I think nearly a year since we last spoke," Valois said, looking out the window reflectively. "He spends entirely too much time in Zurich anyway. Why, it's a wonder the poor man can find a decent meal in that city, when all of Paris would throw open its doors for the baron."

They both laughed, knowing that since the dark days of World War II the two men had maintained a light ongoing polemic over whose cuisine was superior.

"Excellency, I am told I have but a few minutes of your time—so, just for a short while, you must be president of the French Republic and not my godfather," Hana said, half-jokingly.

"Only a few minutes, they told you? Nonsense, you take as long as you wish, my dear—but of course we must set aside familiarities for the official business of *Le Monde*…" His head rocked from side to side as he said this, affecting an air of obliging reluctance. "Would you care for tea?"

Valois reached for the tea set on the side table, freshened throughout the day for visitors, and poured steaming *lapsang souchong* into two gold-rimmed porcelain cups bearing the laurel insignia of the French Republic. He favored the comforting smoky essence of the withered Fukien leaves, believing it set a discerning mood for his guests.

"Oui, merci." Accepting the cup, Hana's demeanor shifted from beloved goddaughter to serious reporter. "As you know, Excellency, this matter of Jewish gold plundered by the Nazis has recently come under fresh and rather intense scrutiny by the world's press, especially in Europe," Hana began, reaching for her notebook. "It seems investigators, both here and in America, have been sifting through newly declassified war records, and rather compelling evidence has been revealed about the degree of France's complicity during the war."

Hana took a moment to sip the tea, breathing in its woodsy fragrance while her mind worked to enforce a dignified bravura she didn't really feel. She knew this was a sensitive matter, not just for the French people in general, but for this leader in particular. She also presumed that, owing to her privileged relationship, she was certainly the only journalist who could ever get this close—and be the first—to discuss the issue in some depth with the president of France. This could surely be the story that would secure her reputation as a hard-hitting journalist, and long-sought independence from her grandfather's influence. The china teacup rattled nervously in its saucer as she reached over to set it on the table.

"So it has," Valois acknowledged. Indeed, he was all too aware of such emerging revelations. But he also knew that it was simply a matter of time before the press started their probing in earnest. He had to ensure that his version of events would be delivered first—with the honor and respect his office deserved, naturally—regardless of its veracity. It was no mere accident that Hana would be the first reporter to scoop the interview. *Le Monde* was strategically vital in establishing preemptive spin on such sensitive matters of state becoming public. Furtive calls had been placed and arrangements were made for the young reporter to be suitably briefed by her editors—all without any appearance of collusion. The fact that *Le Monde* was unaware of her close relationship to the president made it all the more exquisite. If not for that, he considered, this might have posed a much more difficult problem.

"Of course," Valois continued pensively, wandering the memories of his own past, "you must remember those were difficult times for many countries, particularly France. Though most considered Hitler a madman and the Nazi party a despised form of government, its sheer power of intimidation was enormous. As for France, well, despite those Vichy swine we did what had to be done at the time.

"I do not offer this as a form of apology, my dear, not at all," he continued. "But such actions taken by each country in the face of certain invasion must be considered in their proper context." Valois looked directly at Hana as he said this, his heavily lined face a study in somber authority as he recalled a grim history about which he knew too many things.

Hana met the president's eyes with tacit understanding. As an accommodation to years of political expediency, few were aware that Valois and Hana's grandfather, Baron Armand de Saint-Clair, had fought closely together during World War II. Both from aristocratic European families, each could have opted for the relative comfort and safety of some plush headquarters post. Instead, they discreetly used the combined power of their wealth and influence to support the Maquis who, among other noble acts, spirited the assets and the children of French Jews out of their country and into Switzerland.

At the beginning of the eighteenth century, Hana's ancestors founded and had since controlled one of Switzerland's most prominent banks, Banque Suisse de Saint-Clair, concurrent with the emergence of that country's earliest banking laws regarding secrecy. The *Geheimsphäre*, or "sphere of secrecy," was chief among bedrock Swiss democratic principles. Extending the privilege of such privacy to the banks of this small, ostensibly neutral country also served the needs of Europe's wealthy for a cloaked, secure resting place for assets which were deemed by their owners as being within ominously easy reach of whatever shifting political rule their own countries might be suffering at the time—from the Huguenots fleeing religious persecution by Catholic kings, to hiding the royal property of France's Bourbon dynasty on the heels of the French Revolution.

It wasn't until 1934, however, that the Swiss Parliament enacted the stringent laws of today which hold bankers personally liable for ensuring total secrecy in all transactions, regardless of the dictates of other countries. As a result, such an enforced haven became immensely attractive to Jews whose assets might otherwise be in great peril, as Hitler's intentions eventually manifested, and Germany's war machine began to build.

The young Baron de Saint-Clair's banking acumen, bolstered by his family's considerable influence, positioned him well among the financial elite of Europe at the time, and despite countless risks he deliberately used that influence, and his bank, to quietly safeguard a veritable river of Jewish gold and currency assets flowing into Switzerland.

Posing as refugees, agents of the Maquis crossed Swiss borders hauling bags brimming with the goods and chattels of Jews who were forbidden to leave France and Belgium. Agents were accompanied by Jewish children posing as their own—children who otherwise would certainly have ended up in concentration camps, as did their parents. Consistent with the rules of the Geneva Convention, the International Committee of the Red Cross maintained a humanitarian policy of granting refuge to children, thus providing the Maquis with the distinction of rescuing otherwise doomed children while helping to secure their futures with at least part of their family's assets, if not their blood relatives.

Hana arched her back slightly, bringing her chin down while inching herself a bit taller on the sofa, all too aware of her own family's complicity in the situation. She then brushed her hand over the hem of her skirt as she crossed her legs.

"Of course, Excellency," she said, highly sensitive to the moment. "As you say, there are many sides to this story. But I think we have an opportunity here, together, to set the record straight before unfounded speculation takes hold."

Valois was silently grateful for his prescience. It seemed Hana, too, had a vested interest in releasing the story first. Relaxing his guard a bit, he settled back into the armchair.

"I'm especially interested in the observations of Maquis field agents at the time," Hana continued, "but in particular, those involved in the flight of Jewish capital and other assets crossing the border into Switzerland."

Reaching for her valise, Hana produced the aged photos she had been examining earlier.

"I discovered these prints in the public archives of the Bibliothèque here in Paris. These are copies, of course, and as you can see the quality is not very good; most likely they were taken surreptitiously at various border posts." Hana handed the packet to Valois, who studied them intently.

"Since you and my grandfather were so closely involved in the efforts of the Maquis, Excellency, I'm wondering if you recognize any of these individuals. The identity of one man in particular has eluded me—he was a group leader with the code name 'Achille.' Did you know of him? Do you see him in these images?"

As she spoke, Valois leafed through the photos, his eyes playing over the sepia-toned faces and other images of a bygone era. He ran a hand across his neck, massaging folds of skin that had gone fleshy years earlier.

Pausing ever so briefly over one particular photograph, he saw the face of a man he knew. An unmistakable face: one single massive eyebrow cresting dark, deep-seated eyes set over a hawkish nose, featuring at its tip two prominent lateral humps of cartilage. That he encountered the face at the exact moment Hana spoke the man's code name had to be completely coincidental, he knew—but the impact jarred him, nonetheless. Valois wondered if Hana was playing a game with him and looked up at her questioningly as he shuffled other photos on top of the last.

"Why do you seek this 'Achille' person anyway, my dear?" Valois asked pensively.

Hana sensed the man's change in demeanor instantly. She made a quick mental note of which photograph he had been looking at, just before it was mixed among the others.

"I… I'm not quite sure myself," which was the truth, she thought, grasping for words. "In fact, his code name came to me quite by accident, but I have a suspicion his role in the greater scheme of things has been deliberately concealed. I want to find out why and learn if perhaps he's still alive."

The president reached for his teacup, discreetly touching a button hidden beneath the table's edge as he did so. "Well, I'm afraid I can be of little help to you in this matter. None of these faces are familiar to me," Valois said, waving his hand as if to dismiss the pictures. Trying to soften his reaction, he added, "I'm an old man now, Hana, and that was a long time ago. You understand that my memory is not what it was back then. But is there something else with which I might help you?"

As he said these words a dense cloud passed before the sun, plunging the room into a cold grisaille. A chill took hold of Hana's ankles, worked its way quickly up her spine then settled at the base of her neck, where tiny hairs stood briefly on end, sending a shiver back down through her whole body—all within a fraction of a second. The impact of the moment startled her.

"More tea, my dear?" the president offered. "You look chilled."

Regaining her composure, Hana sensed the gesture was polite, though not especially sincere. Her reply was rendered unnecessary, though, when the president's aide walked into the room, swinging both doors wide in a grand gesture.

"M'excuser, Monsieur le Président," the man announced with polite determination. "The Italian delegation has arrived."

"Oui, Stefan. *Un autre moment, s'il vous plaît."* Valois looked directly at Hana, smiling as he shrugged his shoulders slightly and tipped his

head. The aide disappeared back into the anteroom, leaving the tall doors open.

Though bewildered by the abrupt and early end to their meeting, Hana gathered up the photographs, tucked them into her valise, and rose dutifully as the president himself stood, glancing at his watch.

"I must apologize, my dear. The affairs of state never rest, even in the presence of my beautiful goddaughter." Valois leaned over and kissed her on both cheeks, then guided her toward the door. "You will please call on me if there's anything else I can do for you, *non*?"

"Well, yes, there is one more request I have, *parrain*," Hana added as an afterthought, using the French endearment for godfather. "Could you arrange permission for me to access the Special Archives in the Bibliothèque? The authorities there have been most uncooperative. After all, I am working for the good of France in this effort, or at least I would hope you think so."

Valois looked at her, his face suddenly betraying the diplomatic façade it had grown accustomed to over the years—in an instant he looked all of his nearly ninety years.

"Hana, of course your intentions are only the most honorable," he said. "You shall have your permission. I ask only that you be especially careful when disturbing ghosts of the past. Let

Voltaire's caveat guide you: 'History should be written as philosophy.' Look for the lessons that can be learned from past mistakes, *mon cher. Au revoir.*" The president turned and walked back to his desk.

"*Au revoir,* Excellency," Hana replied, her voice smaller than she had intended.

The aide stepped back into the doorway, his arm extended to escort Hana out of the office.

Outside the palace, the bustling traffic on the Champs Elysées was a stark contrast to the strange meeting Hana had just been tossed out of. *What was it she had said or done? It all happened so fast,* she thought.

She determined to bring this up with her grandfather on their flight to Rome the next day.

Sitting at his desk, alone now and behind closed doors, Pierre Valois picked up the telephone and wearily punched eight numbers on the keypad. The receiver was picked up after two rings.

"*Oui*?" said the man who answered.

"We may have a problem, Armand."

6

"For your sake, Father Dominic, I trust you have not only a good reason for your presence in this room, but an explanation for being on the floor of it."

Cardinal Dante, already tall and imposing face-to-face, was now positively towering from Dominic's perspective. Getting to his feet, his mind racing for the expected answer, Dominic returned the man's riveting gaze while assuming a deferential posture.

"Your Eminence!" Dominic said in a tone of a surprised greeting. "What brings you down here? I know this must look—"

"Do not question my presence anywhere, Dominic," Dante cut him off abruptly. "Answer me: why are you in the Riserva?"

Dominic felt the back of his neck burn, the starched collar below his Adam's apple feeling even more constricting. It was the same humiliating feeling he recalled when faced with the militant little thugs in Catholic school. Back then, though he was fully capable of handling himself, he chose the less defiant course of passive resistance. Now, after years of battle-scarred Jesuit discipline, both physical and mental, all of his senses came together in a poised, synchronous defense as his mind reasoned for the best non-combative response.

"May I explain, your Eminence?" Dominic asked submissively. Dante paused just long enough to demonstrate control before motioning for an answer.

Dominic continued. "You see, I arrived earlier to find Brother Mendoza struggling under the weight of a heavy volume he was attempting to retrieve from inside the *armadio.*" He gestured vaguely to the upper shelves of the massive cabinet while holding the cardinal's gaze. "The effort got the better of him, I'm afraid, so I took him back to his apartment to rest. I simply came back to straighten up the room and secure the door."

Dante's tense, volatile countenance gave way by degrees to restrained irritation. His eyes bore into Dominic's, searching for the slightest glimmer of deceit. Finding none, he looked around the room for the first time since entering, surveying the strewn disorder with obvious repugnance. Dominic continued to gather the beribboned packets and loose parchments while Dante slowly walked around the chamber, gauging his own version of reality.

"Ah, yes. Mendoza's condition," he mumbled

with little trace of concern. "Are you aware, Father Dominic, that no one is permitted in the Riserva outside the presence of the prefect?"

"I *was* asked by—" Dominic began, only to be cut off again.

"Whether you knew or not is really beside the point, and polishing your apology will not help. Pick up these materials at once, then leave the room. I'll return Brother Mendoza's key to him myself, if you please." Dante held out his hand expectantly. Dominic produced the brass key, but instead of placing it in the man's hand, he simply extended his own, deliberately holding it in mid-air for the cardinal to take hold of. It was a momentary test of wills, and they both knew it, but Dominic had decided long ago he would give people an opportunity to meet him half-way. Still holding his eyes, Dante reached for the key, his thin, dry lips forming the crack of a smile.

"You are a bright but willful young man, *Mister* Dominic," Dante began quietly, emphasizing the plebeian form of address given to novitiates before ordination. "But," he continued, "do not for a moment presume that your relationship with Cardinal Petrini will excuse you from the rules that exist within these walls. Far more capable men than you have tried and failed—the evidence of their collapse is all around you." Dante's arms rose and flourished, as if the whole of the room's contents were testimony to his statement. The irony was not lost on Dominic.

"Now, let's get this mess cleared up so you can get on with your duties." Dante stepped back toward the door but remained at its threshold, carefully observing Dominic but with no intention of assisting him, the *"let's"* part of his remark clearly rhetorical.

On cue, Dominic went back to restoring the dispersed parchments to their leather case, careful not to expose the hidden compartment to the cardinal's field of view, then returned the heavy volume to its original position high inside the *armadio*. Picking up the broken table leg, he glanced at Dante with a slight awkwardness, then laid the wooden brace next to what remained of the table and started toward the door.

The cardinal, however, held his ground, blocking the exit. It brought to mind Dominic's first meeting with this insolent man. The subtle menace in Dante's voice had returned.

"Do we have an understanding, Father Dominic?"

The younger man found himself physically at odds with the moment. His reflexive response—not to mention the rekindled heat around his collar—willed him to push his oppressor up against the wall. Wisdom, however, cautioned against creating a situation that might reflect poorly on Cardinal Petrini, his own career notwithstanding. He considered his words carefully.

"Of course, Your Eminence," Dominic began, his dark eyebrows furrowing the center of his forehead. "With your consent, I'll go check on Brother Mendoza and inform him of our meeting."

A perceptible sneer spread across Dante's angular face. The cardinal stepped aside, the rustle of his red-trimmed cassock and the jangle of the chained pectoral cross encircling his neck echoing in the cramped chamber.

Dominic walked past the man without looking at him. Stepping into the darkness of the Gallery, he felt the burn of Dante's gaze on his back as moving pools of dim amber light guided him to the distant elevator.

7

Back in his apartment at Santa Marta, Dominic locked the door, slid on his cloth gloves, then pulled out the concealed packet of two small folded documents from the inside breast pocket of his cassock and gently laid them out on the small table next to his bed, switching on the reading lamp.

Torn between his slight guilt at having removed these from the Riserva and the greater pleasure of having discovered hidden papers that, with some likelihood, might not have been seen by anyone in several hundred years, he broke the wax seal and gently unwrapped the purple satin ribbon, his hands trembling with eagerness.

Unfolding the first document, written on parchment in what appeared to be late medieval French cursive, Dominic began reading.

Un fléau charnel fend le siège épiscopal,
Un ciel noir pleut à travers les frontières:
La tache du péché abondante,
Déchirant les fidèles qui gémissent.

From the drawer beneath the table he pulled

out his notebook, roughly translating each sentence as he read:

A carnal blight cleaves the See,
Black skies rain across borders:
The stain of sin abundant,
Tearing asunder the faithful, who wail.

He stared at the obscure four lines, finding no particular meaning at first. There *was* something here, though… he just couldn't place it. Moving on, he translated the other two verses.

In the thirteenth year of a century new,
The vicar shall withdraw:
And in his shadow will come
A sovereign hewn from silver.

The Albigensian truth is summoned,
As the final shepherd of Rome flees:
Mother sacred breathes her last,
The flock wanders in the gloaming.

Why do these feel so familiar? Dominic mused, his eyes playing over the verses as if to conjure some significance out of what seemed to be gibberish. It wasn't so much the words themselves as their cadence. Almost as if he'd read them before.

Turning the document over he noticed an integral leaf folded against the back of the manuscript, on which was penned a large bold signature next to a date: *Michele de Nostredame – 2 Mars 1566.*

Nostradamus? Original quatrains handwritten by Nostradamus?!

Dominic's pulse quickened as he considered what lay before him. The sixteenth century French astrologer and renowned seer had fostered close ties with the Church in Rome, that much he was familiar with, but of the man himself Dominic knew little. The date of March 1566 put this during the mid-Renaissance, a period in which astronomy and astrology were both widely accepted as valid scientific pursuits, especially among Church leaders intent on keeping a tight leash over their flock. Pope Paul III, among Nostradamus's high-profile benefactors at the time, was obsessed with astrology, as were several popes long before and after Paul's papacy. But it was also around that time, the late 1500s, when the Church began to separate the two disciplines, distancing itself from astrology and alchemy as having heretical leanings, with unfortunate timing that Galileo—an astrologer in his earlier years—would come to experience firsthand.

Now aware of their authorship, Dominic recognized why these verses were so familiar.

Nostradamus's poetic quatrains were crafted with a typical coded ambiguity, chiefly to evade close scrutiny by Church authorities seeking to root out heretics of the faith.

Putting the parchment aside, Dominic perused the second document, this one a more recent handwritten letter on a small sheet of ivory classic laid paper. It was addressed to Cardinal Mariano Rampolla, Vatican Secretary of State to Pope Leo XIII, and was dated 12 June 1902. The writer was one Abbé Bérenger Saunière from a French village called Rennes-le-Château. Dominic glanced over the letter quickly, translating as he read. It appeared to be a request for a tranche of outstanding payments due some several months prior, relating to "our matter of special importance to the Holy Mother Church."

Curious, he thought. What 'matter of special importance' would the Vatican be making payments for?

The fact that both documents were found together, hidden in the false bottom of a box made to appear as a book, was more than puzzling.

Though captivated by his discovery, Dominic had little time to deal with it now, since he told Dante he would check on Mendoza's condition.

He spread out the two documents on the table, reversing the folds so each laid as flat as possible, then reached for his iPhone, opened a digital scanning app, and photographed both sides of each page for automatic upload to the cloud, along with his handwritten translations. He would review both again later. Gathering up the papers and returning them to his pocket, Dominic left his room and set out for the prefect's apartment.

Apparently recovered from his earlier exertion, Calvino Mendoza now stood at the entrance to his office chatting with a tall man wearing a black cassock with a scarlet fascia and black shoulder cape with red piping—the distinctive garb of a cardinal—whose back was to Dominic as he approached the two men.

As Dominic drew near, Mendoza extended a welcoming arm. "Ah, Miguel, of course you know Cardinal Petrini...."

Enrico Petrini turned to Dominic, a broad smile creasing his face as he reached out to embrace his protégé.

"Your Eminence!" Dominic beamed, clearly surprised. "It's so good to see you. When did you arrive?"

"I flew in from New York just yesterday, last night in fact, on a red eye," Petrini said, his weary face revealing the effects of a long trip. "How's your work here going, Michael?"

For a man of his age, Petrini was remarkably fit, a neatly-trimmed beard of pure white paired with a shock of matching hair falling beneath a red skull cap. Possessed of a natural leadership aura, Petrini had earned the respect of nearly everyone he encountered, a notable attribution in a domain where gossip and backbiting were standard practice. Throughout the Vatican, Petrini was known as a capable arbiter, someone uniformly approachable and engaging, dispensing seasoned advice when and where needed, which was one reason the pope valued him as a member of his inner circle.

"I couldn't wish for more," Dominic obliged. "Being here, at the center of the medieval world's finest art and manuscripts, is a dream come true. I'm more grateful than I can express."

Still buzzing from his encounter with the Nostradamus manuscript and the Saunière letter, Dominic had a thought. "There *is* something I'd like to discuss when you have some free time, though."

Petrini arched an eyebrow, intrigued. "I'm settling into Domus Santa Marta for the week, and I do have several meetings while I'm here, but we'll find time, Michael. Perhaps dinner tomorrow?"

"Perfect. See you then, Eminence."

Petrini excused himself and walked off toward

the Apostolic Palace.

"How are you feeling, Cal?" Dominic inquired of Mendoza. "Better now, I hope?"

"Oh, Miguel, I'm fine, really. Some of these volumes are impossible for me to manage. I should have avoided such an ill-considered task without your help," he said sheepishly.

Mendoza then looked around, alert to the presence of anyone nearby. "Dante returned my key to the Riserva, by the way, with a brief lecture on my allowing your being there unaccompanied," Mendoza lamented. "We are so short-staffed, and since you were brought in to assist me, I'm going to try to get you full access. Pray my plan works, Miguel. We must still finish our work there."

Dominic paled as he was reminded of the broken table. "I should mention, Cal, that I was so engrossed in something I was reading that the table in the Riserva collapsed under me when my leg fell asleep. It does need a bit of repair now," he confessed.

Unconcerned about Dominic's curiosity, Mendoza waved it off. "That table, indeed much of the furniture here, has seen too many years of use. I'll have one of the *sampietrini* attend to it this afternoon," Mendoza said airily. "Shall we meet there again in the morning?"

"Sure," Dominic replied. "Say ten o'clock?"

8

Business was brisk at the Pergamino Caffè after Dominic's run the next morning. The air in the crowded room was rich with the aroma of roasted coffee beans as Signora Palazzolo steamed espressos for the chattering gaggle of patrons queued up at the bar. While Dominic savored the welcome iciness of a *caffè freddo,* his mind turned to the letter he'd found by Bérenger Saunière the day before.

Opening the browser on his phone, he did a search on "Berenger Sauniere" to learn more about the man, finding with some surprise that he'd earned a fairly detailed listing on Wikipedia. Dominic skimmed the page—then stopped cold when his eye caught an astonishing entry toward the end:

> **François-Bérenger Saunière** (11 April 1852 – 22 January 1917) was a Roman Catholic priest in the French village of Rennes-le-Château... He would be virtually unknown today if not for the fact that he is a central figure in many of the conspiracy theories surrounding Rennes-le-Château...

> Saunière built a grand estate between the years 1898–1905 that also involved buying several plots of land. This included the Renaissance-style Villa Bethania, the Tour Magdala (that he used as his personal library) connected to an orangery by a belvedere with rooms underneath, a garden with a pool… all in the name of his maidservant, Marie Dénarnaud… Saunière's renovation of his church and ostentatious construction in a small hilltop village attracted hostile reactions, with complaints passed on by various sources to the Bishopric of Carcassonne, who had warned Saunière about his selling of Masses… ***The controversy around Saunière originally centered on parchments that he is said to have found hidden in the old altar of his church… and that this was the theoretical source of his income… speculation that Saunière engaged in financial transactions… and his income could have originated from the Vatican "which might have been subjected to high-level political blackmail….*"

Despite the heat of the room, Dominic shivered as a chill gripped the back of his neck. Had he discovered proof of the blackmail Saunière was suspected of? What about those parchments the priest had found in his church altar, and where were they now? And what could be so damning that the Vatican might pay off a simple French cleric to avoid having it disclosed?

If any of this were even remotely possible, the implications could be staggering. Finding the facts might be no easy matter, but the attraction of such a pursuit fueled Dominic's imagination. There was no way he *couldn't* look into it further. He needed to speak with someone about this. But who? He would start with Petrini at dinner tonight.

After changing into his cassock in the restroom, Dominic thanked the signora, then stepped out into the morning heat and made his way to Saint Anne's Gate.

After stopping by his apartment to retrieve the documents he had discovered earlier, Dominic headed down to the Riserva to meet Mendoza. It was ten o'clock sharp when he entered the open room, finding the monk sitting at the reading table, now gratefully repaired, waiting for Dominic to fetch the same large volume he had attempted the day before.

"Good morning, Miguel," Mendoza said cheerfully. "How was your run this morning?"

"Terrific, Cal, and now I'm ready for the day.

What's on our agenda this morning?"

"If you'll be so kind as to hand me the large portfolio that nearly put me in the hospital yesterday," Mendoza said with an exaggerated sigh.

Dominic opened the heavy *armadio* and pulled the stepladder over. As he mounted the steps, he furtively reached inside his cassock, removed the packet of documents he'd secreted there, and with Mendoza's back conveniently turned to him, lifted the lid of the box, quickly tilted the false bottom and tucked the papers inside their original hiding place. He then seated the bottom flush, closed the book and pulled it down from the high shelf where it rested, all in one graceful action cloaked by the long drape of his cassock. Descending the stepladder, he set the book on the table.

"Miguel, you should also find up there a volume marked '*Papa Gregorius VII*' with register indexing on the spine; please bring that down as well. Cardinal Dante needs references from Pope Gregory for a papal encyclical he's working on for His Holiness, something to do with adherence to vows and asserting the preeminence of the papal office—as if we don't have enough of that already."

Back up on the stepladder, Dominic searched among the remaining books and, finding the desired codex, hefted it out from the shelf and stepped down, setting it next to the previous volume.

As Mendoza pawed through the loose documents inside the book box, apparently searching for something in particular, Dominic held his breath, hoping the monk wouldn't discover the false bottom.

"Ah, here it is," Mendoza said with some satisfaction. "Feast your eyes on this, Miguel."

Mendoza gently unfolded a yellowed papyrus beautifully illuminated with gigantic red initials and colorful illustrated marginalia featuring regally dressed bishops and playful cherubs, all as bright as the day they were drawn 800 years earlier. Dominic decided not to mention he'd seen it before, right before breaking the table at which they sat.

"This is one of the great registers of Pope Innocent III documenting the Fourth Crusade of just a few years earlier, which began in 1202. The pope ordered an armed expedition in efforts to recapture the city of Jerusalem which, at the time, was held by the Muslims. As you may recall, that crusade solidified the Great Schism between the Catholic Church and Eastern Orthodox Churches.

"Miguel, would you please take this up to one of our patrons? It was requested by Dr. Simon Ginzberg, a scholar in the truest sense and an old friend of the Archives. He knows the rules. You should find him in the Pio XI Reading Room, adjacent to the Index Room.

"I'll be leaving shortly myself," Mendoza added, "since I found what Dante needs. If you don't mind, we'll leave these books on the table and attend to them later. I've learned my lesson."

9

Having made his way back through the Gallery of the Metallic Shelves and up the elevator, Dominic headed for the reading rooms. He chose to take the scenic route through the Vatican museums, up the *Sala degli Animali* containing scores of sculpted stone creatures great and small, with majestic fourth-century mosaics peering down over the scenes of fauna throughout the gallery.

The next section, the *Sala Delle Muse,* featured the famed Torso Belvedere, a spectacular fragmented first-century Greek sculpture of a muscular young male, on which Michelangelo based his masculine nudes in the Sistine Chapel. Though this was now his place of work, Dominic felt like any other tourist walking through the world's most valuable collection of historical artworks, his eyes and mind completely taken in by the countless splendors.

Eventually he came to the Apostolic Library and the special rooms set aside for scholarly research. The Pius XI Reading Room was a quiet enclave for accredited visitors overlooking the hushed tranquility of the *Cortile della Biblioteca,* one of the several outdoor courtyards available for secluded meditation in the Vatican Museum complex.

Dominic asked Sister Odette, the nun at the reception desk, where he might find a patron named Simon Ginzberg. There were few visitors in the room, but the polite nun pointed out a short, thin man looking to be in his twilight years, with a mop of gray hair and a neatly trimmed Van Dyke framing a deeply weathered face, sitting at one of the reading tables engrossed in a manuscript. Dominic approached the man.

"Dr. Ginzberg, I presume?"

The old man looked up, blinking at the interruption from his work.

"Yes, I am Ginzberg," the man replied with a heavy Middle Eastern accent. "And you are…?"

"My name is Father Dominic. Brother Mendoza asked that I deliver you the Pope Innocent III register." He laid the parchment on the table and began to turn away.

"A moment please, Father Dominic," Ginzberg said. "I don't recognize you. Are you one of the new carrier pigeons under Mendoza's care?"

Dominic chuffed a muted laugh, turning back to respond.

"I suppose I am," he said smiling. "And might I assume you're among the valued treasures the

Vatican maintains here?"

"Hah! Touché, my friend, a worthy rejoinder." Ginzberg held out his hand. "Please, call me Simon."

"Michael," Dominic said as he shook the man's hand. "May I join you for a moment?"

"Of course, I'd love the company." Ginzberg took off his glasses and rubbed his eyes. "So, this is the tale of the Fourth Crusade, is it?"

"Part of it, anyway," Dominic said. "I expect there are other registers, but Brother Mendoza felt this was what you had asked for."

"I'm sure it is, then," Ginzberg replied. "So, Michael, how long have you been here? What do you think of all this?"

Dominic's eyes widened as he pursed his lips and drew in a breath. "It's all pretty overwhelming, I have to say. I've only been here a couple of weeks, and I'm fairly inundated by the sensory overload. My specialties are medieval paleography and codicology. And I'm also assisting with the digitization of the Secret Archives."

Ginzberg's face screwed up at the mention of technology. "Ah, a waste of time, if you ask me," he said. "I do use text and email, of course, dreadful necessities these days. But I prefer the smell of history, the touch and feel of ancient papers, the physical presence of all that my research entails. To handle the original books and manuscripts prepared eons ago by scribes using feather quills, with native pigments and dyes for ink, is an incomparable experience. You simply cannot get that kind of palpable sensation from a computerized data file, not at all."

"I can't argue with you there," Dominic said. "But from what I understand, thousands of people each year are turned away from accessing the Archives, if not for lack of accreditation, then for scarcity of space and assistance, given our small staff."

"I see your point, of course, Michael. I am only too grateful for the privileges extended to me here, and I intend to keep at it. I've been in this very room for so many years now I do feel, as you implied, like one of the splendid sculptures that grace the Vatican halls."

"What is the nature of your research, if you don't mind my asking?" Dominic inquired.

"I don't mind at all. At present I have two tracks of interest, both for papers I'm writing as professor emeritus for Teller University in Zagarolo, just outside of Rome. What occupies my work today is, as you have seen, the Fourth Crusade and the impact of Muslim and Christian occupations of Jerusalem, a city sacred to Jews as well. This is mostly a personal quest, as I maintain a fascination with the crusades in general.

"My primary scope of interest, however, and the area I am most deeply involved with now, is better understanding the Vatican's complacency during the Holocaust, and in particular the role of Pius XII in collaborating with the Nazis. I have a deeply personal stake in this matter, Michael, as a survivor of Dachau myself. I was but a small child at the time, of course, but I watched as my mother and father suffered all manner of torture. I will never forget the smell of the smoke of my parents coming from the crematoriums after being gassed. No, a child does not forget these things." The old man's eyes glistened as he recalled morbid memories still vivid.

"I'm so sorry, Simon," Dominic offered, as he suddenly felt his own eyes sting with empathy. "I can't imagine how you've dealt with such a tragedy."

"Pius XII has had many apologists over the years," Ginzberg said, returning to his original subject. "Even today he has staunch defenders pushing for sainthood. But he has yet much to answer for in decisions made in the name of the Church. With sixteen million pages of Pius's historical record having just been released to researchers, I think I'll be here for some time yet."

Dominic rose from his seat and placed a hand on Ginzberg's shoulder. "Simon, if there's anything I can do to help you in this matter, please, just ask."

"Oh, I'm sure we'll be seeing much of each other, Michael. And if I can be of service to you, you know where to find me."

Dominic returned to the reception desk and made a routine notation in the Admissions log of which document he had delivered to Ginzberg. Looking back at the old man—sitting there, alone, searching for answers—Dominic's stomach clenched as he considered what was at stake for each of them. For Simon, it was clearly a form of closure on a dark and painful personal journey. For himself, his own work ahead took on new dimensions as he saw, through Simon's eyes, the personal impact past decisions can inflict on real lives. Whatever it was he had yet to discover, others could be deeply affected by it. Just who and how remained to be seen.

Turning to leave the reading room, Dominic made his way to the Vatican employees' canteen where he had arranged to have lunch with his new friend Karl Dengler.

The young Swiss Guard was seated at a long family-style table near the window when Dominic entered the noisy room. After exchanging greetings, they queued up in the cafeteria line, chose meals of pasta, baked cod and grilled zucchini, and returned to the table.

"Tell me, Karl," Dominic said, "what is it like for you being in the Swiss Guard?"

Dengler sat up a little taller, proud to have been asked the question. "It is a great honor. Very few who apply are selected. Each of us must have served in the Swiss military—I was a member of the Mountain Grenadiers, the equivalent of what you would know as U.S. Navy SEALs—and we go through extensive combat and arms training. As a Pikeman, my job is to protect the Holy Father at any cost, as my countrymen have done for hundreds of years before me."

"So you actually carry weapons while on duty?" Dominic asked.

Dengler looked warily around the room, then pulled back the cape covering his blue doublet, revealing a Sig Sauer P220 semi-automatic pistol in a shoulder holster.

"It is on me at all times while on duty," he said soberly.

Impressed, Dominic looked in the young Guard's blue eyes. "We'll have to stay good friends, then."

Dengler laughed, then turned the questioning to Dominic. "I'm curious, Michael," he said. "As a young man yourself, do you find it difficult being a priest in terms of, well, sexual relationships? Surely many must find you attractive?"

Having been asked this many times before, Dominic had given much thought to his response. "Of course it's a challenge, Karl. I think I might have made a good husband and father, since I understand love and sacrifice and responsibility. But I didn't grow up in much of a traditional family, so I didn't envision that for my future. I've always enjoyed my solitude and know that being alone is not the same as being lonely. The Jesuit life appealed to me immensely in terms of the order's dedication to knowledge and scholarship.

"And yes, many have tried and failed to defrock me," he continued, a shy smile forming, "and I mean that in both ways. I'm still a man, obviously, and can appreciate beauty in all forms. Though I do think enforced celibacy these days is anachronistic and prevents many men from joining the priesthood, I did take the vow myself, and feel I need to remain true to that."

Dengler was noticeably inspired by Dominic's answer. "You're a stronger man than I am, Michael. And a most impressive one. I appreciate your candor.

"Say," Dengler added, quickly changing the subject." Are you planning to see the *Festa de' Noantri* this weekend? It's one of the oldest traditions in Rome, and my parents insisted I see it and send them photos. You're welcome to join."

"I hadn't heard about it," Dominic said.

"It is a tribute to the Virgin, with a parade that carries her statue to the church of San Crisogno. Street vendors, dancing and music all join in with the procession."

"Sure, it sounds interesting. Are you going alone?"

"No, my cousin Hana will be visiting, so we've made plans to take in the event. She's a reporter for *Le Monde.* I think you'll find her good company, Michael. Like you, she is very smart. She and her grandfather, my great-uncle Armand, are flying in tonight."

Dominic laughed. "Well, you give me too much credit, but I'd love to meet your cousin and take in the sights with you."

"The procession starts on Saturday at 6:00 p.m. in the Trastevere," Dengler said. "We'll meet at five o'clock and walk there from Saint Peter's Square.

"But for now," he said, looking at the clock on the wall, "I must go back to my duties at the gate. *Ciao*, Michael."

10

The gleaming white Dassault Falcon 900 lifted off smoothly from Paris–Le Bourget Airport, destined for Ciampino Airport in Rome, a comfortable two-hour flight.

"Would you care for a glass of champagne, baron?" the steward asked.

Armand de Saint-Clair looked up as he folded the business section of *Le Monde* in his lap. "Yes, thank you, Frederic."

"And you, Miss Sinclair? Anything I can get for you?"

Saint-Clair bristled at the use of his granddaughter's anglicized name, as he had since she recently adopted it. For her, the reason was simple. More often than not, doors were open to Hana that had less to do with personal achievement and more to do with the influence of the noble European dynasty into which she was born. Adapting her professional name from Saint-Clair to Sinclair was, for her, a liberating action, unburdened by her family's deep historical connections to many of the political events of the day and perception by her peers that a privileged life gave her certain advantages.

"No, Frederic, I'm fine for now," Hana replied, noting her grandfather's discomfort.

Sitting opposite the old man, the two of them alone in the spacious cabin except for the crew, Hana was grateful for this rare captive audience. As she formulated her thoughts and how best to present them, she looked out the window as the jet turned to the southeast, banking high over the City of Light, the Eiffel Tower casting a long shadow beneath the late afternoon sun.

"President Valois sends his best, Grand-père," Hana began. "Did you know I met with him yesterday?"

"Oh really, my dear?" Saint-Clair said, with a hint of derision. "And do you think any other reporter not having your family's name would have had the advantage of arranging such a meeting?"

"Oh please, Pépé, let's not go into this again. You know I'm proud of my family, but there are times when I find the name professionally cumbersome. I want my achievements measured on their own merits, not on the basis of influence or intimidation.

"As for my *parrain,*" she affirmed with satisfaction, "he's always insisted I treat him as family, which I do."

Saint-Clair sighed, knowing this was an argument he would not win. Like her late mother, his beloved granddaughter was headstrong, and little would change her mind once it was fastened on such ambitions.

"So, what business might Pierre have helped you with?" he inquired.

Hana responded as she withdrew the packet of photos from her valise and set them beneath her folded hands. "My assignment is a series regarding the depth of France's complicity with the Nazis during the war, especially as it dealt with the plunder of Jewish assets. The American CIA and Britain's MI6 have recently declassified documents describing the actions of French authorities in the arrest of some 13,000 French Jews—of which 4,000 were children, Pépé—and deporting them to Auschwitz. That was just a two-day sweep in Paris alone, but altogether over 76,000 French Jews suffered the same terrible fate."

Saint-Clair listened intently, surprised by the newly released numbers but not by the actions themselves, given the Nazi's occupation of France and its puppet Vichy government nominally ruling the country at the time.

"In the process," she continued, "some 80,000 Jewish bank accounts in France were frozen. Less than 3,000 of the Jews arrested survived the camps, and of the remaining 77,000 accounts, relatives of murdered Jews were unable to claim their families' assets, since they could not possibly furnish required death certificates, an impossibility for obvious reasons.

"And the Swiss, as you know, were hardly neutral in these actions," she said, her voice tinged with anger as she shifted nervously in her seat. "German banks coordinated plans to launder billions of U.S. dollars in gold confiscated from the central banks of occupied European countries—including literally tons of tooth fillings and jewelry extracted from the corpses of Holocaust victims—all of which conveniently found its way into Switzerland, whose banks gladly acted as intermediaries by providing loans to the Nazis in exchange for melted gold. These 'courtesies' resulted in extending the war while ensuring that Switzerland was simply performing its duties as a 'neutral' banking capitol."

Hana's agitation had reached a peak. She pressed the call button. "Frederic," she said, as the steward approached, "I will take that champagne now."

Saint-Clair sat quietly, looking into his granddaughter's determined eyes as she spoke. "Hana," he began, "while I cannot answer to the actions of others, first let me assure you that Banque Suisse de Saint-Clair had no such dealings directly with compromised German banks, or indirectly through other institutions in

Switzerland or elsewhere. My father and I took great risks to avoid complicity with the Nazis, even in the face of Hitler's threatened retributions to those who failed to cooperate with his plans. These were perilous times for everyone, not just for Jews and other targeted groups, but also for governments large and small, and other business interests useful to the Third Reich. Switzerland paid a staggering moral price for its charade of neutrality, one that continues to affect how we do business today.

"Even the Vatican has an enormous burden to answer for," he continued. "As Germany began recognizing the war was in its final days, select high Nazi officials seeking freedom from prosecution handed over *half* of their assets—including loot stolen from their victims—to the Vatican Bank, in exchange for the promise of protection from arrest and legal action. We're talking here about the central core of Nazi leadership—names like Adolph Eichmann, Klaus Barbie, Eduard Roschmann, even Dr. Josef Mengele, the 'Angel of Death' at Auschwitz. The Vatican arranged for new identities and passports for those criminals and dozens more, along with guaranteed passage to safe havens like Argentina, Brazil, Australia, even the United States. Apart from those who committed suicide or faced trial at Nuremberg, many of the worst Nazis had escaped culpability for their unspeakable crimes during this terrible period."

Though she was aware of Pope Pius XII's apparent silence on the matter of the Holocaust during and after the war—while evidence of its consequences was exposed for all to see—Hana welcomed these new details as she scribbled notes in her slim steno pad. Then she slid the photographs across the burl wood conference table.

"I came across these photos from the archives in the Paris Bibliothèque. Since you and Pierre served together in the Maquis, do you recognize any of these men."

Saint-Clair took the photos, carefully examining each one as memories of his clandestine service in the French resistance peered back at him. When he came to the third photo, he pointed to one man—a tall fellow with a distinctive unibrow, and mesmerizing eyes set back over a pronounced nose.

"This man," he said. "He was our group leader, a brave young fighter who went by the code name 'Achille.'"

Hana's reaction was visceral, her face fused with elation and surprise. "Do you know his real name, Grand-père? That's the man I'm looking for."

Saint-Clair hesitated before answering. "I'm

afraid I couldn't say, my dear. It was our practice never to use actual names for fear of capture and interrogation. But as far as I know, Achille survived the war, though I couldn't possibly tell you where he might be now."

Hana reached for the photo. It was the same one Pierre Valois had paused over the day before. She looked closely at Achille's image, letting it linger in her memory.

Glancing up at her grandfather, she said, "Pierre looked at this same photo, and I was sure Achille caught his attention when he recognized him, but he feigned unfamiliarity. Why do you think that was?"

Saint-Clair was indifferent to the question, waving it off. "Perhaps he thought he might have recognized anyone in the image, but just not enough to mention it. This was so long ago now, and I'm not sure how it really matters. What is your real interest in this man?"

"In my research I found numerous references to Achille and his actions to track the flow of forfeited Jewish assets, while he helped save many lives. As with many experts reviewing that period, I suspect there are substantial gold reserves yet to be found in French and Swiss banks that should be returned to their rightful owners. These declassified reports make a strong case for it, and I think we can be of help in making the case for further investigation.

"Unfortunately, I am not alone in this quest," she added. "I happen to know another reporter, from *Le Figaro,* is also working his own investigation, so time is an issue. I must follow all the leads I can to break this story first—and do it quickly."

"Well, keep in mind the Vatican Bank has some involvement here, too," Saint-Clair said. "But you have a difficult job ahead of you, Hana. If you think Swiss banks might be a challenge, you'll get no cooperation at all from the Vatican, if not simply outright denial."

Her grandfather was right, of course. Banks like these were notoriously secretive in their dealings, and a reporter would be the last person they would open their books to. And the Vatican Bank itself was answerable to no government except its own. She would have to find another way.

The rest of the flight was spent in silence as Saint-Clair turned back to his newspaper and Hana reflected on her work in the days to come. She sat back in the leather seat and looked out the window. *Had he told me the truth about our family's involvement?* she wondered, doubts lingering in her mind. *All banks withered under Hitler's influence. How could his have been spared?*

Soon the jet began its descent, with the broad

expanse of city lights signaling their approach to Rome and, hopefully, some of the answers she was seeking.

As the jet taxied into a private hanger at Ciampino Airport, a white Mercedes S500 papal limousine, its engine idling, was waiting inside, its driver standing next to the open door. Armand de Saint-Clair and his granddaughter emerged from the plane as an attendant stored their luggage in the trunk of the car.

"My meeting tomorrow with His Holiness should only take an hour or so, Hana," the baron said as they entered the car. "Shall I text you when we're finishing up?"

"That's fine, Grand-père. I'm having lunch with cousin Karl. He's been with the Swiss Guard for just a few weeks now, so we'll have much to talk about, I'm sure. I'll give him your regards."

11

The lofty red brick archways inside the Ristorante dei Musei resembled the high-ceilinged galleries of the Vatican itself, apart from the white-clothed tables set with food and chattering patrons huddled beneath them at the dinner hour. Tourists, locals, clergy and nuns from around the world enjoyed Rome's traditional cuisine here, an easy stroll from Saint Peter's just north of the Vatican wall. The smells of freshly baked bread and simmering tomato sauce, potently infused with fresh garlic and basil, greet passersby and arriving guests even from across the street as they near the restaurant.

Father Michael Dominic and Cardinal Enrico Petrini were both dressed in street clothes so they might enjoy a conversation without drawing unwanted attention or recognition. Each ordered the pasta special along with shared servings of *antipasti* and *carciofini,* the small violet artichokes grown in Rome and bathed in peppered olive oil, with a bottle of Chianti Classico that Dominic hoped would fuel Petrini's favorable reception of what he was about to share. While the boisterous din of the restaurant made conversing difficult, it also served to prevent nearby tables from overhearing sensitive topics.

"Rico," Dominic began, "I've run across something I'd like to get your thoughts on. But first, let me give you some background." He told Petrini of his episode in the Riserva with Mendoza and helping him to his apartment, then going back to the vault where he spent some time exploring the papers in the box, as well as the table coming apart as he fell on it, and as a result finding the hidden bottom of the box and what it held. He then retrieved photos of the documents on his phone, showing them to Petrini as he discussed his translation of each one and his brief research on Bérenger Saunière.

The cardinal, intrigued enough to stop eating, refilled both their wine glasses before he turned to the images. He enlarged the documents on the phone to better inspect what Dominic had found.

"These are spectacular discoveries, Michael, especially the Nostradamus parchment. Quite rare indeed, I imagine. Have you shared these with anyone else yet?"

"No," Dominic said. "Just you."

Petrini looked squarely at his young ward. "Well, to be honest, I'm a little surprised by your audacity. The Riserva holds the most sensitive papers of the Vatican, and access is restricted for good reasons, I assume. Did you feel this was part of your duties, or was it just curiosity that took hold of you, in the moment?"

Dominic blushed with embarrassment at being called out. "I know, Rico, I probably overstepped my authority, such as it is, but I did return the documents the next day. And Brother Mendoza said he's going to give me my own key to the room, so…" He looked pleadingly at the cardinal.

Petrini took a sip of wine, weighing the situation.

"Alright. Since you asked for my advice, I'll give it to you. I can't say I know much about the quatrains, though they do merit further examination," he said. "But I do know something about Abbé Saunière and the mysteries of Rennes-le-Château. Apart from what you've read about him, there has been no shortage of speculation as to what exactly he found there.

"Some say Saunière discovered documents alluding to the location of the Holy Grail, or the Ark of the Covenant, the reputed treasure of the Cathars hidden during the Albigensian Crusade. Others have theorized the abbé found the treasure of the Knights Templar, or even Mary Magdalene's tomb and those of her Merovingian children. Many books have been written on these topics.

"But what you have here," Petrini whispered

eagerly, "Bérenger Saunière's own letter demanding payment from the Vatican! That would appear to support one of the other theories—that Saunière may have been blackmailing the Church in exchange for keeping secret whatever knowledge he had that might bring harm to the institution. It's said that he did come into a great deal of money for no other apparent reason, using the funds to restore his chapel and rectory and other buildings in the village. If that's the case, Michael, you may be dealing with something quite extraordinary here. Or, it could be as simple as an appeal to the pope for a continuing endowment."

Dominic nervously took back the phone and closed the photos app, pocketing the device. "What do you think I should do, Rico?"

"I'm not entirely sure," Petrini said, thrown off by what he had just read. He poured more wine and poked a fork at what remained of his pasta. "But there *is* someone here who is well acquainted with the Grail legends, and I wouldn't be surprised if he knew more about Nostradamus than I do. He's a respected scholar who can usually be found working on his research in the Archives, a good man named Simon Ginzberg. I have known him for many years and you can trust him."

"I just met him today!" Dominic said

excitedly. "We spoke only briefly, but I found him to be a fascinating character, well versed in history, not to mention his own."

Petrini's expression darkened and his voice lowered as he leaned into Dominic's ear. "Michael, I would caution you to take the utmost care with this information. Depending on Simon's analysis of what it might actually represent, it would be unwise to involve anyone else just yet."

Dominic met Petrini's eyes, nodding in understanding, his mind dizzy with anticipation, heartened by the effects of the Chianti.

After paying the bill, they walked back to Porta Sant'Anna, the heady scent of honeysuckle from the Vatican gardens permeating the warm evening air.

* * *

Early the next morning—before the sun came out in full, before tourists jammed the streets of Rome—Michael Dominic and Karl Dengler met in Saint Peter's Square for a long-planned run together.

Owing to the rigorous athletic regimen of his Papal Guard training, the tall blond Swiss soldier was exceptionally fit, easily able to keep up with the demanding pace of a lifelong runner like Dominic.

Their course started at the Ospedale Santo Spirito near Saint Peter's Square, then up to Castel Sant'Angelo, the towering cylindrical papal fortress east of the Vatican. As they ran northeast along the Tiber River, Dengler, ever curious, was full of questions.

"So, have you ever had a girlfriend, Michael, or anyone you've been especially close to?"

"I did have someone special before I entered the seminary, but when the time came, I broke it off, for obvious reasons. Why do you ask?"

"Was your 'someone special' a girl—or a guy?" Dengler asked.

Grinning awkwardly, Dominic turned to look at his friend as they crossed the bridge at Ponte Cavour. "It was a girl, actually."

"Have you ever been with a guy?" Dengler asked anxiously as he avoided eye contact.

"Well, yeah, sort of," Dominic said hesitantly. "I played lacrosse in high school and the team captain and I were close friends. Very close. I don't know that I'd call it 'experimental' or not, but we were young and had no limits then. He and I had an incredibly tight bond. I've never been as emotionally or physically drawn to anyone else like him. But to answer the question I think you're posing, if my life had taken another course, I'd say I'm straight. It's kind of a moot point now, though."

They ran in silence, each racing the other up the challenging hundred and thirty-eight Spanish Steps to the upper Piazza Trinita dei Monti, before Dengler spoke again, breathing heavily now as they paused to rest.

"I've never come out to anyone before, Michael," he said hesitantly, but bluntly. "You're the first."

Dominic looked at Dengler in a new light, half-expecting the confession. "Karl, I can't tell you how honored I am that you chose to tell me that. To be honest, I would never have thought you to be gay."

"Well, it's not like I'm a card-carrying member of the Lavender Mafia!" Dengler referred to the well-known 'gay lobby' establishment inside the Vatican. "The fact is, I've never been with anyone yet. There were probably opportunities when I was in the army, but I was pretty naïve then and fearful of the consequences. Now I'm 25, and probably too old!"

"Trust me, Karl," Dominic said with a gentle laugh, "a man like you will have no problem finding someone to love. I mean, look at you. You're quite a catch!"

Dengler was contemplative as they picked up their run again, heading toward the Roman Forum and the Colosseum. Soon, he found the words.

"If you were in my position, Michael, would

you find me attractive?" he said tentatively.

Dominic came to a slow stop. Standing in front of the splashing waters of the Trevi Fountain now, he looked gently into Dengler's questioning blue eyes. "Karl," he said softly, "if things were different, I'd be the luckiest guy in Italy to have you in that way." He gave his friend a tight embrace. "Just know there's someone out there for you. You'll find him."

Dengler, trying to remain composed while fending off emotion, hugged his friend fiercely in return.

"Come on," Dominic said cheerfully. "We've got another few miles yet. I want to show you the Suburra, my favorite place in Rome."

12

Simon Ginzberg was in his usual seat in the Pio XI Reading Room when Dominic approached him.

"Good morning, Simon," he said as he took a seat across from the man. "Have you got a few minutes?"

"Michael! Such a pleasure to see you again. Of course, what's on your mind?"

There were only a handful of other patrons in the room, each engrossed in their own work but none sitting close enough to overhear their conversation.

"I had dinner with Cardinal Petrini last night," Dominic said quietly, "and he thought you might be able to help me with a rather sensitive matter."

Intrigued, Ginzberg set down his pencil and folded his arms across his chest, leaning back in the wooden chair. "Petrini? Well, you have my full attention now," he said. "How is it that you know the good cardinal?"

"He's actually been like a father to me since I was born. My mother was his housekeeper when he was a parish priest in New York."

The old man reappraised Dominic, impressed that he was close to one of the more talked-about candidates to be the next pope. "Go on," he urged.

Dominic explained what he found as he had told it to Petrini.

"You certainly have been busy," Ginzberg said with a tone of admonition. "That was some risk you took, secreting those papers out of the Riserva."

Dominic rolled his eyes. "Yes, I got the same reaction from Cardinal Petrini. But the deed is done now, and I'm past the point of no return. Besides, as you'll see, these could have far-ranging implications. As a researcher yourself you must appreciate that."

Ginzberg tilted his head in acknowledgment. "Well, I do understand what drives curious men like us. So enough with the guilt. Let's see what you have."

Dominic called up the images on his phone and passed the device to Ginzberg so he could study the documents.

"These are a bit too small for me to examine properly. You don't have printed copies of them? Can we order the originals from the Archives?"

Dominic blanched at the thought. "I haven't even shared these with Brother Mendoza, and I returned them to the secret box when I had the first chance. Cardinal Petrini was adamant about discussing this only with you."

"I'll tell you what, Michael. Are you comfortable emailing these to me so I can better examine them when I get home? This," Ginzberg said, waving to the phone dismissively, "isn't the best way for me to give appropriate consideration to something you believe may have some importance attached to it. Would that be alright?" Ginzberg wrote down his email address on a sheet of paper and slid it across the table.

Dominic thought about Petrini's caution, then his words about Ginzberg: *You can trust him.* He entered the email address in his phone.

"As long as you keep this between us for now," he said, his brow furrowed with concern. "I don't yet know the implications these documents might have. But Petrini did see them, and I was advised to be discreet."

"My boy, I am the paragon of discretion when it comes to matters of historical importance, especially unvetted discoveries. Have no fear. We'll talk again tomorrow, once I see what you have."

From the open balcony on the floor above the reading room, Cardinal Dante, his arms rigidly crossed, looked down on the two men sitting at the table, observing the exchange. Aware of

Ginzberg's current undertaking—finding blame for the Church, and for Pius XII personally in regard to the atrocities of World War II—he would not be pleased if the scholar were being assisted by one of his own archivists in this matter. He made a mental note to monitor Dominic's activities.

13

Michael Dominic's cell phone vibrated in his pocket during his run through the Suburra the next morning. It was an incoming text message from Simon Ginzberg: **Meet me at Pergamino 0800**.

Perfect, Dominic thought. He was about ten minutes away from Pergamino Caffè, giving him time to cool down and change his clothes before the meeting.

Approaching the coffee shop early, Dominic was surprised to find that Ginzberg had already arrived and was sitting at a table on the sidewalk, deep in thought. After ordering his usual *caffè freddo* he nudged his way back out through the throng of patrons and took a chair opposite the old man. Simon's face was somber, he noted, looking somehow older than he did the day before.

"Well, Michael," he said pensively, "you've certainly come across something of striking interest here. I did not get much sleep last night after reading what you sent. I'm not even sure where to begin. How much do you know about Bérenger Saunière?"

"Not much, really, apart from what little I'd read on the internet and what Cardinal Petrini told me over dinner."

Staring into his coffee, Ginzberg took a deep breath and settled back into his chair. He closed his eyes as if to recall a memory, then began relating what he knew of the enigmatic history of the southern French settlement and its eccentric abbé.

"It all started in June of 1885…" he began. Dominic leaned forward, sipped his iced coffee, and listened intently as Ginzberg told the tale.

At the top of a steep mountain in the Languedoc region of France, between Montségur and Carcassonne, lies the tiny commune of Rennes-le-Château, an obscure but historically rich village at the base of the eastern Pyrenees.

The first day of June marked the arrival of Abbé Bérenger Saunière, the new village priest for the Church of St. Mary Magdalene, an ancient sanctuary consecrated in 1059 but whose Visigothic foundations dated from the sixth century.

A thousand years of weather and war had taken its toll on the run-down church, and the ambitious young priest set about on a modest restoration project that would span several years. With the help of his eighteen-year-old assistant and housekeeper, Marie Dénarnaud, Saunière began remodeling and reinforcing the structure where it was needed most, using a portion of the meager subsistence he received—an annual stipend of less than 60 francs, plus various small donations—to carry out his mission. Most men in their early thirties, especially those possessing the youth, handsome looks, and athletic vigor of Bérenger Saunière, might have quickly tired of the provincial existence such a poor outpost afforded them. But Saunière was born and raised in a village not far from Rennes-le-Château, and he was quite content to spend his time on such a worthwhile project in the familiar environs of his childhood.

In the early days of autumn, Saunière had commenced reconstruction work on the altar inside the church, and in the process, removed an altar stone straddling two ancient marble support columns from the Visigoth period. He was surprised to discover that one of the columns was partially hollow—but even more astonished when he found several cracked wooden tubes inside, each preserved with sealing wax. Carefully removing the wax seals, Saunière extracted several sturdy but aged parchment and papyrus scrolls. Two of the manuscripts were dated four hundred years apart, one from 1244 and the second dated 1644; both depicted ancestral lineage of some sort, genealogies extending back a thousand years or more. Two other documents, apparently composed in the late eighteenth century by an earlier abbé, appeared to contain a complex series of meaningless references—possibly codes or ciphers.

Excited by his discoveries, in March 1892 Saunière took the scrolls to eminent Church authorities in Paris, who then referred him to local specialists in ancient texts. The following three weeks changed Bérenger Saunière's life virtually overnight.

During his brief time in Paris, the simple village priest from Rennes-le-Château suddenly became a central figure among the city's social elite and its celebrated esoteric subculture. He was toasted by some of the most famous luminaries in Paris, including composer Claude Debussy, the opera singer Emma Calvé—even the French secretary of state for culture.

Little else is known of those three weeks in Paris, but shortly after returning to Rennes-le-Château, Saunière plunged into his restoration project with renewed vigor—only now there seemed to be no limit to his resources. He began spending extravagantly on village road improvements, a new tower for the church, a lavish house for his assistant Madame Dénarnaud, fabulous gardens, imported china, and more.

He began a puzzling but vigorous correspondence with many people in other countries throughout Europe, and entertained a diverse assortment of notable visitors in his humble French rectory—among them Archduke Johann von Habsburg, cousin of Austrian emperor Franz Josef. Later, the Archduke had unaccountably transferred substantial sums of money into Saunière's personal bank account.

The local bishop, alerted to Saunière's unusual largesse, demanded that the priest account for his newfound wealth or face charges of corruption, then suspended him when he refused. Saunière promptly appealed to the Vatican, and, astonishingly, was immediately vindicated of all charges and returned to lead his parish.

By the time of his death in 1917, Bérenger Saunière had spent tens of millions of francs on rebuilding his humble church and village. But his Last Will and Testament revealed that he was destitute. Just prior to his death, it was learned that Saunière had left everything he owned to his loyal housekeeper, Marie Dénarnaud.

For the next forty years, Marie lived a quiet but comfortable life, and made a promise that before her own death she would reveal a "secret" that would make its bearer not only rich but also powerful—the same secret Bérenger Saunière held which had made him an exceptionally wealthy man.

In 1953, however, Marie suffered a crippling stroke that left her incapable of speech or writing, and she died a few days afterward, presumably taking the secrets of Rennes-le-Château with her….

"It's quite possible, Michael," Ginzberg said, finishing his story, "that your letter may be connected to the considerable funding Saunière received from unknown sources. But to think he may have been blackmailing the Vatican is inconceivable! Still, many have tried for years to get to the bottom of what the abbé's secrets might have been—without apparent success—and that those in the Church might have been involved would not surprise me at all."

Engrossed in the story without having said a word, questions now swarmed through Dominic's mind—especially the last thing Ginzberg had mentioned.

"What did you mean by 'many have tried for years' to get to the bottom of this?" he asked. "Who, for instance?"

"The Nazis, for one," Ginzberg said without hesitation, prepared for the question. "Many of the highest officials of the Third Reich were deeply involved in the occult, and all manner of mystical practices. Adolf Hitler himself believed the roots of his Aryan master race stemmed from the ancient civilization of Atlantis. Joseph Goebbels was mesmerized by the prophecies of Nostradamus, convincing Hitler that the mystic astrologer had seen the defeat of the British in their coming war plans. By 1943, Nazi headquarters in Berlin even had some three thousand tarot card readers working on troop deployment strategies, hinging their own efforts on what the cards told them about Allied operations.

"Not only were the Allies aware of this, but Britain's MI6 actually hired teams of astrologers to work up Hitler's natal chart and submit reports to the war office, estimating how the Führer's own astrologers might be advising him in terms of tactical planning. It's even believed Churchill ordered that knowledge of the Nazis' occult interests be kept top secret, in the event criminals appearing before the Nuremberg trials be declared insane, thus escaping prosecution.

"But then we come to Heinrich Himmler," Ginzberg added, a far off look in his eyes. "Himmler had invested heavily in a peculiar mix of pseudo-science and the occult. As architect of the *Schutzstaffel*, or what was known as the SS, Himmler had accumulated unimaginable powers, and by 1944 nearly a million soldiers were placed under his command. But it was his determined ambition to possess the Holy Grail that brings him into our story.

"As a medievalist yourself, Michael, you're aware of the Knights Templar and the Cathars of southern France, yes?"

Dominic nodded mutely, entranced by Ginzberg's retelling of history.

"Well," the scholar continued, "in the thirteenth century the Cathars were reputed to be in possession of a great treasure. Many believe that to be the Holy Grail itself, or some variation of earthly riches and mystical knowledge of profound religious significance.

"It's also worth noting that the Cathars conferred great importance to the role of Mary Magdalene, certainly much more than the Church did. She was a prominent teacher in her time, which affirmed the Cathars' belief that women could serve equally as spiritual leaders. And though they venerated Jesus Christ, they flatly rejected the Resurrection, believing it to be more along the lines of reincarnation. One must assume they had some basis of understanding for taking these positions.

"When the Cathars were wiped out at the end of the Albigensian Crusade in the thirteenth century, several Cathar priest-soldiers known as *parfaits* descended in secret from their hilltop fortress at Montségur and are believed to have buried their treasure in one of the many nearby caves of the region.

"Indeed," Ginzberg continued, "the Grail legend has even been linked to the Nazis and Rennes-le-Château, which is only 30 miles from Montségur. The Nazi party held in high regard the disciplines of the Cathar movement: their sophisticated way of life, the stringency of their diet regimen and physical prowess, their innovative Gnostic beliefs—all elements of Nazi goals and aspirations toward the ideal Aryan race.

"During the Nazis' occupation of France, Reichsführer Heinrich Himmler sent an ambitious young SS lieutenant named Otto Rahn to the Languedoc region in a frenzied search for religious artifacts, first and foremost the Holy Grail. Rahn was a capable and published historian, deeply immersed in Wolfram von Eschenbach's *Parzival* legend, and spent several years exploring the whole region in and around those two key villages. Nazi soldiers who assisted in the excavations were even billeted at Villa Bethania in Rennes-le-Château, the lavish home Bérenger Saunière had built for his assistant Marie Dénarnaud, and where she lived for many years."

Dominic was overwhelmed with the rich and complex history that was somehow connected to the simple letter he had found. He glanced at this watch.

"Simon, I have so many questions now, but Brother Mendoza will be looking for me. Will you have more time this afternoon? I assume you'll be in the reading room?"

"Of course, Michael, my apologies for going on like this. Yes, find me this afternoon. There are a few more things I must yet explain."

The two men rose and shook hands. Dominic went inside to retrieve his cassock from Signora Palazzolo, changed, and left the café, his mind racing with theories.

14

Calvino Mendoza was standing impatiently at his desk when Dominic entered the prefect's office.

"Where *have* you been, Miguel? I've been looking for you all morning!"

"I'm really sorry, Cal. I bumped into Dr. Ginzberg at the Pergamino after my run, then lost track of time as we chatted over coffee. That guy sure has some interesting life stories."

"Yes, I'm sure he does," Mendoza said brusquely, a hint of jealousy in his tone. "Cardinal Dante asked about you earlier, by the way, wondering what you and Ginzberg might be up to."

Dominic groaned. *What is it with that guy?* "We aren't 'up to' anything, Cal. We just have mutual interests. So," he said, shifting the subject while clasping a hand on the monk's shoulder, "what is it I can do for you today?"

Mendoza, now slightly flushed, smirked and shook his head. "I told Dante you were doing some task for me this morning, and I didn't know anything about you and Ginzberg, which is the truth. It's not as if we have to punch time clocks around here. Oh, speaking of time—I've enrolled you in the Symposium on Medieval and Renaissance Studies in Paris next week. It's the place to be in our line of work, and they have an important workshop on digital codicology I want you to attend in my place. I've already booked your train passage." Mendoza handed him the tickets and the conference brochure. "I assume you have no other plans?"

"None at all!" Dominic said enthusiastically, eager for a road trip.

"Until then," Mendoza added, handing Dominic a stack of completed requisition forms, "here are the requested material lists for patrons in the Pio and Sisto reading rooms. They are waiting for them now."

Dominic took the requests, checked the locations of the needed documents in the index, and set about his work for the morning.

After he had retrieved and delivered all requisitioned materials to that morning's visiting patrons, Dominic found Simon Ginzberg sitting at his usual place in the Pio Reading Room.

"I've got a little break now, Simon, if it's a good time for you," he said, taking a chair opposite the man.

"Of course, Michael, this is as good a time as

any," Ginzberg said, setting aside the document he was working on. "There are two more things I wanted to pass on to you. I neglected to mention that Otto Rahn, the German archeologist, was believed to have discovered *something* of importance in the Languedoc, either at Montségur or Rennes-le-Château, but the identity of whatever he found was never revealed to anyone except Heinrich Himmler.

"Shortly afterward, Rahn, who was openly homosexual and never fully in line with the Nazi agenda, was assigned as a guard at Dachau in some form of punishment—yes, the same camp my parents and I were confined in, a repulsive coincidence. Anyway, at some point the Gestapo approached him and 'suggested' he commit suicide, supposedly as a consequence of his anti-Nazi behavior. He died in 1939, found frozen to death on a mountainside in Austria. Though his death was ruled a suicide, it's quite possible he was murdered by the Nazis for knowledge of what he had discovered. Himmler was fanatically secretive about his cultish museum of artifacts at Wewelsburg Castle, which is where Rahn's discovery was rumored to have been kept."

Ginzberg's rheumy eyes were now clear with conviction, obviously persuaded that Rahn's demise was not a suicide.

"I suggest you find a translation of

Eschenbach's *Parzival,* Michael. I recall it mentioning something about an '*unreachable castle*'—which could very likely allude to Montségur. There may be something more for you to find there, since *Parzival* was one of the chief motivations for Otto Rahn's own work," Ginzberg said.

"Secondly," he added, "as to your quatrains. These are most intriguing and, as you will find, more than mildly surprising. Nostradamus wrote in cryptic stanzas, leading people to believe his prophesies were the result of arcane wisdom delivered to him by higher powers. And who really knows, perhaps they were.

"But the fact is, he wrote in coded form mainly to evade the attention of the Church, which would brand him a magician or heretic, two sins warranting excommunication. Now, if I'm right in understanding the quatrains you found, they contain rather startling revelations which may have already come to pass."

Ginzberg had printed out the email Dominic had sent him, one quatrain per page, and laid out the first one in front of him:

A carnal blight cleaves the See,
Black skies rain across borders:
The stain of sin abundant,
Tearing asunder the faithful, who wail.

The old man's voice was nearly a whisper as he asked with a glint in his eyes, "So, Michael, does '*carnal blight*' bring anything to mind over the past two decades?"

Dominic hadn't given much thought to Nostradamus's words since finding the sixteenth-century parchment, but he now stared at the four lines before him, reading each one silently. '*The See*' seemed obvious, referring to the jurisdiction of the pope. But '*carnal blight*'?

Suddenly the answer to Ginzberg's prompting came to him like a bolt of lightning—*the sexual abuse scandals that publicly rocked the Church starting in the 1990s!*

"My God, I can't believe this!" he whispered back. "It's as clear as day to me now, if that's the assumed interpretation."

"Of course," Ginzberg replied, "there's no way of really *knowing,* apart from hypothesizing Nostradamus's meaning. But if history is any measure of his uncanny predictions, we may have further evidence here of truly prescient abilities.

"Now," he continued, "let's take a look at this second quatrain."

In the thirteenth year of a century new,
The vicar shall withdraw:
And in his shadow will come

A sovereign hewn from silver.

"I had some trouble with this one," Ginzberg admitted, removing his glasses to rub them clean with a handkerchief, "until I spent some time on that last line.

"You will, of course, recall that Pope Benedict retired in 2013—which could be referred to here as '*the thirteenth year of a century new*' and '*The vicar will withdraw.*' Yes? Well, it was the fourth verse I couldn't make sense of, until I realized that '*A sovereign hewn from silver*' might not mean a silver coin at all, which was the obvious first impression. So, when I took its alternate meaning in Italian, then put other factors in place, new significance began to emerge."

Words now tumbled out of Ginzberg's mouth as he tried to describe his methods.

"I realized the name *Argentina* is not etymologically Spanish, it's Italian, meaning, in its masculine form—*argentino*—'made of silver, or silver-colored.'"

Ginzberg paused a beat to let Dominic absorb this detail.

But the younger man wasn't following. "What does Argentina have to do with anything?" he asked.

"First consider what a sovereign is, if not in terms of coinage?" Ginzberg prompted.

Dominic thought a moment. "A king, or maybe the ruler of a nation?"

"And where does our current pope hail from?"

"Argentina...*No way!*" he nearly shouted. Other heads in the room turned in their direction to see what the commotion was, then went back to their work.

Ginzberg smiled, pleased with his companion's enlightenment.

Dominic was shaken by the implications. "So you're telling me Nostradamus predicted Benedict's retirement *and* Francis's ascension to the throne of Saint Peter?!"

"If we are to believe these interpretations, it would appear that Nostradamus had thus predicted two major historical events that have occurred in our own lifetime," he stated with satisfaction.

Dominic sat staring at Ginzberg, mesmerized by the revelations.

"This last quatrain, however, remains a mystery, although I have some suspicions as to what it may mean." Ginzberg laid out the third and final page.

The Albigensian truth is summoned,
As the final shepherd of Rome flees:
Mother sacred breathes her last,

The flock wanders in the gloaming.

"'*Albigensian*' obviously refers to the Cathars of southern France. As to their '*truth*,' one might assume that could have a bearing on their lost treasure—which isn't necessarily of a physical form, remember. It's also been suggested to be of profound spiritual magnitude." Ginzberg pointed to the second verse.

"The '*final shepherd of Rome*' seems to me to be quite specific, a reference to the last pope. In his 1139 book, '*The Prophesy of the Popes*,' Saint Malachy, the twelfth-century Irish archbishop, had laid out a set of predictions based on a vision he had when visiting Rome, claiming he had been given the names of 112 popes to be elected from that day forward, up until the very last pope to head the Church. He seems to have had some success with his prophesies up to and including Benedict XVI, who was identified as the 111th pope, and if the math is correct, either Francis is currently the 112th pope, or there is another yet to come—one identified as *Peter the Roman*. The final prediction is a bit unclear there."

Ginzberg searched for the Malachy document he had prepared among the papers on the table. Finding it, he laid it out for Dominic to read.

In the final persecution of the Holy Roman Church,

there will sit… Peter the Roman, who will pasture his sheep in many tribulations, and when these things are finished, the city of seven hills [Rome] will be destroyed, and the dreadful judge will judge his people. The End.

"This is the actual translation of Saint Malachy's prophesy," Ginzberg said, "which alludes to the final days of the Church of Rome, and indeed, the end of the world. But Nostradamus could not have seen Malachy's work since it was not published until 1595, and your document is dated 1566, so there seems to be some independent overlap here."

Ginzberg leaned back in his chair and stretched his arms. "The only thing I can make of this is that Malachy and Nostradamus, both seers of a sort, predicted the same event using different contexts. And in Nostradamus's case, it would seem to relate to whatever treasure the Cathars had hidden away.

"I do find it curious," he went on, "that these two documents, bound together and hidden in your secret false-bottom book, both appear to speak to apocalyptic events: Saunière's reference to possessing some knowledge of vital importance to the Church—essentially based on the events surrounding him and his proximity to the lost treasure of the Cathars—and Nostradamus's third quatrain here, preceded by two others that seem to hold some validity. It's quite a lot to ponder, isn't it?"

"Yes, it is. But why do you think they were hidden together?" Dominic asked. "Who would have even done that?"

"Well," Ginzberg said, pleased that Dominic had asked the question, "some four hundred years ago one of your predecessors here in the Secret Archives, an overly-vigilant archivist named Gonfalonieri, was known to have come across many provocative documents he believed might bring harm or embarrassment to the Church. Reluctant to destroy them given their historical importance, he simply bound the various documents and hid them away, or intentionally mislaid them, so as to prevent their being easily found. It's quite possible he, or someone else, secreted the Nostradamus parchment inside your book—though that doesn't explain Saunière's letter wrapped with it, which was written centuries later.

"So," Ginzberg smiled, "what we have here is the classic riddle, wrapped in a mystery, and literally hidden inside an enigma.

"The only thing that remains," he continued, "is to try to find out what Bérenger Saunière had in his possession for which the Vatican may have been paying hush money. And I expect you may find leads to that answer in the French National Library in Paris, where Saunière's documents have been archived."

Dominic's face lit up. "As it happens, Simon, I'll be in Paris next week for a symposium Mendoza asked me to attend."

"Marvelous! The French Bibliothèque is a wondrous place, Michael. I only wish I could go with you, but my work here is too pressing."

"Thanks for your help on all this, I really appreciate it," Dominic said. "I'm sure I'll see you before I leave next week."

As Dominic rose from the table and turned, he observed a tall, lanky priest standing behind him at the near end of the reading room, his long arms folded behind his back. The man was staring directly at him. Quickly averting the surprise eye contact with a bow of his head, the priest turned and walked to the door leading to the Vatican gardens. And then he was gone.

15

Cardinal Fabrizio Dante sat at an imposing 19th-century Tuscan walnut desk in the center of his opulent office quarters on the fourth floor of the Government Palace, the dome of Saint Peter's Basilica dominating the view outside his windows. A sprawling tapestry featuring the ancient Roman Senate in session hung on the wall behind him, and the inlaid dark crimson leather on his desktop was spare but for a few personal mementos and an amber Murano glass ashtray in the far corner.

Opposite him, in a guest chair fashioned like a throne, sat a tall, thin priest, his spindly arms crossed in front of him, a cigarette clenched between the bony fingers of his right hand.

"Both of them were having quite the animated discussion, Eminence," Father Bruno Vannucci said with a pronounced lisp that echoed off the walls in the tall-ceilinged room. He tapped an ash into the glass bowl. "I couldn't hear everything, but I did catch several names: Nostradamus, the German author Otto Rahn, and I believe I heard them discuss a place called Rainy Château, or something like that."

"Rennes-le-Château?" asked Dante, a single eyebrow arching with interest.

"Yes, that could have been it. Father Dominic seemed very excited by what Dr. Ginzberg was telling him, apparently associated with certain documents they were looking at. It was hard to make out much more. Oh, and Dominic mentioned he's going to Paris next week."

"I see. Alright, Father Vannucci. Thank you," Dante said, handing the priest a slip of paper. "Here is my private cell phone number. Do text me if you see or hear anything else."

"Of course, Your Eminence. Is there anything else I can do for you?"

"No, that will be all," Dante said as he waved him out.

Vannucci stubbed out his cigarette in the ashtray, fluttered a hand to disperse the lingering wisps of smoke, and smiled nervously at the cardinal as he turned and swept out of the room, gently shutting the door behind him.

Dante picked up the telephone receiver, punched in a series of thirteen numbers, and leaned back in his chair.

"*Gović*," said the answering voice with a heavy Slavic accent.

"Petrov, I may require your services. Can you be in Paris next week? Good. I'll be in touch."

16

The thunderous bells above Saint Peter's Square had just struck five o'clock when Michael Dominic spotted Karl Dengler sitting beneath Bernini's columns, engaged in animated discussion with an attractive woman seated next to him on the steps of the basilica. Seeing his friend approach, Dengler waved his arms as both he and the woman stood up.

"*Ciao*, Michael!" Dengler said, grinning as Dominic joined them. "This is my cousin, Hana Sinclair. Hana, this is Father Michael Dominic."

"Good to meet you, Father Dominic," Hana said as they shook hands.

"Please, it's just Michael when I'm wearing jeans."

Hana laughed, giving him an appraising look. "I'm sure you get this a lot, and I mean no disrespect, but in school we had a name for handsome priests like you: '*Father—*'"

"*—What-A-Waste?*" Dominic finished for her, rolling his eyes. "Yeah, I've heard that one before." Hana and Dengler laughed at the quip as Dominic, blushing, stood a little taller and ran a hand through his hair. "Trust me, it's more of a burden than a blessing."

Parting the sea of tourists around them in Saint Peter's Square, Dengler led the way as the three headed toward the Trastevere. The late afternoon warmth was more pleasant than tolerable, and as they walked in the shade of the trees lining the banks of the Tiber River, Hana and Dominic talked about their backgrounds while Dengler was busy with his camera, taking shots of anything and everything. As they entered the crowded area, Hana described the origins of the festival.

The annual *Festa de' Noantri* celebration, she explained, dated back to 1535 when local fishermen discovered a cedar statue of the Virgin Mary bobbing in the waters of the Tiber during a fierce storm. They donated the statue to the Church of Sant'Agata, where it remains venerated throughout the year, removed only for these week-long events in July. Bedecked in white finery, the statue of the Madonna Fiumarola is carried by a cortege of porters visiting all the churches lining the route of the procession, as well as by boat along the river where a small flotilla of watercraft reenacts the statue's discovery.

"The best place to see the river procession," Hana explained, "is on the Ponte Sisto, an ancient pedestrian bridge crossing the Tiber. There are lots of restaurants nearby so we can have a bite of dinner afterward."

Crowds of locals and tourists had already begun assembling on the Ponte Sisto when they arrived. Accustomed to the rigors of crowd control, Karl Dengler nudged his way through the throngs of people, forging a path for Hana and Dominic to a spot midway along the south side of the bridge, where they planted themselves for the events to come.

Mingling furtively among others in the crowd, Father Bruno Vannucci, also dressed in civilian clothes and wearing a Team Roma soccer cap, had discreetly followed them from Saint Peter's, staying close enough to hear their conversation while blending into the crowd around them.

"You seem to know a lot about Roman culture, Hana," Dominic said. "Have you spent much time here?"

"I was born and raised in Switzerland, but I lived here for five years when I was in boarding school at St. Stephen's. And my grandfather has been an informal advisor to many popes over the years, so I often join him on his trips to Rome. But these days my work keeps me mostly in Paris. In fact, I'm going back there next week to do some research at the Richelieu Library."

"There's a coincidence!" Dominic said. "I'm going to Paris next week by train for a symposium at the Park Hyatt Paris-Vendôme. And I, too, have some research I need to do at the Richelieu library."

Hana thought a moment, then said, "Listen, Michael, why don't you come back to Paris with me on our plane? It's much nicer than a 12-hour train trip, and it would be good to have the company. My grandfather is going on to Castel Gandolfo with His Holiness next week, so he won't need the jet."

"You have your own *jet?!*" he asked, clearly impressed.

"Well, it's his bank's, actually, but he won't mind our using it while he's away."

"That would be *great!* I'd love to take you up on it, thanks."

A flotilla of colorful boats, with the statue of the Madonna Fiumarola in the lead barge, was making its way toward the bridge while Dengler was occupied taking photographs of all the pageantry. Turning to Hana, Dominic asked if she knew anything about a little French village named Rennes-le-Château.

"Actually, I do. We have a large family that's spread out across Europe. My great-grandmother lived near Rennes-le-Château, in a historic town called Carcassonne, and I visited her there in summers when I was younger. There's a lot of history in that part of France, and a number of mysteries tied to Rennes-le-Château in particular. I sort of grew up on the legends."

"So you must know about Bérenger Saunière!" Dominic said eagerly.

"Of course. Saunière practically drives the whole tourist industry there by himself, or in his memory, anyway. Why?"

Dominic thought carefully about whether he should reveal the contents of the abbé's letter, and of Simon Ginzberg's analysis.

"How about I tell you more on our way to Paris? It may be rather sensitive, so this will be off the record. Are you okay with that?"

"Sure, Michael, off the record it is. If a Vatican scholar of your caliber is researching Bérenger Saunière and it's sensitive, well, you have my interest."

After taking in a bit more of the parade, Dengler, Hana, and Dominic walked into town and settled themselves in a pizzeria off the Ponte Sisto.

Bruno Vannucci, thinking he might be recognized by Dominic in the close confines of a *trattoria,* stayed on the bridge while texting a brief report of what he'd heard back to Dante. The adrenaline rush of his spy mission for the cardinal dissipated, he slipped into the nearby Garbo Bar for a beer to cool off from the evening's warmth before heading back to the Vatican.

17

Croatian Special Liaison Petrov Gović sat in his office at Interpol headquarters in Lyon, France, sifting through a stack of Blue Notices targeting suspected Serbian and Croatian nationals involved in potential terror threats for which the agency had been alerted. Distinguished from Red Notices, which sought the arrest of certain individuals for specific crimes, a Blue Notice served to identify and locate certain subjects, making them susceptible to surveillance for any purpose a member nation requested, though usually connected with a criminal investigation.

As he studied the reports, Petrov smiled at the irony. He unconsciously rubbed the band on his right ring finger, smoothing his thumb over the skull that emblazoned the modified SS-Ehrenring—the mystical Death's Head Ring. Cryptically fashioned with a modified steganographic swastika and symbolic runes, it signified his membership as a faithful servant of one of the very organizations that Interpol sought to identify from its Blue Notices.

In a recently published report, the Council of

Europe had expressed alarm over looming extremism by neo-fascist groups linked to the Ustasha, the Croatian ultranationalist puppet government originally formed in league with the Nazis during World War II. While the Ustasha had supposedly melted away after the war ended, authorities in Balkan states were now troubled by the specter of its possible resurgence. And they had good reason to be.

The Ustasha was deemed a terrorist organization not unlike the Nazi party. During the war, the fiercely Roman Catholic Ustasha persecuted hundreds of thousands of Jews, Serbs, and Roma gypsies to ensure a more racially pure Croatia under a regime of forced Catholicism.

Ustasha camps housed as many as 700,000 prisoners at their peak, most of whom were savagely exterminated with a brutality that shocked even the Nazis.

Much like their German allies, the Ustasha had plundered vast amounts of gold and currency from Jews and Serbs, and it had been recently revealed that the Ustasha had sent 200 million Swiss francs directly to the Vatican, presumably with the complicity of Pope Pius XII.

The Vatican had maintained full diplomatic relations with the Ustasha, and after the war ended, had facilitated the escape of Nazi war criminals to safe havens through ratlines operated by Catholic priests, notably those of the Franciscan order.

Although the war had long been over, the Ustasha still maintained secret underground militia factions peppered throughout the Balkans and South America, still in pursuit of creating the ideal fascist Catholic nation through political influence and even ethnic cleansing, if it came to that.

Among Petrov Gović's primary goals now was the establishment of "gladiator bootcamps" throughout eastern and western Europe, beacons of hope for young conservative activists spurned by liberal democratic principles of the West. For years the "Novi Ustasha" had been buying up abandoned convents, monasteries and vineyards in Italy, France, and Germany, refitting them with classrooms and training camps—academies for shaping the minds of a new generation of ultra-right Catholic leaders who embraced the Ustasha's worldview.

Petrov's father, Miroslav Gović, had been a field marshal in the Ustasha militia during World War II, but with the capable intervention of Ustasha sympathizers in charge of official personnel files, nothing linked Petrov to the new Ustasha. Nothing except the secret Ehrenring known only to those within his organization. As regional cell leader for the Novi Ustasha in France,

Petrov Gović issued similar rings to compatriots under his command. And membership was growing.

Petrov Gović's unique role at Interpol provided him with the perfect cover for vetting lists of qualified fascist recruits for Ustasha affiliation, leaving the unwitting leg work to other international agencies inside Interpol member countries for identifying far-right contenders.

Sorting the Blue Notices into stacks, Gović placed suitable Croatian candidates into one pile, and all Serbian subjects into another. Names and location details of the Croats would be passed on to his recruitment lieutenant, Roko Sirola, as potential conscripts, and their Blue Notices would be downgraded to mere informational petitions. The Serb notices would remain Blue and in full force. Those weren't his problem.

Augmenting his covert Ustasha activities, Petrov Gović also provided singular mercenary services to select clients whose influence could be useful to his more furtive nationalistic mission. Among those clients was the Vatican Secretariat of State. In exchange for Gović's own discreet personal assistance, Cardinal Fabrizio Dante had offered the agent funding and other confidential services provided by the Vatican Bank, including limited access to gold reserves from long-dormant accounts—accounts linked directly to former

Ustasha constituents dating from World War II. It was a perfect arrangement, and one which both men depended on frequently.

Dante's assigned mission for him this week seemed simple enough. First, Gović logged onto Interpol's ECHELON terminal, accessing the classified Nominal Database and placing email intercept directives on Michael Dominic, Hana Sinclair, and Simon Ginzberg, whose details had been provided by Dante. With the intercepts now in place, Gović would be notified by text the moment any messages sent by or to the three subjects were transmitted through the global internet.

At Dante's insistence, Mendoza had provided details of Dominic's itinerary in Paris, which the cardinal passed on to Gović. Turning to his desktop computer, Gović logged on to the French rail system TGV's website and booked first class passage for the two-hour trip from Lyon to Paris for the coming week.

Then he arranged for a room at the Park Hyatt Paris-Vendôme.

18

Michael Dominic had just settled into the richly upholstered leather seat of the Dassault Falcon when the steward appeared, asking if he would like a glass of champagne before takeoff. Dominic opted for coffee instead.

"It's hard to grasp how people live like this," he said to Hana, who took the seat opposite him, champagne flute in hand.

"My grandfather travels a great deal," she said. "Like many high net worth individuals, he is scrupulous about controlling his time, and the plane serves that purpose well for him. But today, it's working out quite nicely for us, while he's slumming it with the pope!" Hana pressed the reclining button in her seat and leaned back, smiling.

"Now, Father Dominic," she said slyly, "do tell me more about your interest in Bérenger Saunière. What are you up to?"

Though still uncertain about the consequences, Dominic had decided he could trust Hana with his discovery. Her obvious influence and access could come in useful to both of them.

Still, he wanted to keep the circle of intimates small.

"What I'm about to tell you, Hana, could have far-reaching implications that I don't yet fully comprehend, so I'll have to ask that what I say remains between you and me."

"You have my word," Hana promised, raising three fingers of her right hand in a mock girl scout pledge.

As the jet lifted off from Ciampino Airport heading toward Paris, Dominic took a deep breath and began his story of both Bérenger Saunière and the Nostradamus quatrains.

"I can see why this might be disturbing to some, Michael, not least of all you," Hana said soberly, her investigative journalist's radar now fully engaged. "I don't know too much about Nostradamus, but I'm fascinated by his legacy and eager to learn more.

"As for Rennes-le-Château," she continued, "others have searched for years trying to find Saunière's treasure, or some more reasonable understanding of what he actually found. I wonder if someone else has taken over Saunière's role since his death. Do you think the Vatican is still making payments to anyone?"

"Now there's a thought," Dominic said,

intrigued. "Hopefully we'll discover more at the Bibliothèque. Simon told me Saunière's papers were archived there. In which case, though, who could possibly be making *and receiving* payments for this kind of knowledge?" The mere suggestion of an ongoing modern blackmail conspiracy set his mind onto new possibilities.

"As long as we'll be in France, perhaps we should also visit Rennes-le-Château," Hana offered. "I have an aunt who lives near there, in Montazels. She is quite involved in the community and may know someone who might be able to help. We'd have to take the train from Paris, but the trip is only a few hours. I'll give her a call if you'd like."

"We'll make the time," Dominic affirmed. "Apart from our research, I just need to put in an appearance at the symposium at the Park Hyatt, but that won't take more than half a day."

Hana looked at Dominic with concern. "Are you sure this is a path you want to take, Michael? It could be nothing, of course, that's always a possibility. But if it *is* what you suspect—and I'd be inclined to agree that there may be something there—then we're talking major stakes in terms of the Vatican's involvement. Although, truth be told, this would hardly be the first scandal they've gotten themselves into."

"Are you referring to any scandal in

particular, or just generally?" Dominic asked with a sarcastic chuckle. "And if you don't mind my asking, what does your research next week involve? Are you onto a big story?"

Hana briefly described her current work on the Church's complicity with the Nazis during World War II and the flow of Jewish assets through French and Swiss banks.

"Well, now, there's a scandal worth exploring! But it can't be making you any friends in the Vatican. And since your grandfather is in banking, what does he think of this particular assignment?"

"That's another story entirely," Hana replied, shaking her head. "We have our differences, but he's assured me our family's firm had no involvement with the Nazis.

"But back to my question earlier—do you feel the risks you're taking will be worth the potential reward? I'm curious."

"Well, I'm too invested now to just leave things where they are," he said. "I've been trained to dig deep into mysteries like this. If there is even a remote chance that Saunière came into possession of ancient documents, and they're anywhere to be found, I must know more. I realize it may be a long shot, but since we're starting with where it all began, why not let it play out?"

Hana appreciated her new friend's predicament, and his determination in getting to the root of an unsolved problem, much like her own interest in puzzles. It was also similar to her personal drive and ambitions. *We make a good team for this kind of adventure,* she thought.

Hana opened her purse and, finding her address book, looked up her aunt's phone number in Montazels. Reaching for the satellite phone installed next to her seat, she dialed the number. While she spoke to her aunt, Dominic stood to stretch, marveling at how the one-percent lives as he looked around the plush cabin.

"We're set," Hana said enthusiastically. "My aunt actually knows the niece of Marie Dénarnaud! They both belong to the Languedoc-Roussillon Garden Society. She's quite old now and pretty much a recluse, but she's going to make arrangements for us to meet."

"Hana, I don't know how to thank you!" Dominic said, enthused at the prospect. "This is beyond any expectations I had. I just hope we're doing the right thing."

"Can't back out now, Michael. The fun is just beginning."

Having descended over Paris, the pilot announced they would be landing shortly. The Falcon's wheel gear extended as Hana and Dominic looked at each other with eager anticipation, then buckled their seatbelts for the adventure ahead.

19

The Richelieu Library, one of four Paris locations of the expansive *Bibliothèque National de France,* is a grand neoclassical structure in the heart of the 2nd Arrondissement, a district of Paris just north of the opulent Palais-Royal. Originally built in the mid-eighteenth century, the Richelieu houses, among other vast holdings, over 225,000 manuscripts dating back to the Middle Ages—many plundered from the Vatican during Napoleon's invasion of Rome in 1798.

Having secured their accredited research credentials from the French Ministry of Culture, Hana and Dominic situated themselves in the spacious Labrouste Reading Room, a breathtaking atrium featuring sixteen arboresque cast iron pillars supporting a network of terra cotta domes, and walls frescoed with elaborate paintings of clouds, trees, and squirrels peering down on countless rows of black leather-topped reading tables. Five stories above them, skylights bathed the room in a light so natural it gave the impression patrons were sitting outdoors.

When they checked in at reception, both were

greeted personally by the chief curator of medieval manuscripts, Monsieur Bernard Duchamp, who accepted their prepared material requests for retrieval from the stacks: for Dominic, the official papers of Abbé Bérenger Saunière from Rennes-le-Château, the journals of German archeologist Otto Rahn, and an early copy of Wolfram von Eschenbach's *Parzival* manuscript. Among Hana's selections were archived photographs from the French Resistance, and microfiche from the extensive Gallica database for newspapers from 1943 to 1945—anything mentioning the '*Maquis*' in search index keywords for both requests. Using her newly-won access to the Special Archives section, she also requested a specific set of documents from the *Quai d'Orsay*—the French Ministry of Europe and Foreign Affairs office—relating to later investigations of Jewish gold in the French banking system. Though not otherwise government classified, these were marked "*Confidentiel,*" and were to be treated as context sensitive. Had she not gotten direct permission from President Pierre Valois, Bibliothèque personnel would certainly not have permitted a journalist access to such documents.

Hana's newspapers were immediately accessible at the microfiche desk, so while she began her work there, Dominic remained in the Labrouste Reading Room with his first selection—

a 13th-century parchment codex of the Bavarian knight Wolfram von Eschenbach's Grail legend *Parzival,* its stunning full-color illuminations and three-column text handwritten in Middle High German, depicting a spectacular rendition of von Eschenbach's masterpiece of medieval literature.

The epic poem tells the story of Parzival, a naïve young man who was raised in the forest, isolated from the ways of the world. He sets out on an odyssey to become a knight and is eventually granted a seat at King Arthur's Round Table. Following a long journey and spiritual quest, Parzival returns to court and, having correctly answered a vexing question, is hailed as the new Grail king.

Parzival was believed by many to be more authentic than apocryphal, passed down from oral traditions through the centuries. In fact, scholars have long debated whether the Holy Grail was actually part of Solomon's Treasure, which included a reliquary casket—an ossuary—captured by the Visigoth King Alaric in 410 CE, and later moved from Rome to Carcassonne in Gaul.

Von Eschenbach also described a particular cave in the south of France, an allusion to where the Grail might be found. Although the epic poem is comprised of 25,000 lines of verse, Dominic recalled from his first reading at the Pontifical

Institute the general location of Ginzberg's recommended passage—something about an *"unreachable castle,"* Simon had mentioned. Paging through the codex he finally came to the passage, translating it into English:

In a distant land unreachable by your steps
lies a castle, called Monsalvat,
A luminous temple stands in the middle there.
So costly, as nothing known on earth:
In it a vessel of miracle-working blessing
is guarded there as highest holiness,
is tended by the purest human beings.
Each year a dove from heaven draws near
to newly strengthen its magical power.
It is called Grail and purest blessed faith
is imparted through it to its knighthood.
Whoever has been chosen to serve the Grail
Him it will arm with super-earthly power
on him is every evil person's deception lost
When he sees it, the night of death gives way.

I can see why Simon thought "Monsalvat" could be considered Montsegur, Dominic mused. That would also be consistent with the views of many Grail scholars. The *"luminous temple…so costly"* could refer to the Cathar treasure, and the mention of the *"purest human beings"* and *"its knighthood"* surely meant the Cathars themselves. More pieces of the puzzle coming together.

Monsieur Duchamp arrived with the archives for both Bérenger Saunière and Otto Rahn and set them on the reading table. Finished with *Parzival* for now, Dominic handed it back to the curator and began going through Saunière's parcel first.

It was surprisingly spare, mainly administrative ledgers and parish baptismal records. But one document that stood out was most revealing—Bérenger Saunière's Last Will and Testament from April 1912, prepared five years before he died.

> *I, the undersigned, Bérenger Saunière, priest, former Curé of Rennes-le-Château, declare that this document is my last Will and Testament and that it represents my last wishes. First of all, I hereby revoke all and any former Wills that may exist and that may be produced.*
>
> *I leave to Marie Dénarnaud, my neighbour, all my goods, movable and immovable. I leave to her all the furniture, linen, and utensils contained in the presbytery, the Villa Bethany, and the relevant outbuildings. I leave to her all the provisions of the household,*

wines, wood, silver, and valuables.

Marie Dénarnaud will replace me, in consequence, in the possession of all that shall belong to me at the time of my death.

I give all these goods to Marie Dénarnaud without the need to produce an inventory, a necessity against which I wish absolutely to protect her as my sole legatee.

Since Saunière had left everything to his housekeeper, Marie Dénarnaud, it was certainly possible her niece might know something about what the supposed treasure was, or if her aunt Marie had even received a portion of it in the abbé's bequest. Though he expected his chances were slim, Dominic could hardly contain himself. He looked forward to meeting the niece later in the week, grateful for Hana's timely assistance, and becoming even more appreciative that he had met her in the first place. She was an ideal partner in this quest.

Putting the Saunière material aside, Dominic moved on to Otto Rahn's journal, which revealed a fascinating account of his exploits in Montségur and Rennes-le-Château, among the many sites he had excavated while searching for the Grail in the

Languedoc region of southern France.

Rahn was a gifted historian and, by the time he died at age 35, had written two books: *Crusade Against the Grail* and *Lucifer's Court*, both explorations of the Grail legend, and each detailing his life's work trying to find the mystical treasure. Nazi SS chief Heinrich Himmler had named Rahn his *Obersturmführer*, or senior storm leader, and chief investigator for all things occult, which gave the young lieutenant ample time and opportunity to exercise his vision, along with the SS troops needed to carry out his mission.

Consistent with Ginzberg's assessment, Rahn, too, believed that Monsalvat and Montségur, the Cathar fortress high atop the French Pyrenees, were one and the same. His journal went on to express his certainty that the Cathars were the last to possess the Grail, and that it "vanished" with them at the end of the Albigensian Crusade, when the last of the Cathars were burned to death by command of the pope. But even Rahn did not know what form the Grail actually took: Was it the chalice from the Last Supper? The Lance of Longinus that pierced Christ's side while he was on the cross? Or was it some form of spiritual relic that could ensure eternal youth? The legends were many and varied.

As he sat reading, Dominic's imagination wandered back to the twelfth century, his favorite period in the history of human events, and in particular the trials and tribulations of that most fascinating of Gnostic revival movements, Catharism. Violently persecuted by the Roman Catholic Church, the Cathars were a peaceful and highly principled sect who called southern France home. They espoused two opposing deities in eternal conflict: *Amor*, representing the Good God of the New Testament and creator of all things Spiritual, and *Roma*, the Evil God of the Old Testament who created the Physical World and all things Material. As the Cathar movement grew, the Roman Church—whose dogma allowed for only one God—viewed the Cathars as heretical outcasts that must be destroyed, especially since Cathar theology was spreading like wildfire throughout the Languedoc, threatening the Church's tight hold over shepherding its obedient flock.

Another of the Church's grave historical tragedies, thought Dominic. It was reminders like this that caused him to question why he had chosen the priesthood in the first place. It wasn't like he could be all that proud of his employer's institutional legacy, that much was a given. One could argue that these events happened long ago and under the aegis of more deplorable leaders. But the fact was, such political decisions were still being made, just in a more modern context. Despite its sheer historical relevance for two thousand years, and the abundance of its treasures—treasures he now had personal charge of!—the Vatican itself was still colonized by forces of often malicious intent, where flagrant careerism was the principal avocation sought by everyone, regardless of station.

Dominic knew he should not pursue this line of thinking, not now. He must keep his mind focused on the one current and very engaging task before him, grateful he was largely detached from the interminable political machinations of those above his humble position as a *scrittore*. He returned to Otto Rahn and his search for the Holy Grail.

"Michael!"

Dominic looked up to find Hana standing next to him, a look of sheer delight on her face. It was a welcome relief to the remorseful place he'd let his mind stray off to.

"You won't believe what I found!" she said, handing him an aged sepia-toned photograph in a Mylar sleeve. "You know how much I love puzzles. Look at these two men…." Her finger pointed to two individuals standing together in a row of four others, behind them a formidable S35 French cavalry tank covered in camouflage paint.

"Who are they?" he asked.

"The one on the right is identified simply as

'Achille,' the Maquis group leader I've been trying to track down. I was shocked to find him, to be honest; it's like looking for a black cat in a coal mine. But then I was stunned when I recognized the man standing next to him." Hana pointed to the man on the left, still jowly in his youth, with a receding forehead, hollow cheeks, and clearly identifiable eyes.

Dominic was unfazed. "I don't recognize him. Who is it?"

"That," Hana said, "is my godfather—Pierre Valois. The president of France."

20

Several seats down from where Michael Dominic sat under the high domes of the Labrouste, a man reading the daily *Le Figaro* turned a page, the broad newspaper serving as cover from the approach of a woman who was about to join the sitting priest.

Petrov Gović stood up, inconspicuously sauntered a few tables away, then circled back to take a seat at the table directly behind Dominic. Reaching into the breast pocket of his dark blazer, he removed an iPhone, activated the recording app, and set it screen-side down on the table in front of him, the microphone a mere four feet away from the couple behind him. He returned to reading his newspaper.

"Valois told me he didn't see 'Achille' in a similar photo I showed him, so he had to be lying, or at least putting me off" Hana said. "I'm mystified by why. My grandfather easily recognized him."

"Maybe it was just too long ago. I imagine he'd be up there in age now, wouldn't he?" Dominic asked.

"Well, he may be long in the tooth, but one

doesn't get to be leader of such a nation if he's mentally confused or doddering in old age." Hana was frustrated when faced with duplicity, especially by someone she was close to. "Have you had any luck in your own research?"

"I wouldn't call it luck so much as serendipity," Dominic said optimistically. "Everything points to Rennes-le-Château or Montségur in one way or another." He described his findings in the Otto Rahn material, *Parzival*'s surprise reference to the mountain fortress, and finally, his delight at finding Bérenger Saunière's Last Will & Testament.

"He left everything he had to Marie Dénarnaud! I'm anxious to meet her niece. I wish now I didn't have this symposium to go to, though I was looking forward to it. I'm obsessed with this whole Saunière mystery."

"Like the long line of conspiracy theorists before you…" Hana said, smirking. Dominic laughed loudly, then ducked his head and blushed, forgetting he was in a library.

"I have yet to get the *Quai d'Orsay* materials from the Special Archives. You saw the look on Duchamp's face when he recognized who authorized my access. They are very particular about who gets to see what here," Hana said, looking up. "Speak of the devil…."

Monsieur Duchamp was walking toward

them, a single folder in his hands. "Thank you for your patience, mademoiselle," he said, handing her the documents. "This is all we could find for your request."

Hana accepted the folder, which was about half-an-inch thick, thanking the curator for his efforts. She sat down across from Dominic and began poring over the documents, uncertain as to what she was actually looking for, but nonetheless content that she at least had this.

Later, her neck aching, Hana looked at her watch. The many hours she had been in the Bibliothèque, especially squinting at the microfiche screen, had left her weary. She stretched her neck and arms, took a few deep breaths, and adjusted her distance vision, taking in the beauty of the grand building and its many patrons busy with their own research.

It was then she noticed the man sitting behind Michael, reading a newspaper. She had seen him arrive earlier, when they first sat down. But he was sitting at the far end of *their* table before, still reading a newspaper. *Odd that he would change seats,* she thought. *And was it the same paper?* She was tired. It likely meant nothing.

"Michael, I'm spent," Hana said. "Let's finish this in the morning, before your workshop at the hotel. Then while you're away I can continue with these documents on my own."

"Good idea. Feel like having some dinner?" Dominic asked.

"We're in Paris! Of course we're having dinner," she said.

Packing up their materials, they returned the items to the assistance desk, indicating they would return in the morning to continue their work.

As they headed toward the exit, Hana looked back at where they were sitting. The man who had been behind Dominic was gone.

21

The spacious fitness center in the Park Hyatt Paris-Vendôme was exceptionally well-equipped, as would be expected from one of Paris's finer conference hotels. Dominic had awakened early to get in a workout before joining Hana for breakfast but was surprised to find her already in the gym, vigorously climbing a StairMaster, her hair tied back in a ponytail, her lithe body glistening with sweat. *No wonder she's in such good shape,* he observed, tempering his thoughts.

Grabbing a fresh towel from a stack near the door, Dominic picked out a treadmill in front of Hana's machine, set the timer for thirty minutes, and started his run.

"Our train to Montazels leaves at six in the morning, putting us there in the early afternoon," Hana said as she buttered a flaky croissant while Dominic sipped his French roast coffee. "Rennes-le-Château is only two miles from there, so we'll rent a car at the train station."

"Has your aunt already contacted Marie's

niece?"

"Yes! Her name is Élise Dénarnaud, and she's expecting us. She has lived in Rennes-le-Château her entire life, so I imagine she knows as much as anyone about the goings on there. I've emailed details of our train trip to my aunt and when she can expect us."

Dominic picked up the symposium brochure, surveying the various sessions scheduled for the day. "I've pretty much got what I need from the Bibliothèque. I'll just stay here and pick up a few of these talks and that symposium workshop while you finish up your work there. Sound good?"

"Sure," Hana replied. "I shouldn't be more than a few hours. I'll just meet you back here, and we'll have an early dinner, then call it a night."

The morning air was warm and humid as Hana set out on the fifteen-minute walk to the Richelieu library, peering into shop windows as she made her way along the Rue Casanova.

Her thoughts turned to Michael Dominic, what a gentle man he was. Intelligent, witty, disarmingly attractive, and impossibly fit. *What makes a man like that become a priest, for God's sake? He could have any woman he wants—unless, of course, he preferred men.* But she didn't get that vibe from him, something she was pretty well-attuned to.

Enough of that, she scolded herself, *the man is out of bounds.* It had been some time since she was with any man, much less someone she could see spending a life with. Like her grandfather incessantly reminded her, she was indelibly wedded to her work. But she loved her job; it's what made her get up in the morning, made her creative juices flow.

Still, a girl could dream....

Monsieur Duchamp was attending the reception desk when Hana entered the Richelieu. Signing in and showing her pass, she retrieved the same folder of documents held aside for her from the previous day and made her way to one of the long tables under the bright domes of the Labrouste Reading Room.

The documents, dated from 1949 to 1999, comprised mostly official investigative reports for three of France's most prestigious banks before they were nationalized after the war: BNCI, CNEP, and Crédit Lyonnais. The investigations summarized complex arrangements with other banks throughout Europe and North America in the wrongful seizing of accounts and safe-deposit assets of Jewish customers during France's occupation by Germany, among them J.P. Morgan and Chase Manhattan, two behemoths of the American banking system that were involved in a class-action lawsuit.

Hana paged through the reports, looking for threads of connection, names of individuals who might stand out. Too convoluted to take in in one sitting, she took an iPhone out of her bag and subtly began scanning images of each page, uncertain of the library's policy on such mundanities but muting the shutter sound and flash just in case. When she was finished, she returned to the assistance desk, handed over the materials, then turned back to use one of the computer workstations on the side of the large room.

As she turned Hana nearly collided with a burly man heading toward the exit—*the same man who was sitting behind Michael yesterday!* She looked directly in the man's eyes, eyes that avoided her gaze as if she wasn't even there. He looked to be north of fifty, bore dark Slavic features and black crew cut hair that was obviously dyed, and he was wearing the same jacket he had on the day before. She kept watching as he walked out the door with the assertive stride of a man used to having people move out of his way.

What are the odds? she wondered.

* * *

Back in his room at the Park Hyatt, Petrov Gović

checked email on his laptop. Sitting in the inbox was a brief transcript of Hana Sinclair's email message to her aunt intercepted by ECHELON.

Opening a browser, he logged on to TGV and booked first class passage on the train to Montazels. It would be a long day.

22

Even at that early hour, the Gare du Nord train station was bustling with swarms of tourists and commuters, most clutching tickets and Starbucks coffee cups, many running with wheeled baggage trailing behind them through the crowd of travelers, desperate not to miss their trains. High-speed French TGV trains are scrupulously punctual, lest the company pay passengers a hefty rebate on the ticket price for even a 30-minute delay.

Hana had reserved two rooms at the Maison Beausoleil, a quaint Bed & Breakfast in a village near Montazels, so as not to inconvenience her aunt. Since they were only planning an overnight trip, each carried a backpack containing a change of clothes, plus fruit, packets of nuts, and bottled water for the seven-hour trip. They had left the remainder of their luggage with the hotel concierge for their final night in Paris when they returned.

Dominic had chosen dual facing seats in the first-class section ahead of the cafe-bar car, with a small table separating them. He stowed their backpacks on the overhead racks as the train began pulling out of the station. As it gained speed, they both settled in for the duration: Dominic reading Otto Rahn's *Crusade Against the Grail,* while Hana busied herself with a crossword puzzle.

"You like crosswords, eh?" Dominic asked her.

"I'm fiendishly good at puzzles, something I picked up as a child but refined as an investigative reporter." As she looked up at him, a thought crossed her mind, something she'd been meaning to ask him. Now seemed as good a time as any.

"Tell me, Michael," Hana began, "why did you choose the priesthood? What makes a man like you opt for a life of service and solitude and, well, celibacy?"

"*'A man like me'?*" Dominic laughed self-consciously. But he knew what she meant. "Well, I lived in a parish rectory growing up. My mother and I had separate living quarters in the rectory, of course, but I've been around the priesthood all my life, with Enrico Petrini as the only man I could really look to for guidance.

"The truth is I never really thought of doing anything else. It wasn't as if I had a particular calling to do this work, though, which might set me apart from most men who enter the priesthood. What I really found compelling was the singular fulfillment of being in service to people and being a part of the historical institutions of the Church. I went into seminary thinking, '*Yeah, I could be good at this.*' Traditionally—apart from the Church's sexual abuse scandals—being a priest was an important and respected, even admired career—and I needed that bit of elevation of my status, or maybe I should say elevation of my self-esteem. I suffered a bit of bullying in my early life because of being the son of a single mother. And, admittedly, the church felt like a bit of a sanctuary from that bullying as well. That I could also chase a life of scholarly pursuits with history's most sacred treasures was the real bonus."

As she watched him speak, Hana saw in Dominic a rare and incredibly genuine man, one she knew she could trust and depend on. Her eyes grew misty as she listened.

"As for the celibacy issue," Dominic continued, "That's a hard one…."

Hana burst out laughing at the imagined innuendo, bringing her hands up to her eyes as much to hide her embarrassment as to wipe away the emotion gathered there.

"No! I didn't mean it *that* way!" Dominic said quickly, laughing with her over the unintended phrasing. "You naughty girl.

"I *meant*," he went on, "that loneliness is the most challenging aspect to deal with. We all have natural doubts and anxieties about the real consequences of commitment, and those may or may not ever go away. I struggle with them daily—especially when meeting someone like you. You're a remarkable woman, Hana. You really are." Dominic reached across the table to squeeze her hand.

Taken aback, Hana blushed and turned to look out the window. The landscape was speeding by at nearly two hundred miles per hour, as fast as her mind was working to come up with a response to what this unobtainable man just said to her.

"I can't imagine how difficult that must be for you," she said quietly. "But I *can* tell you how much I admire you for it. Your self-discipline and restraint are models anyone can aspire to. To be honest, I'm envious. And not a little disappointed."

They looked at each other, their faces a blend of melancholy and obliged acceptance.

Hana abruptly excused herself and got up to use the restroom. She made her way back to the cafe-bar car, thinking about Michael, when, looking up through the door window of the adjoining car, she saw a man walking away from her, entering the second car beyond the bar.

It can't be! The same man from the Bibliothèque is on this train? Once is chance. Twice is coincidence. But a third time? That's a pattern. Hana decided to follow him.

She passed through the door from the cafe-bar car but didn't see him now. She walked down the aisle, glancing at each passenger as she moved through the car to the next door of the adjoining car. He wasn't there either, nor in the last car. *He couldn't just disappear!* She tried the door to the restroom, but it was occupied. She waited.

After a few minutes she knocked on the door.

"Zauzeto!" a Slavic voice said sternly. *"Occupé!"*

Hana took an empty seat near the toilet door, prepared to confront the man when he emerged. But after another ten minutes she felt a bit foolish and walked back to join Michael three cars up. On her way back she stopped to use another restroom.

"It's the strangest thing," she said, returning to her seat. "When we were in the Bibliothèque the other day there was a man sitting at the end of our table, reading a newspaper, before he moved to take a seat right behind you. Then I saw him again when I was there the next day. I bumped into him in the aisle at the reception desk, but he didn't even acknowledge me, just kept on walking out the door. And now, I just saw him again on this train! Don't you think that strains the bounds of coincidence? He's been in the restroom for at least fifteen minutes. I was going to challenge him but thought better of it."

Dominic looked perplexed. "I can't imagine our lives are so interesting as to be followed by someone, do you?"

"I suppose not," Hana replied. "Still, it seems unusual."

Dominic thought back to that tall, thin priest watching him in the Pio Reading Room, but dismissed it as not worth mentioning. A lot of priests wander the Vatican.

It was a little past noon when the train began to slow, and a voice came on the loudspeaker announcing their arrival in Montazels. Dominic gathered up their backpacks from the overhead rack while Hana made one last trip to the restroom.

As they stepped down from the train onto the platform, Hana looked around at the disembarking passengers, curious to see if the man got off as well. Not seeing him, she and Dominic headed to the car rental counter, such as it was—a local one-off company with just two older Citroëns, one black, one white—but it suited their purpose. Hana handled the paperwork, putting it on her *La Monde* business account, then they drove to Hana's aunt's cottage not far from the station.

After introductions and light conversation over a lunch of charcuterie, olives, and freshly baked baguettes, Hana took directions from her aunt to the home of Élise Dénarnaud in Rennes-le-Château. They said their thanks and goodbyes and headed to the historic village.

23

The French commune of Rennes-le-Château stands on a hilltop overlooking the lush Aude valley, a vast region located between the Mediterranean Sea and the Pyrenees mountains north of Spain. Thick riparian forests of oak, beech, fir and chestnut dominate the countryside, with deep-canyon rivers nourishing the drylands, chaparral, and mountain grasses native to the area.

Few regions in France are as historically fertile as the Aude. Traces of human civilization date back 1.5 million years BCE, with the oldest human skull in Europe found in nearby Carcassonne, itself one of the most perfectly preserved fortresses of the medieval period. The Romans had built strategically important settlements and mercantile ports by 200 BCE. Later it was ruled by the Visigoths and later still by the Cathars. Through it all, the small village of Rennes-le-Château sat on a rocky plateau with commanding views of mountain peaks and jagged ridges leading up to its limestone hillside.

As Dominic drove the white Citroën up the main road leading into the village, Bérenger Saunière's prominent Tour Magdala dominated the skyline, its crenellated tower symbolizing architectural embattlements of an earlier era. As Hana had read from a brochure she picked up at the train station, Saunière built the neo-Gothic structure in 1906, dedicating the tower in the name of Mary Magdalene, for whom he had shown great affection.

Parking the car in the village, Hana and Dominic walked to the Church of Saint Magdalena, a venerable air of intrigue surrounding its sharply arched doorway. Entering the narthex, they were startled by a brilliantly colored statue of Asmodeus, a terrifying demon supporting a holy water stoup on its back while crouched on one knee, its anguished face and wild eyes not an uncommon sight in older French chapels.

"It may surprise you to learn," Dominic said to Hana, "that traditionally, Asmodeus, one of the seven princes of Hell, guarded buried treasure."

Eyeing the demon, Hana winced. "It's rather off-putting, isn't it?"

For a small village church, it was a surprisingly opulent homage to Mary Magdalene, with elaborately-carved statues nestled in inset alcoves, tall stained glass windows casting slanted shafts of tinted light throughout the chapel, antique stands of votive candles flickering in dark corners, and an elevated golden pulpit where Bérenger Saunière once preached to his congregation in front of an imposing semicircular apse, its golden altar shimmering in the natural light.

They walked through the small garden outside the church, admiring the Villa Bethany—the former home of Marie Dénarnaud—and the striking Tour Magdala, which Saunière once used as his library and study.

Their brief tour complete, they drove the short distance to Élise Dénarnaud's home.

The car pulled up in front of a pleasant but decaying old two-story cottage with a lush, fulsome garden surrounding it. As they got out of the car, Hana marveled at the wild orchids, tulips, dwarf iris, and narcissus nestled among beds of wildflowers and Mediterranean grasses, clearly the domain of someone who loved the natural splendors of gardening. An old woman wearing an apron, gloves, and rubber boots came around from the back of the house to greet them.

"Bonjour," the woman said cheerfully. *"Mademoiselle Sinclair?"*

"Oui, bonjour Madame Dénarnaud," Hana replied, as the woman smiled and nodded, removing her gloves.

Hana, continuing in French, extended her hand, saying, "Please, call me Hana. And this is my colleague, Father Michael Dominic."

Dominic, wearing black trousers and a black shirt with starched white collar—hoping his appearance as clergy might be helpful in their mission—took the old woman's hand. "Very pleased to meet you, madame," he said in French.

"You have such a lovely garden," Hana said, taking in the scene with obvious appreciation.

"*Merci beaucoup*," Madame Dénarnaud said. "It is much work, but it is all I have to do in the passing days. It fulfills me." She beamed proudly at the arresting landscape. "Please, come inside. I'll make tea."

"My aunt Marie was quite *la femme* in her day," Madame Dénarnaud said as the three settled in her sitting room, steaming teacups in hand. "I was just a child at the time, but I remember she often walked around the town dressed in the latest Parisian fashions, wearing jewels fit for a queen. The other villagers called her *La Madonne,* but I think that was more to the appeasement of Abbé Saunière, who idolized Saint Mary Magdalene." The old woman tilted her head and winked knowingly. "Though I think he also loved my aunt a great deal. They were the talk of the village. Would you like some tea?"

Hana and Michael, who were both nursing full teacups already, looked at each other in confusion. "No, madame, but thank you, the tea is very good," Hana said. "Can you tell us about Abbé Saunière? Did you know much about him?"

"Well, he died long before I was born," the woman said, her glazed eyes looking into the distance. "But my aunt spoke of him all the time; she cared for him a great deal. From his photos the abbé was such a handsome man. Much like you, Father Dominic."

Michael blushed as both Hana and Élise Dénarnaud looked at him. Hana smiled as if she were thinking, *'See what I mean?!'*

Changing the subject, Dominic said, "Madame, we are mainly interested in what Abbé Saunière might have been in possession of that may have brought him a great deal of attention, which I understand helped him with building his church, the Villa Bethania, and much of the village. Might you know anything about that?"

The old woman looked bewildered. "Why, yes, the abbé built us a fine church. Have you seen it yet? It's very charming. But too many tourists come to visit it now.

"In her will," she continued, "my aunt left everything to a family named Corbu, to whom she had also sold the property left to her by Abbé Saunière. But before she died, she gave me many small things which she valued personally. I keep them in the attic."

She then stood up and said, "I'm so sorry, I should have offered you some tea." She headed into the small kitchen.

Hana looked knowingly at Michael. *"We need to see the attic!"* she whispered.

Dénarnaud returned to the room with a fresh teapot. "Oh, I see you already have tea. Goodness, where is my mind these days? You know, perhaps I should show you the things my aunt left me years ago. Abbé Saunière bequeathed everything he possessed to her when he died, but she gave me some things shortly before she passed that I haven't seen myself in many years. Please, come with me upstairs."

Sensitive to the woman's senility, but grateful she had finally gotten to the point of their visit, Dominic and Hana set down their teacups and followed her up the old narrow staircase. Framed photographs of her aunt Marie, Bérenger Saunière, and other people of an older age were hanging on the wall, peering down on them as they ascended the steps.

At the end of the upstairs hall, Madame Dénarnaud opened a door to another narrow staircase. She switched on a light and they climbed up into a cramped attic, filled with years of memories and detritus—old chairs, a couple of lampshades and a bookcase, a large rusty birdcage, a tarpaulin covering a stack of paintings leaning against the wall, and several boxes containing everything from clothing to books.

"I'm not sure which of these was my aunt's, but they've got to be here somewhere."

She moved about the room glancing in boxes until finding one that looked familiar. "This may be one," she said.

"Here," Dominic offered. "Let me give you a hand." He lifted the heavy box from its place under a slanted eave of the house and set it on a dusty table under a bare lightbulb hanging from the ceiling.

The box was filled with old newspapers, books, a couple of photograph albums, and other remnants of life long ago. Dominic sifted through its contents but didn't find anything of particular interest.

"There's another one, over here," Élise said from a far corner. Dominic fetched that box and brought it back to the table.

"If you don't mind, I'm going downstairs," the woman said. "The air up here is too musty for me. Take your time looking at whatever you like." She slowly made her way back down the narrow staircase.

Protruding from one corner of the box was an old wooden tube about twelve inches long.

Beneath that were packets of correspondence and postcards bound by frayed twine, another photo album, and assorted odds and ends from an earlier age.

Dominic sorted through the packets of letters, all of which seemed to be routine correspondence or other documents dated well after Bérenger Saunière died in 1917.

He pulled out the wooden tube, a curious container, he thought. It was sealed at both ends with old newspaper caps and twine, as if it hadn't been opened in decades.

"This wood is quite old, Hana," Dominic said, noting the wax-sealed cracks repaired over the ages. "And the shape is rather odd, too."

He looked at Hana questioningly, his eyebrows raised in interest.

"Well," Hana said mischievously, "she *did* say we're free to look at anything…."

Carefully unfastening the twine and peeling away a cap from one end, Dominic peered inside the tube beneath the light. He could see there was some kind of paper object rolled up inside it, but instinct cautioned vigilance in trying to extract it. He gently shook the wooden tube to shift the contents toward the open end of the container, then again when he saw the success of his efforts. Its content was now accessible. He gently tested the document's resilience and, feeling confident it wouldn't chip or tear, began rolling it more tightly inward with two fingers, so as to free its grip from the wood surrounding it, then slid it out of the tube.

Stunned, Dominic instantly knew what he was holding: an ancient papyrus manuscript.

That feeling came over him again. The one he so often felt when coming into contact with paper antiquities. His hands were trembling, and he regretted not having his archivist's gloves with him in the moment. Setting the document down, he picked up a piece of old cloth he found in the box, then wiped his hands as best he could, removing any dirt or residual oils from his skin. Hana looked on as he gently unrolled the papyrus, her eyes wide with interest.

Dominic's face turned ashen as he surveyed the document in his hands. It was unquestionably of ancient origin, at least as old as the Nag Hammadi codices or the Dead Sea Scrolls. He took a deep breath and turned to look at Hana, his face pale but euphoric.

"What is it, Michael?!" she asked, seeing his face drain of color. "Are you alright?" She pulled over one of the wooden chairs in the attic. Dominic slowly sat down, visibly shaken.

"Whatever it is, it's significant in age alone," he said. "It appears to be written in Koine Greek, consistent with a few first- or second-century biblical manuscripts I've seen. Papyrus became too rare and expensive for general use in that era so most scribes turned to parchment and vellum—meaning this may have been written by or for someone of means. I'd need some time to translate it, but it's in remarkably fine condition, especially given its apparent age. I've never seen anything like this outside of a museum or the Vatican Library."

Dominic looked up at Hana, searching her eyes for comprehension. "We *must* get permission from Madame Dénarnaud to take this with us," he said. "At minimum it belongs in a controlled environment, not in a damp and moldy attic. And its value to scholars could be of immense historical significance."

"Do you think this is what Bérenger Saunière had that the Vatican was sending him payments for?" Hana asked.

Dominic stared through her, his mind reeling with possibilities. "Hard to tell yet, but it certainly could be. We'll know more when I'm able to spend time analyzing it.

"First, I'll take a scan, so we at least have that." He wiped any dust particulates off the table with the cloth, then unrolled the document, anchoring its four corners with books he pulled out from the box. Taking out his phone and opening the scanning app, Dominic took several shots at high resolution for safe storage in iCloud. Carefully removing each book and allowing the papyrus to roll up naturally, he delicately reinserted it back into the wooden cylinder and resealed the end.

He rechecked other boxes in the room for anything else resembling a similar container or other documents. Finding nothing more, he returned the two boxes to the floor. Turning off the ceiling light, they headed back downstairs.

"Madame," Dominic said when they rejoined the old woman in her sitting room, "we've found something that could be quite important to our historical work in the Vatican." He held out the wooden tube. "Have you any objection to our taking this with us for analysis? Rest assured it will be in very good hands."

Madame Dénarnaud stared at the wooden cylinder, then up at the priest, a warm smile crossing her timeworn face. "Oh, yes. That was given to my aunt by Abbé Saunière himself. Like me, she had no children of her own, so before she died, she handed it to me, saying it contained a secret that must be preserved…something that was quite important to the abbé's work in the village, I think. But that was so long ago, and I have never opened it, having no need to, really. I prefer to spend my time in the garden…." The woman turned to look outside the window, her distant gaze seeing far beyond the landscape.

She turned back to Dominic. "For that matter, Father, I have no need for anything in this house. I have no one to leave things to," she spread her arms around her, taking in the entirety of her home, "so all that I have will go to the church when the Lord takes me. No, I have no objection at all, Father Dominic. Please do take it. I hope you find it helpful."

"Madame," Hana began, "has anyone ever approached you before asking about your aunt?"

"Oh no, my dear," she said, somewhat perplexed. "Few people know who my aunt was, or, I mean, that we were related at all. Only a few of my friends in the Garden Society in Montazels—your own aunt, in fact—know of my aunt's relationship to Abbé Saunière. I prefer to keep the details of my life private, you see, so it's just as well."

Dominic couldn't believe his good fortune. Straining to mask his exuberance, he said, "God bless you, madame. You are very generous. We appreciate this so much."

The old woman blushed and smiled, then turned to Hana and gently kissed each of her cheeks. "I need to return to my garden now before the sun goes down," she said. "Would you care for more tea?"

Hana took both of the woman's hands in hers,

smiling warmly. "No, madame, thank you, you've been too kind. We must be going now as well."

Waving goodbye, Hana and Dominic got in the car and slowly pulled away from the curb. Neither of them noticed a black Citroën parked two cottages down from Madame Dénarnaud's, the man inside having seen the priest put an object of some kind in a backpack in the trunk.

Both Dominic and Hana were silent as they drove down the hill toward Montazels, each contemplating what had just occurred, and the potential significance of what might be in that manuscript.

Hana turned to Dominic, a mix of reflection and astonishment on her face. Dominic met her eyes, and they both just stared at each other.

"What do you suppose it could be?" Hana asked.

"I couldn't begin to speculate," he responded. "But if it's in any way related to that letter Saunière sent to the Vatican—and to the unusual largesse he came into—I'd say we need to be very careful what we do with it, and whom to trust. I *do* know we can rely on Dr. Simon Ginzberg, a scholar I met in the Archives. That might be a start."

As dusk began to fall, Dominic drove straight to Maison Beausoleil, where they checked into their rooms, then met for dinner at a quaint bistro next door to the inn.

The black Citroën was now sitting in the shadows of the parking lot outside the bistro, inside of which sat Petrov Gović, smoking a cigarette.

24

The next morning Élise Dénarnaud had just finished eating breakfast and was about to begin her gardening for the day when she heard a knock at the door. She got up to answer it.

"*Bonjour,* madame," said the husky man standing there, his black pomaded hair shining in the morning sun. "My name is Anton Dominic, and I was hoping to find my brother here, Father Michael Dominic? He said he was going to pay you a visit?"

"*Oui,* monsieur, your brother was here just yesterday, with a colleague. But you have missed them. I imagine they are on their way back to Rome now."

His face showing dismay, Petrov Gović sighed heavily. "*Mon Dieu,* he is a difficult one to keep up with. I hope he was able to find what he was looking for...."

"*Ça alors,* I do not know if what I gave him will be of interest or not, monsieur. He seemed quite curious about something he found in a wooden cylinder, something left to me by my aunt. Perhaps you can call him?"

"*Merci,* madame. I will do just that. Thank you

for your time."

25

Cardinal Dante set the iPad down on his desk as he stood at the window, gazing out at the gardens below. Petrov Gović's encrypted report from Rennes-le-Château had been transmitted through ProtonMail's email servers stored deep beneath the Swiss Alps, secure servers that worked well for the Church's benefit.

"Our Father Dominic seems to be off on an adventure, Calvino."

Brother Mendoza sat uncomfortably in the tall throne of a guest chair, his sandals dangling in midair, not even touching the floor. He was reasonably certain Dante preferred his visitors to feel intimidated in his presence, like small children.

Fabrizio Dante's lips twitched as he considered his options. When he had stepped into the role of Vatican Secretary of State, Dante had studied the highly-classified *Dossier Segreti*—secret internal dossiers going back to the start of the twentieth century, those containing distinctly sensitive matters of ongoing concern to the Church. He was keenly aware of extraordinary payments made from "Peter's Pence"—the pope's private reserve fund, handled by the Vatican Bank on behalf of His Holiness, but without accountability—including those to the village priest of Rennes-le-Château between 1897 and 1917, the year Bérenger Saunière died, and also the year payments appear to have stopped. A report indicated that in 1896 a special papal legate had been sent by Cardinal Lucido Parocchi, the Vatican Secretary of State at that time, to meet with Abbé Saunière, in an effort to substantiate what the abbé possessed that might have been of such grave concern to the Church. But no subsequent report mentioned what kind of damaging information or provocative materials might have been involved. Yet payments commenced that year. Dante found this omission highly unusual, especially in such tightly controlled documents to which few had access.

Like many, Dante had for years been aware of the various conspiracy theories attributed to Bérenger Saunière and the supposed treasure of the Cathars. But there was nothing that might lead him to believe these stories were actually true—except for the suspicious payment transactions made to Saunière himself. The *Dossier Segreti* also revealed that Vatican emissaries had tried to obtain Saunière's personal papers from Marie Dénarnaud after the abbé's death, to no avail. Even later, efforts were made to extract information from the Corbu family after Dénarnaud's passing; again, without success.

This was an unsettled mystery, and one Dante needed to resolve in order to ease his mind. If Dominic had stumbled onto something of this nature, Dante wanted to know about it.

"Brother Mendoza, I'd like you to find for me the personal records of Cardinal Lucido Parocchi. They should be in the Secretariat's archives during Pope Leo XIII's papacy. I'm especially interested in any activities dealing with an Abbé Bérenger Saunière in the French parish of Rennes-le-Château, and in particular a visit by the papal legate at the time. Let me know what you find as soon as possible, will you? I want you to handle this personally, and do not mention it to anyone else, including Father Dominic."

"It may take some time to find such materials, Eminence," Mendoza replied, dreading the task, "but you will have them." The monk grasped the desk in front of him for leverage and dropped to the floor from the high chair, then left the room, closing the door gently behind him.

Dante picked up his iPad and sent a secure Telegram text message to Petrov Gović: Still waiting for intercepts of Dominic and Sinclair emails. Send copies of anything to me immediately.

26

After a mutually fitful night of sleep, Hana and Dominic boarded the morning train back to Paris, retrieved their luggage from the Park Hyatt concierge, and took a taxi back to Le Bourget airport to board the waiting jet for their return to Rome.

After takeoff, Dominic settled himself at a large conference table in the cabin and carefully withdrew the papyrus from its wooden repository. Anchoring the top and bottom edges with magazines, he began inspecting the manuscript, a notebook and mechanical pencil at his side.

Hana had taken a seat across the aisle from Dominic, allowing him the time and solitude she knew he would need for such a focused task. While he worked, she reviewed the investigation records of the French banks, copies of which she had scanned into her iPhone in the Bibliothèque.

"Would you like something to drink, Michael?" Hana asked.

"Not yet, thanks. Best not to have liquids anywhere near the papyrus while I'm working with it," he cautioned. "But, depending on what I can make out here, we may have something to celebrate later." He looked up at her enthusiastically.

Dominic well knew that translating ancient manuscripts was not an easy task. In the seventeenth century it took seventy men in six committees more than four years to translate the Old Testament into English. Fortunately, the Saunière document was just a single page written in Koine or "common" Greek of an older era, which Dominic knew fairly well. But for a full transcription, he would need specialized dictionaries and other essential references. Fortunately, his smartphone was equipped with an Ancient Greek translator app, which would suffice for the moment.

Complicating a systematic translation of Ancient Greek was the typical profusion of diacritical marks, diphthongs, digraphs, and all too frequently the lack of punctuation and spacing between characters. Early New Testament manuscripts were composed without much punctuation at all, but in English, punctuation could have a dramatic difference on how any given document was interpreted. Knowledge of common syntactic structures, prepositions and conjunctions, word roots, and suffixes and prefixes—all were key to understanding the original writer's intent.

Despite that, Dominic was keen to dig in, given he had a two-hour flight ahead of him. This first draft would be the most generic version possible given his basic knowledge. He opened the translator app and slipped on his cotton gloves.

Inspecting the document closely now for the first time, he counted some 700 characters. The first line was fairly short, so he began with that.

ἐγώ εἰμί Μάριάμ ἐκ Μάγδαλα

Dominic knew the pronoun "ἐγώ" translated as the pronoun *"I,"* which excited him. *Could this be written in the first person?* he pondered. As such it might be a personal letter, as opposed to the recounting of a story by someone else in the third person.

Turning to his device, he input "εἰμί." The app returned a translation of the verb *"am." "I am."* Adrenaline now coursed through him. *Was an actual name forthcoming?!*

The next several glyphs were more complex. He had to input one character at a time to observe what appeared in the translator, and after five letters nothing tangible had been returned—until he added the sixth character. Then a word appeared. A woman's name. The six characters "Μάριάμ" translated as "Mariam."

Dominic was exuberant. "Mariam," and its variations of Miriam, Marian, Marie, and Maria, or more frequently, Mary, was the most common name for women in the ancient world, especially as found in biblical texts.

"Hana, this is fantastic!" Dominic turned and said to her, a look of elation on his face. "So far I've translated the first line as '*I am Mariam.*' There are a few more characters to go here, but you might want to get the champagne ready."

Returning to his work, Dominic knew the next characters, "ἐκ," represented the preposition "*of.*" He had now transcribed four words in his notebook: *"I am Mariam of…."*

He stopped for a moment and stared at the next set of characters, and in doing so the pit of his stomach tightened up, the tension making him lean forward. The next two characters "Μά" were identical to the first two of "Mariam." *It couldn't be!* he thought, thinking ahead frantically. What ran through his mind seemed an impossibility, which, if correct, would be of truly extraordinary importance, and a first in the history of ancient documents. Trembling now, he finished the translation.

M = M
ά = a
γ = g

$\delta = d$

$\alpha = a$

$\lambda = l$

$a = a$

was correct. "Μάγδαλα" translated as *"Magdala."* The lead sentence of the manuscript now read:

I am Mariam of Magdala.

His face drained of color, Dominic turned to Hana. Feeling his gaze, she looked up. "I've seen that look before," she said hesitantly. "What is it now?"

"Come over here!" Dominic said excitedly, turning his notebook around so she could read the translation.

Hana got up and sat in the opposite chair facing him. She read the five words.

"Who is Mariam of Magdala?" she asked, not yet comprehending its significance.

Staring directly into her pale green eyes, the shock on his face apparent, Dominic answered. "You may know her better as Jesus Christ's most beloved disciple, Mary Magdalene."

27

Hana Sinclair sat bolt upright in her seat and shivered at the profoundness of what she had just heard.

"What does this mean, Michael?" she asked, folding her arms across her chest.

Dominic was lost in thought over his discovery. "If Mary Magdalene actually wrote this manuscript, it would be the first recorded instance of *anything* written by her personally. Apart from several references to her in the gospels, there was a papyrus discovered in an antiquities market in Cairo in 1896—a Gnostic text called the *Gospel of Mary*—which was translated into Coptic Egyptian by a scribe in the fifth century. And although it wasn't written by the Magdalene herself, it describes in great detail her interactions with the Savior and other apostles, clearly revising much of what the Church had permitted to be published about her in Scripture.

"This could undoubtedly be one of the most important discoveries in history, Hana. But I can't do much more here without my reference books to transcribe the rest of it," he added, agitated he could go no further. "I'll have to finish the balance when I'm back in the office, and definitely on my own. I want to know what else she has written here before deciding whom to share it with, and what to do with it."

Fidgeting in his seat for the rest of the flight, all Dominic could do was stare at the papyrus, contemplating the profound significance of what more it could possibly contain.

It was nearing sunset when the Dassault Falcon touched down at Ciampino Airport and taxied into its private hangar near the Signature Flight Center, twelve miles southeast of Rome. The pilot had arranged for a taxi to meet them, and after porters loaded their bags in the trunk, they departed for the Vatican to drop off Dominic.

"My grandfather maintains a suite at the Rome Cavalieri Waldorf Astoria, so I'll be staying there if you need me," said Hana. "And please, call me the minute you know more about this Magdalene affair. If there's anything I can do to help, you know how to reach me."

Dominic had another idea. "Actually, I think it's wiser for you to keep the manuscript for now, Hana. If I take it inside the Vatican and it's discovered, it could be considered as already belonging to the Archives, since there's so much there yet uncatalogued. I'll bring my reference materials to your hotel and we'll work on it there. Would that be alright?"

"That's a smart idea, Michael. Rest assured I'll take very good care of it."

Before handing over the cylinder, Dominic stood in front of Hana, thought for a brief moment, then opened his arms and pulled her into a long, meaningful hug. No words were spoken.

Hana was taken aback by his embrace, but also more receptive than she'd expected. She leaned into his body as if the mold of his form was made just for her. She savored the moment.

Slowly separating, Dominic placed his hands on Hana's shoulders. "Thank you so much for your help on this. The whole thing is a bit overwhelming, frankly, and I'm glad to have someone I can trust to share the experience with."

Startled, but now finding her breath, Hana looked into Dominic's dark brown eyes, trying to find something there. What she found, or what she was even looking for, she wasn't quite sure. His face was a pastiche of sincerity, self-assurance, and genuine caring. She would leave it at that.

"I'll text you when I'm able to break away, and we'll continue this later. Okay?" Dominic said.

"I'm looking forward to it," was all Hana could muster, and she meant every word of it.

28

"The symposium was everything I'd hoped it would be, Cal. You should have been there."

As Michael Dominic spoke, Calvino Mendoza glanced through the notes and materials his assistant had brought back from the Paris event, noting in particular some of the newest advances in digital codicology and manuscript watermarking methodologies.

"Peter Townsend wasn't able to attend either, so I'm sure he'll appreciate seeing these," Mendoza said. "How was the rest of your trip, Miguel?" The monk looked at Dominic, eyebrows arched, aware that he had two days unaccounted for while in Paris. Dominic was prepared with a response, just in case.

"Well, after evaluating all the talks and workshops available, there were only four sessions that applied to my work, or to my interests overall, and they were all on the same day," he reported. "And since we had set aside three days for the trip, I spent some time with a new friend while I was there, someone I met who was involved with ancient manuscripts and who

might be useful to us in the future."
Uncomfortable with outright lying, Dominic had fashioned a truthful explanation suitable to both himself and the kindly monk.

"It's always good to build a network of colleagues, Miguel. You never know when they might be needed.

"Now, I need you to do something for me, and in secrecy, please. Dante asked me to locate the old archives of one Cardinal Lucido Parocchi from around 1896, during Leo XIII's papacy. Now, I must tell you, Miguel, that the cardinal specifically asked me not to tell anyone, even you. But this is a cumbersome task and a waste of my time, though *he* seems to think it's a priority. Why we need to go that far back for anything is a puzzle to me, but, '*Ours is not to reason why....*'"

"Sure, Cal, I'll get on it right now. Anything in particular I should be looking for?"

"Oh, yes," Mendoza remembered. "He wanted to know more about a papal legate visiting a priest named Bérenger Saunière in a French parish called Rennes-le-Château."

Dominic stood there, speechless, his whole body frozen. *This cannot be a coincidence!* he thought. All of a sudden Hana's story of someone following them flashed through his mind. *But why? This made no sense! Am I being paranoid? Or is Dante the one who's paranoid?*

Without betraying his fractured composure, Dominic left Mendoza's office and headed down to the Miscellanea section in search of the Parocchi archives, trying to reason whether this presented a new predicament or not. He swiftly decided this was not happenstance. *Dante had to know we were in Rennes-le-Château!* But he couldn't possibly know why—*or could he?* Regardless, Dominic had to assume this added a new dimension to his discovery, one that warranted complete discretion in their activities, especially if Dante's spies were watching.

His mind preoccupied, Dominic wandered through the Gallery of the Metallic Shelves as if he were lost in the desert, eerie pools of illumination, like moonlight, following his every footstep as he walked slowly, aimlessly, assessing the situation. Surrounding him were millions of pages of Church history tucked into folios and codices, in journals and binders of every sort, documents no one had any particular need to read after they were prepared, many of them going back to the ninth century. And yet for hundreds of years the Vatican's policy had been absolute—to maintain the Secret Archives as its repository for every document it generated or acquired. A frequent thought crossed Dominic's mind again—*What must be hidden here…silent time bombs waiting to enlighten or destroy people and institutions…?*

He had reached one of the index stations positioned throughout the subterranean Gallery, and logging onto the computer terminal there, searched for the Leo XIII section, then the Parocchi subsection. Finding the location details, he walked down another twenty or so aisles until he came to the designated area, then to the numbered folio containing Parocchi's archive for 1896.

Cardinal Lucido Parocchi was, in his time, a very important prince of the Church. Following a succession of honors and promotions, he eventually became the head of all cardinals in the Catholic Church. Just eight years later Pope Leo XIII appointed him Secretary of the Supreme Sacred Congregation of the Holy Office, the same department in the Vatican that had been responsible for the terrible Inquisitions three centuries earlier.

Dominic sifted through scores of reports and forms and doctrinal dissertations, none of which seemed relevant to his quest. Then he came to a folder labeled *"Gallia"*—Latin for *"France"*—which, he reasoned, would be a good place to start.

Paging through the sequentially-dated papers—silently grateful to his predecessors hundreds of years earlier for their thoughtful organization—he came upon three neatly handwritten onionskin pages the color of wheat, stapled together and titled in Italian, "Report of Activities at Rennes-le-Château, France." It was marked *"Privato e Confidenziale."*

His anticipation peaking, Dominic took the entire folio to the nearest reading table and sat down, turning on the table lamp lest he find himself in total darkness when the overhead lighting sensed a lack of movement.

The report itself was written in Italian, in the graceful cursive hand of its author. He began reading and translating.

Report of Activities at Rennes-le-Château
Private and Confidential

This account is submitted on 11 June 1896 by Monsignor Franco Moretti, papal legate of the Holy Office, at the request of Cardinal Lucido Parocchi.

I met personally with Abbé François-Bérenger Saunière of the communal parish in Rennes-le-Château, Aude, France, on 2 June 1896. Abbé Saunière had written to the Holy Office in regard to a manuscript he came into possession of and which, he believed, might bring grave harm to the Church.

Saunière informed me that upon

discovering this manuscript in one of the old chapel's hollow altar columns, he had been sent to Paris by Monsignor Félix-Arsène Billard, Bishop of Carcassonne, to resolve the document's meaning and value. On his return to the village, he wrote his letter to the Holy Office requesting this audience.

When I asked that he show me the manuscript, he at first declined, instead presenting me with a translation of it which he procured from experts in Paris. The substance of it is, I must say, considerably frightful, and I shall relay its content in person when requested to do so. In the interest of vital security, I do not think it appropriate to lay such details down in written form.

Once again I insisted Saunière show me the manuscript to prove its existence. It was only then he agreed. He proffered a wooden cylinder from which he extracted an ancient papyrus document. To my seasoned eye, I believe it to be fully authentic. It was written in Koine Greek and is apparently by the hand of an individual having profound historical importance—a name of which we are all familiar. Again, I shall reveal this in person, for reasons stated.

I inquired as to why the abbé contacted the Holy Office in this regard. His reply was direct and to the point, constituting nothing short of extortion. Saunière is requesting substantial funding to restore the church and other buildings under his domain, in exchange for conserving the document securely protected and hidden from public revelation. He also informed me that arrangements had been made for release of the information should any ill-timed misfortune befall him.

Given the circumstances and the apparent legitimacy of the manuscript I witnessed, and its exceedingly damaging content, I recommend surrendering to Abbé Saunière's audacious petition. The requested funds pale in comparison to the harmful desecration, indeed, the possible destruction it could bring to Holy Mother Church.

I believe this is a matter in which the Holy Father must be informed immediately, and I recommend convening appropriate individuals to further discuss details I have omitted here. This affair should be treated with extreme urgency and the highest confidentiality.

Signed / Msgr. Franco Moretti, S.J.

Dominic sat back in the wooden chair, galvanized by what he had just read. With mounting anxiousness, translating the rest of the Magdalene document now became of vital importance. He *had* to find out what Moretti learned from Saunière.

His thoughts turned to Dante. Should he turn over this devastating report to the man who was very likely having him followed, for reasons unknown? Should he hide it away in a box, like his fellow *scrittore* Gonfalonieri did a few hundred years ago? Or maybe he should keep it himself, and just give Mendoza the rest of what was left in the folio for Dante's purposes? He had to make a decision *now*. First, though, he scanned the report and uploaded it to the cloud.

Professional ethics compelled him to leave the

document intact, but after saying a quick prayer—a fitting Act of Contrition—he chose to place the damning report into another folder, as if it had been misfiled by accident. A large folio next to "*Gallia*" was labeled "*Anglia*," Latin for "*England*." Dominic pulled out the folio, found a suitable place to bury the Moretti report, and returned the "*Anglia*" folio to its place on the shelf. He decided to deliver the remaining "*Gallia*" folio to Mendoza for Dante's review.

He suddenly had a desperate desire to speak with Hana, to share the report with her. To plan their next steps. To calm himself down. Until he could get to her, however, he decided he would email the Moretti report to her for review. He added a brief message:

> Hana – I found the attached report on Berenger Sauniere from a papal legate who visited him at Rennes-le-Château in 1896! Read it and we'll discuss when I see you tonight – M

That task finished, he pocketed the phone, extinguished the table lamp, grabbed the folio for Mendoza and Dante, and returned upstairs to the prefect's office.

29

The Send button on Dominic's email app initiated its normal sequence of events. His message and the attachment were transformed into bits of electronic data and routed to the Vatican's central mail server, which immediately dispatched it to the shared internet backbone at the U.S. Aviano Air Base in northern Italy. Before being routed to their final destinations, though, all incoming messages routinely passed through an innocuous device the size of a small attaché case, which some years before had been secretly installed by the U.S. National Security Agency to monitor all internet traffic into or out of Italy—public and private. As they were programmed to do, logic circuits embedded in the device fed all words contained in the message through its Dictionary. The Dictionary was continuously updated by the NSA with particularly meaningful words relating to such activities as terrorism, assassination, and political coups. It was also known that the Dictionary flagged words relevant to commercial interests, aviation and private space ventures, for example, along with customized searches, and in hundreds of languages.

At the earlier intercept request of Interpol's Petrov Gović, the keywords *"Rennes-le-Chateau"* and *"Berenger Sauniere"* were applied as legitimate Content for Disposition, and Dominic's original message and attachment containing those words was held on a backburner chip, where it would remain, undelivered, until released with proper authorization. Triggering a classified router, the entire message was then scrambled and uplinked on an ultra-secure channel to a Vortex communications satellite currently in low orbit over Libya. Onboard transponders relayed the message through two adjacent satellites in the linear fleet, until it was downlinked to one of several giant white radome listening posts at Menwith Hill, a major NSA communications intelligence hub situated in a cow pasture on the remote Yorkshire moors of England, part of the "Five Eyes" network involving the United States, Australia, Canada, New Zealand, and the United Kingdom. Identified as a Priority One transmission, the message was immediately rerouted to Fort Meade, Maryland, headquarters of the NSA, where a soft alarm sounded at the ECHELON command console.

Built during the Cold War, ECHELON was now mainly used to filter all foreign telephone, fax, and internet communications having any relevance to the interests of the United States. The orderly manning the console was accustomed to many such alerts each day—email sent, for example, between Airbus executives and various European government agencies discussing ways to outmaneuver Boeing—these were routine intercepts, and were generally sent on to the Office of Intelligence Liaison at the Department of Commerce, inevitably finding their way to Boeing Headquarters in Chicago. Only rarely did the orderly encounter one originating from within the Vatican, and as a Catholic himself, he felt a momentary rush of added privilege in performing his duty for God and country. Interpreting the route coding ID assigned to the message at the ECHELON hub in Menwith Hill, the orderly dialed the Officer-in-Charge for Minor State Relations, alerting him to an incoming message just forwarded to his console. Scanning its content, it took the OIC less than a minute to locate and input a forwarding address to the message and tap the Send button.

Back at the orderly's console, a flashing icon appeared next to the OIC's forwarded message on the outgoing traffic log. A new code had been generated for disposition of the original message. The orderly entered a sequence of characters and executed a command that allowed the original message to be sent on to Hana Sinclair, then retraced the path of Dominic's message as far back as the backburner chip in Italy, instructing it to wipe clear its contents.

A few seconds later a subtle, two-toned chime announced the arrival of an encrypted message on a computer located in the office of the Vatican Secretariat of State. It was from Petrov Gović.

At the moment, Fabrizio Dante was not there to read it. But it would wait.

30

Back at his Interpol office in Lyon, Petrov Gović had just finished reading the intercepted Moretti report sent by Father Dominic when his private cell phone vibrated.

Tapping the green button, he held the device next to his ear. "*Gović.*"

"Petrov, this is Sirola. Is this a good time to talk?"

"Roko, my friend," Gović said. "Of course, now is fine. Where are you calling from?"

"I am on assignment in Zagreb this week," Roko replied. "But I believe you have some names for me?"

Gović reached for the stack of Croatian Blue Notices he had set aside as recruitment candidates. "Have you got something to write with?"

Gović read the names of several Croatian nationals whose fascist undertakings had flagged them for action by Interpol. Roko Sirola, one of his most capable agents in the expanding Novi Ustasha, was charged with the discreet enlistment campaign for new soldiers.

"Roko," Gović added, considering what he

had just read. "A rather interesting opportunity has come to light which may require your assistance. There is a priest in Rome, no one of particular importance, who may have acquired something that may be of value to us. Once I know more, I will provide further details. Until then, *Za dom–spremni!* Gović out."

Ending the call with the traditional Ustasha salute—meaning *'For the homeland–ready!'*—Gović weighed the consequences of his considered duplicity. Whatever it was that Dominic obtained from the Dénarnaud woman, the Church—at least according to the Moretti report—may deem it of vital importance to possess at all costs. Something that valuable to Cardinal Dante might prove of equal value to the Ustasha. If Saunière was able to trade on the knowledge, so could Gović.

Sitting in his office, Cardinal Dante had finished reading the entire "*Gallia*" folio Mendoza had given him. Finding nothing of significance regarding Bérenger Saunière or Rennes-le-Château, disappointment clouded his mind.

He opened his iPad to draft a message to Petrov Gović when he found an unopened ProtonMail message from the agent sitting in his inbox. Logging onto the secure server, Dante read the forwarded message Michael Dominic had addressed to Hana Sinclair, then read the attached scanned report from the papal legate, Monsignor Moretti.

Seething with rage after he read it, Dante was infuriated with Mendoza at his breach of protocol, ignoring his explicit instructions not to involve Dominic.

Dante had to assume Dominic was in possession of *something*. It was clear he had found the Moretti report and had willfully withheld it from the folio he gave Mendoza. Dante would deal with that later. But the more important question was—*What else did he have?* Why the interest in Rennes-le-Château? What had he obtained while visiting the Dénarnaud woman?

As he considered the predicament now facing him, an unsettling sense of vulnerability began to form. Circumstances were getting out of control. His control.

He needed to tread very carefully. Unsure of the stakes involved, but assuming they were extraordinary based on Moretti's assessment, Dante needed a plan.

31

His work done for the day, Dominic had arranged to meet Hana at her hotel. He tossed his reference books into a backpack and hailed a taxi from Porta Sant'Anna.

On arriving at the Rome Cavalieri, he entered the grand hotel lobby and took the elevator to the Palermo Suite. Hana answered the doorbell, a look of astonishment on her face.

"Michael! Were you as shocked as I was after reading the Moretti report?!"

Still standing at the door, Dominic said, smiling, "Can I come in…?"

"Sorry," Hana confessed, shaking her head. "I'm too flustered by all this to remember my manners."

Dominic entered the foyer and looked around. It was by far the largest hotel suite he had ever seen. A complex of rooms, actually—5,000 square feet comprising four bedrooms, an intimate dining room for eight with its own privately stocked wine cellar, maharajah seats and Empire bronzes making up the sitting room, fine Oriental rugs on rich walnut floors, columns of green marble and polished wood supporting inset ceilings from which hung grand crystal chandeliers, with Old Master oil paintings gracing every wall. And all of it overlooking the evening splendors of Rome through floor-to-ceiling windows.

Taking it all in, Dominic turned to Hana stoically. "As if the private jet wasn't enough. International banking must pay very well these days."

Hana was nonplussed, showing a flash of embarrassment in the sumptuous extravagance surrounding them. "My family's wealth goes back generations, Michael. I rarely let others into this part of my life. It can be overwhelming for most people, so please don't judge me by it. I fight hard to separate myself from the trappings as best I can."

"No judgment, I promise," Dominic said. I am just grateful for a safe place for our research. Especially now. So, what about that Moretti report? I couldn't believe what I read, either."

He laid out for Hana how he came to find the report, at Dante's request through Mendoza, giving her a visual description of the Miscellanea and a general impression of the difficulty locating anything there. "Honestly, it's a wonder I found it at all.

"It's also worth noting, by the way, that Dante told Mendoza he didn't want *me*, specifically, to be involved in searching for that document!

Thankfully for us, Mendoza thought it would be a waste of time to go searching for it himself. But excluding me from the equation can only mean that Dante is on to us. I don't do well feeling paranoid, Hana.

"But," he added, "I think we must assume Dante knows about you and our trip to Rennes-le-Château. I'm certain now that we *were* being followed. All this makes little sense to me—unless Dante suspects we have something he wants. What if we were even being watched while visiting Madame Dénarnaud?"

Hana reached over and squeezed Michael's hand. "Well, there's not much we can do about that now, except be more careful going forward. Meanwhile, let's get to work on the Magdalene manuscript. I locked it in the safe, let me get it."

As she left the room, Dominic retrieved the reference books from his backpack and took a seat at the dining table. He had also brought four small leather sandbags for securing the corners and archivist's gloves for handling the ancient paper. Returning with the wooden cylinder, Hana handed it to him. He slipped on the gloves and carefully withdrew the manuscript, then transferred the document into an acid-free archival sleeve of Type D Mylar, itself secured inside a stiff archival folio for stronger and safer conservation. They would no longer need the wooden tube.

"This may take a few hours, so if you have anything else you need to do, I'll let you know when we have something."

"Take your time," she said as she walked back to the sitting room. "I'm still working on those financial reports from the Bibliothèque."

Though the content of the manuscript was relatively short, the work was tedious. Translating ancient languages isn't just about interpreting what the original author wrote, word for word. It also involves attempting to unravel what the writer actually meant to convey, the challenge of communicating idioms, ancient grammar, and cultural figures of speech, not to mention the lack of punctuation creating run-on sentences.

Dominic turned to one of his reference books for comparable examples of first-century Koine Greek in the Byzantine era, with which to analyze the Magdalene manuscript. He noted one of them was quite similar.

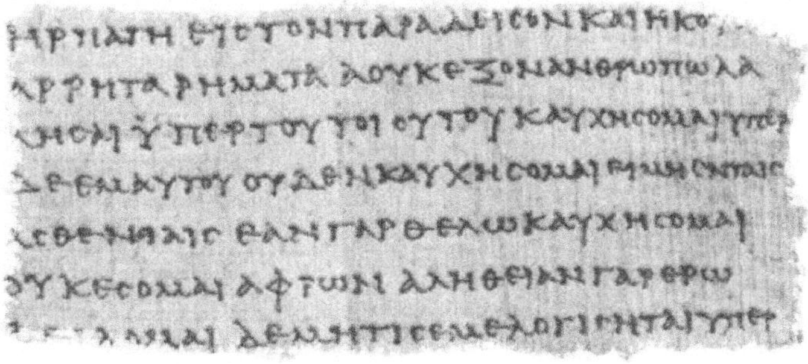

Using earlier published translated documents such as these—and an indispensable reference titled *Synopsis Quattuor Evangeliorum*—assisted Dominic considerably in detecting unique linguistic and textual indicators useful to most ancient Koine Greek-to-English transcription projects.

First, he examined the entire document several times in order to distinguish identifiable concepts or key sentences, or repetitive words that stood out. Then he visually scanned the text for specific names of historical people or places he might recognize, to help contextualize the writing.

One name and place caught his attention immediately: *Jesus* and *Nazareth!* Then he recognized two more geographic places, *Jerusalem* and *Gaul*—Gaul being the archaic name attributed to France. These words he had encountered before and often in his work dealing with biblical scrolls.

Progressing slowly but steadily on his first draft, the result was an incoherent hodgepodge of words with indistinct meanings, a common result with early translations. Then came time for using the dictionary to identify more distinct meanings, remaining mindful of overall context.

After some two hours of effort, Dominic had completed a first paragraph—one that promptly refocused his worn-out mind.

> *I am Mariam of Magdala. This is my account of Jesus of Nazareth.*
>
> *To stave off those who might seek to defile our Lord's remains, in haste I have departed Jerusalem, the land which holds the misery of our Lord's persecution, and in secret I have taken my husband's body to Gaul, where his remains shall be buried next to mine when my own time comes.*

The impact of this statement alone staggered him. Mary Magdalene unequivocally asserted that Jesus was her husband!? And she took his body to France!

Dominic was aware of the many legends claiming that after Christ's death, Mary Magdalene, Joseph of Arimathea, and several other disciples were cast adrift in a boat without oars or sails—expeditiously sent away from

Jerusalem by fellow Jews to protect them from the Romans—which eventually landed on the shores of southern France, where they built churches and preached the gospels.

He also thought back to the stories of Magdalene having brought an ossuary—a chest made for holding bones of the deceased—along with her in her travels. *Could that be the reliquary spoken of in the legends of the Cathars' treasure? One containing the bones of Christ?*

His hands quivering now, Dominic set about working on the rest of the manuscript before telling Hana of this first mind-boggling discovery. Better accustomed to Mary Magdalene's hand now, the remaining translations came a bit easier. After another two hours he was finished, and what he read, now in full context, left him lost for words.

> *After his crucifixion, the Lord came to me as in a vision, "Mistake not my resurrection as being of the body, my beloved, for it was only my spirit that ascended into my father's kingdom, as will yours when you depart this life."*
>
> *Then I said to Peter, "Peter, do not tell the others, but it was the spirit of our Lord which left this world. His body did*

> *not ascend as the others believe… Joseph of Arimathea helped me move our Lord's body from the cave and take it to safety, for when we fled the Romans."*

Dominic read it over again and again, making sure he had gotten the most crucial components correct. In the end, he was confident the translation was as accurate as one could make it. There had to be more pages, somewhere, continuing her story. But as with the *Gospel of Mary* and other texts, there were often pages missing from those which were found. Rarely were ancient manuscripts discovered in their entirety, leaving scholars to add their own interpretations of what might be missing, or just suffering with the loss and taking what remained at face value.

He stood up unsteadily, took a deep breath and stretched, removed his gloves, and went into the sitting room where Hana was working on her laptop.

"There's that face again," she said, looking up at him questioningly. "So, what have we got? Is it important?"

"Hana," he said, his face pale and drawn, "this is the single most consequential document the Christian world will have ever known. Full stop."

He escorted Hana to the table and handed her his notebook. She sat down and read it.

"My *God,* Michael. This is *extraordinary!* What does one even *do* with knowledge like this?!"

"There's the problem." Dominic acceded, still shaken. "The Roman Catholic Church, indeed all of Christian theology, is predicated on the death and *bodily* resurrection of Christ as among its most basic foundations of faith. Most messianic prophesies view the Resurrection as God's promise that all believers will ascend bodily into heaven after the Second Coming, as Jesus's body was believed to have done after the crucifixion. If that *didn't* happen, there's a problem with the whole Christian eschatology. Jesus would have been a mere mortal, thus challenging his divinity.

"The empty tomb," he continued, "has long been debated by scholars as to whether Christ's body actually resurrected, or if it was merely a spiritual ascension and the body itself was either stolen or moved elsewhere within the three days following the crucifixion. These parables have been analyzed and interpreted in countless ways by scholars and theologians for centuries, but no one actually knew for sure. Until now."

Dominic couldn't believe he had said those words, much less that *he* was the one to rediscover long-hidden proof contradicting not only oral tradition but accepted biblical scripture.

"It's no wonder the Vatican may have paid Bérenger Saunière to keep this information suppressed," he said. "If this ever got out, it would bring the Church to its knees. Everything would have to be reconsidered, Hana. Faithful Christians the world over would question the basis of their own faith, not to mention the motives of Church leaders throughout time."

Still standing, Dominic put his head in his hands, his mental faculties spent from the efforts of translating, his mind swimming with ramifications. Sensing his exhaustion and what this new and profound knowledge must mean to him, Hana got up and reflexively embraced him. Giving in to an unexpected need for comfort, Dominic fell into her arms, trembling, tears suddenly falling onto her shoulder.

"It's alright," she whispered, "It's a lot to take in."

"But this changes everything," he muttered. "The basis for my own faith. One of the reasons I became a priest. It's all a lie."

They both stood there, embraced in silence, Michael giving in to fatigue, undone by his work and the resulting myriad conflicts ahead.

32

Twenty miles outside of Rome lies the historical town of Zagarolo—a medieval commune with roots in the nearby ancient city of Gabii, on the hills of an extinct volcano crater—and the host location of Teller University, an undergraduate college focused on Jewish Studies including Hebrew, Talmud, and Jewish history.

Professor Emeritus Dr. Simon Ginzberg was sitting in his office in the Caprioli Palace on the Teller campus when an email came in from Michael Dominic's Vatican server.

Simon – Please see attached, your eyes only. Will share original manuscript in person. When and where can we meet? – Michael

Intrigued, Ginzberg opened the attachment and began reading. When he finished, he felt as if he had been gut-punched. He read it again, breathlessly but with renewed vigor, dumbfounded by the obvious consequences. *What in God's name has young Michael discovered here?!"* he pondered.

Realizing this was not something they could very well discuss inside the Vatican, Ginzberg promptly sent a text message to Dominic: **I suggest meeting here in my office. Are you available tomorrow evening?**

The reply was immediate: **Yes. We'll see you then.** Ginzberg texted back directions to his campus office.

* * *

Petrov Gović sat with his back to the wall at a corner table in Chez Antonin, a popular lunch bistro in the heart of Lyon just off the Rhone River. He had just dug into a tender Bresse Chicken cutlet when his phone buzzed. Setting down his spoon with a sigh and putting on his reading glasses, he found another intercepted message from Michael Dominic sitting in his inbox. He took a sip of the chilled Beaujolais he'd ordered and read the message sent to Simon Ginzberg, then opened the attachment.

As he reread the translated Magdalene manuscript, he picked up his spoon, taking small bites of the fish stew as he considered the impact of what was reading. He set the spoon down and stared out the window, not really focused on anything in particular, as his thoughts turned to what this knowledge might mean. And then it struck him.

Standing up, he threw down a twenty euro note on the table and quickly left the restaurant, abandoning a perfectly good meal.

There were things to do.

33

After Simon Ginzberg had welcomed his guests to the Teller campus, he invited them to sit, then locked the door to his office and closed the vertical blinds on all windows. The room turned shadowy, with what remained of the setting sun casting an orange glow on the white blinds, lending a moody atmosphere to the meeting. Dominic introduced Hana and gave Simon the basics of her background and her help thus far.

"Would either of you care for coffee or tea?" Ginzberg asked.

Both of them declined. For a few moments no one said a word. The atmosphere in the room was tense with anticipation. Ginzberg spoke first.

"I expect this manuscript has turned your world upside down, no?" the old man said, grinning knowingly.

"I was about to say, '*You have no idea,*' but I think you do, Simon," Dominic said. "Not many things intimidate me or move me to tears. But this exercise has done me in. I honestly have no idea what to do about it, which is why we've come to you."

"Well, let's start with seeing what you have here," said Ginzberg. "I haven't been this excited since being allowed private access to the Gnostic Gospels from Nag Hammadi a few years back. Did you know the Dead Sea Scrolls from Qumran were even declared Israeli *state secrets* when they were discovered in the early 1950s?! A preposterous appellation, of course, and so typical of power-hungry men trying to exact ownership over every rare object of value.

"Considering which," he added, looking directly into Dominic's eyes, "can you imagine how zealously the Vatican would try to quash this, given their historical chauvinism? Not to mention the impact they might consider its contents could have on its global congregations!"

Dominic had no answer, though not as if he hadn't already considered the questions.

He withdrew the folioed manuscript from his backpack and handed it to Ginzberg, who switched on the reading lamp over his desk and gazed at the extraordinary papyrus.

Thoroughly proficient in translating Koine Greek, the scholar read each of the glyphs, and in a short while concluded that Dominic's transcription was accurate, or close enough, to the original.

Ginzberg took off his glasses and rubbed his hands across his face. "I cannot express how privileged I am that you bring this to me, Michael," he said, his eyes glistening with emotion. "Of all the antiquities I have dealt with in over sixty years of scholarship, none has affected me like this Magdalene message. It is profoundly important on a number of levels.

"Apart from the obvious first—that being the only extant writing by the Magdalene herself—this is the earliest direct witness report of Christ's crucifixion ever to be found, and from his own wife, no less! Which in itself is an important observation, that this bears proof of Christ's marriage to Mary Magdalene. From that one might assume the existence of the *Desposyni*, or descendants of Christ, as many scholars and researchers have imagined based on the Lost Gospel in the British Library, with further corroboration implied in the *Gospel of Philip* from New Testament apocrypha.

"But most crucially," Ginzberg added, words now tumbling out of his mouth, "there's the obvious absence of the presumed resurrection! My God, the entire Christian belief system is based on Christ's bodily ascension into heaven, and his promise to the faithful that they too will ascend. To think that such a charade has been played out for two thousand years is nothing short of breathtaking. But, as Otto Rahn himself once wrote, 'Intense faith finds attentive ears in a suggestible people.'

"As I seem to recall there's even mention of the consequences of Christ *not* being resurrected in the New Testament itself… in 1 Corinthians, I believe." He reached for his bible, found the passage in Chapter 15, and read it aloud:

> *"And if Christ has not been raised, then all our preaching is useless, and your faith is useless. And we apostles would all be lying about God—for we have said that God raised Christ from the grave. . . . And if Christ has not been raised, then your faith is useless and you are still guilty of your sins. In that case, all who have died believing in Christ are lost! And if our hope in Christ is only for this life, we are more to be pitied than anyone in the world."*

Ginzberg took a deep breath, leveling his gaze back onto the manuscript. "And lastly, we have the Magdalene having taken Christ's bones to France. Now, this knowledge has been posited long before in many oral traditions. Which brings to mind the Cathars and their rumored 'holy' treasure. Perhaps it wasn't the Grail 'cup' they possessed at all, but something more consistent with sacred knowledge, as has been widely speculated. This would certainly constitute that kind of discovery. And if those stories have any substance, that ossuary could very well be buried in one of the deep caves at Grotto de Lombrives in France, or the Caves of the Sabarthès at nearby Montségur, according to Cathar legend.

"In any event, Bérenger Saunière certainly had something that the Church, in the person of Monsignor Moretti, believed to be of sufficient enormity to pay for its concealment. I'm surprised they didn't try to obtain the manuscript themselves, by any means possible, to ensure its 'safekeeping.'"

Dominic stood up to stretch his legs. "I haven't found anything to substantiate the Church's attempts at such an undertaking, if there even was one," he said, pacing the small office. "So, what's your advice on what we should do with this now, Simon?"

Ginzberg, pensively steepling his fingers as he sat in his chair, paused for several moments before answering. "First, the manuscript must be protected at all costs, and not in the Vatican. If you have access to a secure place, keep it there for the time being."

"I have a safe in my hotel suite, which is where it's kept now," Hana said assuringly.

"Good. As for what to do, I believe we need to think on this for a while," Ginzberg said.

"Meanwhile there's also the matter of determining the document's authenticity, which would call for, among other things, a carbon-14 dating analysis. We can do that here, of course, but we'll need to extract a small piece of the papyrus for testing. Are we in agreement on that?"

"Absolutely," Dominic said. "We should also do a molecular spectroscopy while we're at it. Toshi Kwan can help me with that back at the lab. When will you have results, Simon?"

"It shouldn't take more than a couple hours or so, provided I can get access to the accelerator mass spectrometer without raising interest by others in the lab here. I'll do it tonight when everyone's gone."

"Well, apart from Bérenger Saunière's obviously profitable dealings with the Vatican, the manuscript has been kept in hiding for two thousand years. It can wait a bit longer for us to reflect on our next moves. My inclination is to carry out the tests and just to sit on things for now. Would you agree?"

Dominic breathed a sigh of relief. "Yes, that gives us time to consider the consequences and determine how its exposure might play out—*if* we ultimately decide exposure is the best option. Right now, I can barely form a cohesive sentence, much less make plans on changing the course of world history."

Ginzberg laughed. "Don't take this on as an undue burden, Michael. This is a monumental adventure! These things have a way of working out, do they not? Take the *Gospel of Thomas* and the *Gospel of Mary*, for example, Gnostic texts the world never knew of before their fairly recent discovery—they also changed history, though each is still being examined and interpreted decades after being found.

"In any event, rest assured," the old man added with a twinkle in his eye, "your privileged role in history is guaranteed, whether you like it or not."

"There's one more thing that just occurred to me," Dominic said with a far-off look. "Remember that third Nostradamus quatrain, about the '*Albigensian truth*' being summoned, and '*Mother sacred breathes her last*'? If this *is* the treasure of the Cathars—the Albigensians—could release of this manuscript spell the end of the Church? Or the end of the world?"

All three of them sat in silence, thinking the unthinkable.

34

Perched high atop a broad hill overlooking Italy's Lake Albano, the Papal Palace of Castel Gandolfo serves as the summer residence and weekend retreat of the pope, as it has for hundreds of years and dozens of popes. Built in the early 17th century, the entire Apostolic Palace complex is larger than all of Vatican City itself, comprising 135 acres of ornamental gardens and building complexes ensconced in a sleepy village in the Alban Hills, some sixteen miles southeast of Rome.

Seated at a magnificent Red Verona marble table in the spacious Sala del Concistore, the palace's conference room for visiting dignitaries, four of the pope's closest advisors had assembled to discuss a delicate matter involving the Church's financial assets: Cardinal Enrico Petrini, the most trusted member of the pope's *Consulta;* Cardinal Fabrizio Dante, the Vatican Secretary of State; Bishop Klaus Wolaschka, president of the Institute for Religious Works, also known as the Vatican Bank; and Baron Armand de Saint-Clair, president of Banque Suisse de Saint-Clair and also a member of the pope's *Consulta.*

"Gentlemen," said Wolaschka, "I remind you this gold has been sitting in our vaults now for nearly seventy years. No one with acceptable proof of ownership has laid claim to it, so I submit that it belongs to Holy Mother Church. That has been my position since I took this post and remains so to this day."

"Of course no one has claimed it, Klaus," Petrini said with annoyance. "Most of it belonged to Jews and Serbs and other unfortunate souls who lost it during the reprehensible Nazi purges. We *must* accede to requests by international Jewish groups representing Holocaust survivors and work out an acceptable form of restitution. To ignore their pleas goes against the fundamental work of the Church."

"I'm not so sure I would agree, Enrico," Dante countered. "To even acknowledge the Vatican Bank's being in possession of it would exacerbate the already injured reputation of Pius XII, one we can hardly afford to aggravate this year." Though he didn't have to clarify the issue, Dante referred to the millions of newly released papers of Pius XII's papal reign, a cache certain to bring unwanted attention to the Church's role during World War II.

"How much are we talking about, Klaus?" Dante asked.

"At current market rates—and this is not for

public consumption—we're looking at around 200 million U.S. dollars in gold bullion alone," Wolaschka said casually, not meeting anyone's eyes as he glanced out the windows over the palace gardens.

Saint-Clair was taken aback. "That is a shocking figure, Klaus! Is that on the books as being a Church asset? Or has it been held in abeyance in some form of concealed account?" he demanded.

The banker was indifferent to Saint-Clair's outburst, not answering the question directly. "From my understanding, Armand, we acquired those reserves legitimately, acting on behalf of European central banks whose assets were being seized by the Nazis on a regular basis. And many of those were forced out of business by the Reich's actions. Who's to say what actually belongs to whom now? With no official transfer paperwork proving such transactions, and no permissible heirs showing proper documentation, such as death certificates, there's really nothing we can do."

"How can we possibly justify requiring death certificates for the millions of Jews who were slaughtered in concentration camps?!" Petrini asked, appalled at the very concept. "It's inhumane to even require this of survivors who were children at the time, from whom everything had been taken. What proof could they possibly have now? The Nazis never bothered with *death certificates!*"

At that moment two Swiss Guards opened the double doors of the room and snapped to full attention as the pope walked in, a crystal bowl of fruit in his hands. The four men at the table stood and bowed their heads.

"Good morning, Your Holiness," they said in unison.

"*Buongiorno,* my friends," said the pope brightly as he entered, suddenly aware of the tensions in the room. "I thought you could use some refreshment from the garden… ripe Giallone peaches from our orchard. I picked them myself, just now." He set the bowl down on the marble table, conscious that things were likely being discussed here which should not concern him.

"Please, don't let me interrupt your work. We are leaving Castel Gandolfo later this afternoon, I thought you should know."

After giving the group his blessing that their work be fruitful, the pope left the room, and the Swiss Guards quietly closed the door.

Saint-Clair looked down at figures in a report he was holding. "Quoting *The New York Times,* 'The Swiss have estimated that from September 1939 to June 1945, Germany's Central Bank acquired or disposed of some $909 million worth of gold at wartime prices,'—which today, gentlemen, would equate to roughly 12 billion U.S. dollars at current exchange rates."

"Armand, your own bank must have vast stores of gold bullion from wartime accounts," Wolaschka asserted. "Everyone knows Swiss banks were the safest havens for the Nazis. Are you yourself not a subject of current investigations by the British and American governments?"

"At no time did my family's bank have any dealings with the Reich!" Saint-Clair declared hotly. "My father resisted their appeals and their threats successfully, though others weren't as fortunate—or should I say, as shrewd—in negotiating with Hitler. Indeed, we came to the defense of those whose fortunes were in serious jeopardy—foremost, the flight of significant Jewish capital—and every cent has since been properly accounted for and returned. And that's the responsible way it should be handled by every banking institution." He turned and looked directly at Klaus Wolaschka as he said these last words.

Enrico Petrini came to Saint-Clair's defense. "Are you aware, Bishop Wolaschka, that hundreds of thousands of Holocaust survivors' families still living have yet to see any compensation thus far? *Over seventy years after the fact?* How can the Vatican Bank possibly avoid charges of complicity now?

"My friends," Petrini continued, looking around the table, "the Holy Father is depending on us to make the right decision in this important matter. And soon."

Dante looked at his watch. "I'm afraid we're out of time today, gentlemen, so this matter will have to be tabled for now. Klaus, I'd like to meet with you in my office tomorrow so we can discuss internal implications. And Armand, may I have a word with you? Let us take a walk in the gardens."

The centuries-old, immaculately maintained papal gardens of Castel Gandolfo's Villa Berberini, once the site of Roman Emperor Domitian's first-century country villa, have served the meditative needs of popes for generations. Umbrella pine trees, towering cypresses, and blue-green age-old cedars line shaded walking paths amid geometrical parterres that rival the natural beauty and grace of the gardens of Versailles. Ancient grottoes and fountains featuring classical aquatic deities and statues of the Virgin Mary and other saints look out over exquisitely manicured lawns and hedges.

Fabrizio Dante and Armand de Saint-Clair ambled along the myrtle-lined paths built by Pope

Urban's architects in the 17th century, as each savored one of the Giallone peaches the pope had brought them from the adjoining orchard.

"Armand," Dante began, "I have come to understand that your granddaughter has been collaborating with one of our Archives personnel, Father Dominic, in a matter that may be of some concern to the Church." He paused to take another bite of the peach, its juice dribbling onto the pebbles of the path.

"I don't have the full particulars as of this moment," Dante continued, "but I would think it in both our best interests that whatever their little scheme is doesn't appear on the front page of *Le Monde*. Or any page, for that matter."

"Hana?" Saint-Clair asked, surprised. "I can't imagine what she might need from your Archives, Eminence. I do know she is working on this matter of Jewish gold and the complicity of Swiss banks during the war—surely a timely topic given the focus of our meeting today—but I don't see how that requires the assistance of your staff. I will certainly ask her about it, if you wish."

"That would be kind of you, Armand. As you may know, Father Dominic has been, more or less, a ward of Cardinal Petrini's since he was a child. But as Dominic works under my supervision, I'm sure I can keep things in order in our own house."

"Back to the matter at hand," Saint-Clair said,

"why is Wolaschka so intractable on his view of the Vatican's gold holdings? At least some of those reserves cannot be claimed as Church assets. It's illogical to think otherwise."

"Klaus is a hard-headed man of figures, and German to boot, so efficiencies run deep in his blood. Let me work on him further. This is a delicate matter for the Church at a perilous time—given the release of Pius XII's papers, as you know—but the Holy Father does want it brought to an amicable conclusion."

"As do I," Saint-Clair concurred, as both men returned to the cool embrace of the Apostolic Palace.

35

From his window seat in the last row of Croatia Airlines flight 5434, en route from Zagreb to Fiumicino airport in Rome, Roko Sirola sat staring at the billowy white clouds the jet was now passing over, absently twirling the silver Ehrenring fastened on his left hand as he looked at photographs of Dominic and Hana for his new assignment.

A priest and a woman journalist, a rich one at that, he pondered. Gović wants this mysterious document pretty badly, suspending my recruiting work until this mission is complete. But for a five-thousand-euro payday, who's complaining?

Among his other talents—the only legitimate one being a gift for smooth lip service, useful in his enlistment efforts for the Novi Ustasha—Roko Sirola was also a master thief and safecracker. Gović's directive: obtain a document in a wooden cylinder from the safe in Hana Sinclair's hotel suite. *Easy work, easy money,* he thought, smiling as the pilot announced their final approach to Rome.

Two hours later, Hana Sinclair had finished her

work for the day, no closer to finding "Achille," but having learned much more about the flight of Jewish gold and the Swiss and French banking systems, work she would continue tomorrow.

Closing her laptop, she went into the master bedroom to pick out something suitable to wear for dinner with Michael—a dinner over which they would discuss options for handling the Magdalene manuscript.

Eyeing her wardrobe, she chose a smart black Armani pantsuit with a white Carolina Herrera collared shirt, adding a slender gold chain with a crucifix pendant around her neck.

She glanced at the clock on the wall. Twenty minutes to seven. Michael would be here soon.

"Vodka neat, Akvinta if you have it. Punzoné if not," Roko Sirola said to the cocktail waitress as he sat in the guest lounge in the lobby of the Rome Cavalieri. Every luxury hotel here stocked Punzoné, Italy's own premium vodka. But Roko preferred the taste of home with Croatian Triple Distilled Akvinta. Hell, even Stoli would suffice in a pinch. He just needed a bracing shot to settle his nerves.

Watching people move in and out of hotel lobbies was a pastime of Roko's while he patiently waited to do a job, especially in important world cities. Saudi princes in their flowing white qamis and red-and-white ghutras; titans of industry in their expensive Italian suits; cardinals, priests, and nuns wearing their varied habits; and, least abiding of all, hordes of tourists wearing every conceivable casual-attire atrocity vacations seem to inspire—especially Americans, he thought, who had no sense of decorum for time and place. Plus, they were loud and obnoxious.

His eyes surveilling the elevators and grand staircase for signs of either target, whose faces he had memorized on the plane, Roko sat sipping the Punzoné, grateful for its sultry flush on his palate.

Just then he saw the priest enter the front door, not wearing his habit and collar but tan chinos, with a black polo shirt hugging his fit body. He then went directly to a house phone in the lobby, likely calling the woman, Roko presumed.

Hanging up the phone, the priest made his way toward Roko in the guest lounge and took a seat nearby. Roko pulled out his cell phone and made as if he was consumed with something important, balancing his drink on one hand, the phone in the other, his head down between the two.

A few minutes later the woman emerged from the elevator, and the priest got up and joined her as they both went out through the main lobby doors.

Roko swallowed what remained of the vodka, grabbed the shoulder bag he'd brought with him and headed toward the front desk, where a large group of tourists were checking in. He mingled among them as each received their room keycards. Then, singling out the easiest target—a large woman carrying several shopping bags—Roko bumped against her as his hand dipped inside her purse and extracted the keycard she had just placed there.

He then found and entered the men's room and selected a stall, locking the door behind him and taking a seat on the toilet. From his bag he removed a small handheld device—a specialized conversion unit for hacking RFID components on keycards—and inserted the stolen card, pressing two buttons to activate the conversion. Thanks to known vulnerabilities in the underlying software on many high caliber brands of electronic keycard systems, a few minutes later he had a master key for use with any room in the hotel.

Heading up the elevator, Roko got off on the seventh floor and located the Palermo Suite. He knocked on the door and waited several moments, then knocked again. Confident the room was deserted he inserted the keycard. The lock clicked and the LED turned green. Using the cuff of his jacket to press down on the door handle without leaving fingerprints, he slipped inside.

Appraising the opulence of the luxury suite, Roko hoped he might find more than a document in the safe. A king's ransom in jewels would be a nice addition to an already lavish fee. But with so many rooms, where would the safe be? Time was a factor.

He began searching the most likely place: the closets in the master bedroom. Finding nothing there, he moved to the other bedrooms and an office in the suite. Still nothing. That likely meant a wall safe. Looking around the office, he picked out the most obvious of the smaller paintings and checked each one for side hinges. His intuition paid off. With an easy touch, a faux Modigliani nude painting clicked inward, then swung open, revealing a common safe brand Roko was well familiar with—and one which could be a breeze to open, if he got lucky.

From his shoulder bag he extracted his tools: the all-important safe audio amplifier with earphones, replacing the time-honored stethoscope; a cordless drill with tungsten carbide and diamond drill bits; and a borescope for optically inspecting the internal workings of the safe once a hole was bored.

But first, the test of luck. Nearly all in-room hotel safes have an administrator's super code. When safes are installed, the hotel is responsible for changing those codes, but because of the sheer number of safes most hotels require, and the management's lack of time or technical knowledge, most are often installed as delivered by the manufacturer.

From his bag Roko pulled out a pair of latex gloves and fastened them on. He pressed and held the LOCK button until the BATTERY indicator appeared on the digital display, then he pressed and held ZERO on the keypad until the word SUPER appeared. Next he entered the default manufacturer's code "999999"—and the lock mechanism clicked. Luck having won the moment, he swung open the safe door.

"Oh, Michael, I'm sorry," Hana said, just as they were about to get into a taxi. "I left my phone on the charger. I need to go back to the room. I'll just be a few minutes."

"Not a problem, I'll go back with you," Dominic said. "It's a nice night for walking and I missed my run this morning."

Returning to the hotel entrance, they headed for the elevators.

Roko peered inside the safe. *Where was the wooden cylinder?! Gović will be furious if I don't bring back what he wants.* The only thing he found was a leather folio. Pulling it out of the safe, Roko opened it to find what appeared to be an old parchment encased in a plastic sleeve. *Maybe this is what he wanted. If it's in the safe it must be of some value.* He thought about calling Gović to confirm, but again, time was a concern. He dropped the folio inside his bag, closed the safe, and headed for the exit.

The elevator doors opened on the seventh floor and Hana and Dominic stepped out, heading down the hall toward her room. Just as they turned the corner, Hana noticed a man coming out of her suite.

"Who's that?!" she asked uneasily. Dominic looked up.

Just then Roko spotted them. As he did so, he put his head down, casually turned to take the hallway on his left, then started running.

Dominic raced down the hall in pursuit. By the time he reached the end of the hallway, he could hear the man running, doubling back down the opposite hallway toward the elevators. Turning the corner, he picked up speed, then observed the door to the stairway was closing. Body-slamming the door open, Dominic ran after him down the stairs, gripping the handrails as he flew down two steps at a time. He could hear the man's footsteps below him, clanging on the wide metal steps as he descended.

Out of breath now, Roko had reached the lobby exit door. He could hear Dominic gaining on him just two floors above. Quickly he decided to go down further, to the parking garage. But first he opened the lobby door wide, then let it slowly close on its own as he continued descending, as fast and quietly as possible, making his way down to the first level of the garage. He silently opened the door and slipped through it, gently closing the door behind him.

After seven long flights, Dominic had finally reached the lobby exit door. Seeing that it was just about to close shut, he pulled it open and ran out into the busy hotel lobby, breathing heavily. Placing his hands on his hips while catching his breath, Dominic surveyed the crowded room for the man he'd been chasing.

He was gone.

36

Dominic had taken the elevator back to the seventh floor and knocked on the door to Hana's suite. She opened it, and her eyes told him all he needed to know.

"He took it, Michael!" she said angrily, her eyes tearing up. "That son of a bitch stole the manuscript!"

"Are you okay otherwise?" Dominic asked, embracing her after their ordeal.

"Yes, but how are *you*? Are you hurt? Did you find him?"

"No, he got away from me. And yes, I'm fine."

"How could someone break into my hotel room, and even then, get into the safe?!" Hana was fraught with tension, furious that expected safeguards—especially in a 5-star hotel—could be so easily sidestepped.

"From my experience, people can and will do anything to achieve their corrupt intentions," Dominic said. "As for the manuscript, don't worry about that. I took precautions."

"I don't understand. What do you mean 'precautions'?"

"Remember a few days ago when we visited

Simon in his office, and I left the manuscript with him for testing? Oh, speaking of which, he did confirm both tests indicated a high probability of organic authenticity, with the carbon-14 analysis dating it to the first century."

"Not as if we had any doubts," Hana said, "though it is good to know science backs us up. But go on."

"Anyway," Dominic continued, "I returned the next day to pick up the manuscript, then made a high-res copy of it in the digitizing lab, putting the copy inside a separate folio. I thought about affixing it with an AirTag tracker, just in case, but it was only a copy so it wasn't really necessary. Then I went to the Vatican Bank and opened an account, securing the original manuscript folio in a safe deposit box. I just figured that while we still needed to work with the document, I didn't want to take any chances with such an important treasure—even in a hotel's safe, which is only as good as its most honest employee. And as it turned out, that was a good move."

Hana tilted her head, reappraising him. "Good-looking, smart, *and* piously devious. Your mother would be proud."

"That doesn't resolve the main problem, though," Dominic said. "Now someone else has an explosive document that could bring serious harm to the Christian world, *if* they knew how to translate it. But finding an expert in Koine Greek wouldn't be all that difficult. How they learned about our having it in the first place is a mystery. So far we've only told Simon."

"I'm betting that whoever it was hacked our emails," Hana said. "I've had experience with this in the investigations I've done; it's easier than you might think for someone so motivated. That would be the most logical answer. In hindsight, we should have used *Le Monde*'s secure Sourcesûre system for safely transmitting and storing the manuscript through my account there."

"I'm afraid I have to agree," Dominic added dejectedly, "We'll need to be more careful going forward. I'm such a fool. I should have taken better preventive measures dealing with such an important artifact. By and large I've led a fairly shielded life, and not having experienced many adverse situations, I fail to anticipate them."

"On that I disagree. Replacing the original in the safe was very forward-thinking. But the real question is, who's behind this? Who else knew we even have the document, much less that it was in the safe?!"

"All good questions. I think your speculation about our emails being hacked is a good bet. So we should assume our text messages are also at risk. We should keep this in mind for any communications going forward.

"As for who wants this manuscript so badly as to steal it in broad daylight, that guy in the library and on the train would seem to be our prime suspect. But who is he? Who does he work for?"

Hana stood and walked to the window, looking out over the city. "What about Cardinal Petrini? Think he might be able to help us figure this out?"

Dominic thought for a moment. "I'm not quite ready to bring him into all this yet. But I am having dinner with him tonight. Why don't you join us?"

"I'd love to meet him. Didn't you say he's somewhat of a foster father to you?"

"He's the only father figure I've had in my life," Dominic replied, "and one of the most decent men I know. You'll enjoy his company, I'm sure."

"Back to something you said earlier," Hana observed. "What are those AirTag trackers you mentioned?"

"They're Bluetooth and ultra-wideband tracking devices developed by Apple. You can affix them to most any object you want to keep track of. Then once registered, you can locate them from any distance using the 'Find My' app. All the tag needs is *any* iPhone nearby to relay its low-energy encrypted signal—even a phone belonging to someone else in a crowd. The tag then sends its location signal to the home device using iCloud and *voila!*—your object is found. We're experimenting with these on certain manuscripts in the Archives that move around a lot, especially when they're being digitized."

"I could use one of these to find my wallet!" Hana joked. "Have you got any spares?"

"As a matter of fact..." Dominic reached into his backpack and produced two white disc-shaped objects about the size of a half-dollar. Using his own iPhone he registered one labeled "Hana's wallet," dropped it into a pocket in the pouch, then showed her how it worked using the Find My app. A map appeared showing each of their locations, plus a third icon indicating the wallet.

"This is too cool, Michael, thanks!" she said. "I can see this coming in very handy. You boys have all the fun tech stuff."

"Just don't tell anyone I let you into our clubhouse," Dominic said, grinning.

37

The next day Cardinal Petrini returned from Castel Gandolfo, refreshed in spirit—as the papal retreat does for many of its guests—but troubled by the Vatican Bank president's aversion to a proper accounting of its acquired gold reserves.

He was looking forward to dinner with Michael and his colleague Hana Sinclair this evening, curious as to what might be happening with the Saunière letter they found.

Meeting promptly at eight o'clock at the Ristorante dei Musei north of the Vatican, Dominic and Hana walked in to find Cardinal Petrini already seated at a corner table in the back, an opened bottle of wine set before him. As they sat down Dominic made introductions, and in the midst of the usual small talk they ordered their meals. Petrini was elated to find that Hana's grandfather was Armand de Saint-Clair, the good friend and colleague he had just seen earlier that day.

As they spoke, Hana couldn't shake the

feeling that she somehow recognized the cardinal, but she knew they hadn't met before, nor had she previously seen photos of him. Still, there was something familiar about the man.

While Petrini and Dominic went on talking about Curial matters, Hana studied the cardinal's face. Then abruptly it came to her—*he would be the spitting image of Achille now as an older man!* The heavy unibrow set over deeply embedded eyes; the unusually pronounced ala nasi at the tip of his nose; the age he would now be. A little more flesh on the face, but that would be expected with time. Confident in her suspicion, she reached inside her valise and withdrew the two photos of the groups of Maquis soldiers.

Petrini, conscious that Hana had been staring at him, turned to her questioningly, the corners of his mouth forming the hint of a smile.

"Your Eminence," she asked, "would you indulge me for a moment? May I show you two photographs, to see if you recognize any of these men? These were taken during the war."

"Certainly," said Petrini. He accepted the photographs, and in a flash, a clear expression of recollection came over him. He lifted his head and looked at Hana, a droll smile now in place.

"Given the way you've been studying me, I expect you already know the answer," he said.

Hana smiled back enthusiastically. "It *is* you,

isn't it? *You* are Achille!"

Petrini turned back to the photos affectionately, his thumb brushing over the faces of his former comrades in the French Resistance.

"Yes, Hana. That was my code name during the war. How in heaven's name did you find these? And, more to the point, for what purpose?"

Hana explained her project and the research she'd done so far, lacking only the identity of the Maquis group leader.

"What can you tell me of your role and achievements in the war?" she asked.

"That would take much more time than we have tonight," Petrini said, a distant look in his eyes, "but in short, I was in my teens when the war broke out, living in Italy with my parents. Wanting the best opportunities for me, they sent me to America, and with their political connections I found a job at the Italian embassy in New York. It was there I was picked up by the U.S. Office of Strategic Services, the OSS, and was soon working with both British Special Operations branch and French Intelligence, in a clandestine action known as Operation Jedburgh. There were only about 300 of us 'Jeds,' specially selected for providing liaison between Resistance guerrillas and Allied forces, including the coordination of airdrops of arms and ammunition to liberation fighters.

"Our team was the first to parachute into central France the night before Allied troops stormed the beaches of Normandy. It was the most exciting and terrifying time of my life. In fact, surviving the war—given everything I witnessed—is what compelled me to join the priesthood."

Dominic was spellbound by his mentor's story. "Rico, I never knew any of this. I'm more impressed than I can say. Did my mother know?"

"Oh, yes," Petrini replied, that far-off look returning. "Grace and I shared many such stories in our years together at the rectory. She was quite a woman, your mother." Petrini rubbed his eyes, which had started misting as he recalled old memories.

"Yes, she was," Dominic said reflectively. "God, I miss her so much."

Sensing a change in mood, Hana steered the conversation back to Petrini's wartime activities. "If I may, Your Eminence, did you have any direct experience with helping Jews safeguard their assets, specifically gold? That's the central theme of the piece I'm working on, and whatever you tell me can either be on the record or on background, as you prefer."

"I'll tell you what I can, Hana, but I would prefer it be used on deep background," Petrini began. "As it happens, I did work very closely with Allied efforts to intercept Nazi and Ustasha gold shipments."

"Ustasha?" Hana inquired. "I haven't come across that name."

Petrini laid out the story as best he could recall, given that he was a very young man at the time. He admitted that what he was about to tell her involved the Church to some extent, asking that she treat the knowledge in proper context.

The Ustasha, he explained, was a terrorist movement formed and headed by Ante Pavelić, a man who became the leader of the Independent State of Croatia—essentially the *Führer* equivalent of Adolph Hitler to Germany. In 1941 the Nazis invaded Yugoslavia with intentions of splitting up the country, and turned to the Ustasha to lead their armies in taking over Croatia as well as parts of Serbia and Bosnia. Thus began a major genocide campaign against Jews and Serbs and others who steadfastly refused to convert to Catholicism. Over 500,000 Orthodox Serbs, 80,000 Jews and 30,000 Romany Gypsies were slaughtered between 1941 and 1945. The brutality of the Ustasha regime exceeded that of the Nazis; they set up numerous concentration camps, the most brutal one being at Jasenovac in Croatia, where they knifed, gassed, poisoned, or cremated live thousands of inmates. What the Nazis did at Auschwitz was tame by comparison.

Once the Axis powers came to realize they were losing the war, the Ustasha, much like the Nazis, hid or liquidated as much of the looted gold, currency, artworks, properties, and other stolen assets they could. In an unconscionable betrayal of their holy vows, the Catholic Franciscan order itself became complicit in assisting the Ustasha with its unholy mission. With the approval of the Archbishop of Croatia, Aloysius Stepinac, Pavelić was permitted to confiscate and conceal thirty-six chests of gold—mainly jewelry, watches, and the fillings and dentures ripped from the mouths of Jews, Roma, Serbs, and others in the camps, along with two truckloads of silver—all of which was buried beneath the Franciscan monastery in Zagreb.

This hidden cache of Ustasha treasure ultimately found its way to Naples, where, with the help of the Mafia, the gold and silver were melted into bullion, which was discreetly deposited into Franciscan accounts in the Vatican Bank. From there, no one is sure where much of the plundered assets ended up, but it was a safe bet to assume they found their way to South America and other havens for Nazis and former Ustasha officials. The Franciscans also ran some of the most efficient ratlines for facilitating the escape of war criminals, men who took their plunder with them under new identities and passports provided by the Vatican.

"With the remaining looted bullion we have now," Petrini continued, "we're working to make restitution to survivors of the Holocaust and other groups as best we can. But there are difficult decisions ahead, and we're doing what we can to expedite the process given our lumbering bureaucracy."

At Hana's urging, Petrini spoke for another hour, vividly telling her about his exploits in the Maquis, the tales of bravery he witnessed and the atrocities he encountered.

"What became of Archbishop Stepinac?" Hana asked when he had finished.

Petrini's face darkened. "Somewhat surprisingly, Pope Pius XII promoted him to cardinal. And after Stepinac died in 1960, the Church began the beatification process toward sainthood. That business is still ongoing, but not without controversy.

"As a personal favor to me, Hana, I must ask that you treat this information delicately. And, of course, not to use my name as your source."

"Certainly, Eminence," Hana replied. "I appreciate your sharing all of this with me."

"There is, by the way," Petrini noted, "one name you might look into: Miroslav Gović. He was a ruthless mercenary who became a field marshal in the Ustasha militia and fully earned his sobriquet 'The Butcher of Zagreb.' He worked very closely with Archbishop Stepinac in the matter of that Franciscan gold operation. We tried several times to capture him, without success."

Hana made note of the name, then asked the cardinal, "How much of this gold still remains in the possession of the Vatican?"

"I'm afraid I can't go into specifics at this stage. Should I have anything more I'm able to pass on at some point, I expect we can meet again.

"Incidentally, Michael," Petrini turned to Dominic, "I was wondering if there were any further developments on that Saunière letter you discovered, and the Nostradamus quatrains?"

Dominic thought carefully before responding, not yet prepared to reveal the dramatic events of late. "Nothing to report quite yet, Rico," he said. "But I've got some solid leads to run down and hope to turn up something soon. I'll let you know."

* * *

It was just before noon the next day when Dominic found Toshi Kwan alone in the Vatican digitizing lab.

"Hey, Toshi, have you got a few minutes?"

The young analyst looked up from his computer, surprised at having a visitor. "Sure,

Michael, what's up?"

"I need a spectral analysis of a particular manuscript to determine the origin of its paper. And this needs to stay between us. Can you do that for me?"

Toshi smiled, a conspiratorial look on his face. "A secret mission, eh? I'm in. Peter won't be back from lunch for at least an hour so we're good on time. Let's see the manuscript."

Dominic reached into his backpack and took out the folio containing the Magdalene papyrus, gently removing it from the Mylar sleeve and laying it out on the light table.

"Whoa! This is definitely an old one. And it's in Koine Greek." He looked up at Dominic. "Should I ask what it is?"

"Best that you don't. Actually, it's not part of the Vatican Archives. I found it in France, which is a longer story than we have time for. I'm having a carbon-14 test done at Teller University, but am relying on your expertise in spectroscopic analysis to help identify where it came from."

Carefully turning the manuscript over, Toshi surveyed both sides. "You do realize I'll have to extract a small portion for analysis, right? It doesn't have to be large, just a sufficient enough sample to provide qualitative properties for the spectrometer."

Finding a corner of the papyrus with no

writing on it, Toshi used a mini-plane sampling knife to shave off a small sample. Dominic looked on nervously, cringing as he always did at the destructive nature required of such tests on irreplaceable artifacts.

The extraction complete, Toshi then inserted the shaving into a sample holder, then positioned it into the lab's Excalibur 3000 Digilab Spectrometer and began running the specified tests. Meanwhile, Dominic reinserted the original document inside its Mylar sleeve and back into the folio, which he tucked into his backpack.

Within a few minutes, the spectrometer issued a series of beeps and the attached line printer began issuing a batch of diffractograms, colored line graphs, which Toshi ripped off the printer, then took a seat at his desk and began analyzing. Dominic stood next to him in silence, anxiously awaiting the verdict.

"Well, Michael," Toshi said, "depending on its source, the general composition of papyrus contains between 55–70% cellulose and 33–34% lignin, with the balance of content comprised of ash and bound water. This particular sample has a high degree of oxidation and crystallization, consistent with ancient papyri. It also has a rich carbonyl vibration pattern with high fluorescence and has definitely been well cared for given its approximate age of two thousand years.

"So, with this and what else I see here—plus experience with similar artifacts I've analyzed—we're most likely looking at an origin of upper Egypt at around the first century. Is that what you were hoping for?"

Dominic's face broke into a wide smile as he listened to Toshi's closing revelation. "That's exactly what I was hoping for, Toshi! I don't know how to thank you, this is fantastic. Just remember—between us, right?

Toshi reached his hand out, which Dominic took to shake vigorously. "Our secret," he said. "Let me know if I can be of further help."

38

"Vodka neat, Akvinta if you have it. Punzoné if not. Make it a double."

Roko Sirola sat on a plush barstool in the Monkey Club lounge overlooking the Rhône River in Lyon. The bartender, a voluptuous young woman with a martini glass tattooed on her bare shoulder, poured a short tumbler of Akvinta in front of her customer. Savoring his moment of bliss, Roko let the smooth and creamy hints of Istrian wheat trickle down his throat, silently toasting his triumphant score in Rome.

The door swung open and Petrov Gović entered. Adjusting his eyes to the dimly lit room, he spied Roko sitting at the bar and made his way to him.

"Nadia," he said, addressing the bartender, "a glass of Beaujolais, please." Then to Roko, "Let us move to a table."

Roko fetched his backpack from the adjoining stool and met Gović at a table on the back wall of the bar. The two had just sat down when Nadia appeared, placing the glass of wine in front of Gović.

"*Za dom–spremni,* my friend," he said to Roko. "What do you have for me?"

Roko withdrew the leather folio from his pack and handed it to Gović.

"Did you have any trouble?" Gović asked.

"Nothing I couldn't handle, Petrov," Roko said. "The priest and the woman had returned unexpectedly. They saw me as I was leaving the room and the priest chased me down the stairwell, but I managed to shake him. Otherwise everything went better than I could have hoped. But there was no wooden cylinder in the safe, just this folder."

Gović opened the folio to find the object of his desire—the Magdalene manuscript—the intercepted translation of which had been taunting him for days. "That's fine. They obviously transferred it from the cylinder for conservation purposes."

"What is it, anyway?" Roko asked.

"It could be the answer to our financial prayers," Gović said optimistically, leaving vague the specifics. "Our mission to bring the Ustasha back to its full glory is now within reach, Roko, literally in our hands at this very moment."

Admiring the ancient papyrus, Gović thought he noticed something amiss, but couldn't put his finger on it. The document looked surprisingly fresh to his eye, even in the dim light of the bar.

Holding it up more closely, he inspected the weave of the paper, only then realizing that's what it was—paper. Not papyrus. His jubilation turned to outrage in a heartbeat.

"This is a fucking copy!" he hissed under his breath, his jaw clenched in anger. *"They still have the original!"*

"It's the only thing I found in the safe, Petrov!" Roko said defensively. "I didn't see anything else in the rest of the suite, either."

"The priest must have put it in safe storage somewhere," Gović said, still seething. "Maybe even in the Vatican. This makes matters much more difficult."

He looked Roko in the eyes accusingly, slowly regaining his composure. Reaching into his coat pocket he withdrew a fat envelope, pushing it across the table.

"You did the job I expected of you, Roko. There's no way you could have known this was not the original. But I may call on you again in this matter."

Roko picked up the envelope and dropped it into his backpack, zippering it shut. Shaking hands and uttering the mutual Ustasha salute, each downed their drinks and went their own way.

* * *

Back in his office at Interpol, Gović locked the door and drew the blinds, then extracted the copy of the Magdalene manuscript from its folio and took a photo of it using his phone camera. Though he had since reread and now fully grasped the importance of the translation, he was less impressed with the document itself than he was with the wisdom of its use as a means to a very profitable end.

But first he had to provide Dante with a copy of the manuscript, both to justify his fee and to set the stage for the special plans he had in mind.

Launching a new secure ProtonMail message, he attached the photocopy of the manuscript with a brief note asking Dante to call him as soon as possible.

* * *

As he was reviewing the flood of other messages he had received earlier that afternoon, Cardinal Dante's tablet pinged the unique tone for secure incoming email. He tapped the pending message from Petrov Gović in his inbox, read the note, then opened the attachment. An ancient papyrus of Koine Greek filled the small screen.

Dante was both captivated and terrified by what he was looking at. Surrounded as he was by millions of such manuscripts, this one held a singular fascination, for the very life of the Church rested in its power, in its use or abuse. That thought alone turned his attention to Gović, the mercenary, presumably the only person outside of Dominic and the Sinclair woman to know of its existence. Could he trust Gović? Or was this another nuisance he would have to deal with? And what of Dominic, what was his plan? Certainly he would tell Petrini. Too many people already knew about this—all of which made for a very restless Secretary of State.

He picked up the phone, punched his private line for a dial tone, and called Gović in Lyon.

"Petrov," Dante said tersely when the man answered, "Do you have the original?"

"I'm afraid not, Your Eminence. We were able to get into the safe in Sinclair's hotel suite, but Dominic had apparently taken the original somewhere else, leaving a copy in its place."

"Goddamnit!" Dante shouted, the curse echoing in his vast office. "I want that original manuscript, do you hear me?! Do whatever it takes to get it—and destroy any other copies you have of this document. You must give me your word on that, Gović. I'll make it worth your while."

"I'll take care of everything, Eminence. Leave it to me."

Dante slammed the phone down in its cradle, cursing under his breath.

39

Armand de Saint-Clair was in the sitting room of his suite at the Rome Cavalieri, savoring an aperitif, when he heard the electronic click of the door in the foyer open. Closing the door behind her, his granddaughter walked in.

"*Bonjour,* Grand-père," Hana said. "How was your trip?"

"As to be expected, my dear," Saint-Clair replied with a sigh. "I don't think His Holiness is well-served by certain of those in his circle, but that has been a longstanding problem for many popes, so there's not much to be done about that. Still, it was as productive as one could hope for, though we have more meetings this week in the Vatican. What have you been up to these past few days?"

Hana took the seat across from him. "I just had dinner with a good friend who introduced me to Cardinal Petrini. We had a lovely time. What an illuminating history that man has. You know him, of course."

"I do, yes. As a matter of fact, he and I were at Castel Gandolfo together, meeting with Cardinal

Dante and Klaus Wolaschka, that crook of a banker from the Vatican. They were the problematic fellows I had alluded to.

"By the way, Dante took me aside and asked about your involvement with a 'Father Dominic'? Is that the good friend you mentioned? What can you tell me about him, and perhaps what you're up to?"

"Well, I wouldn't say 'involvement' is the right word, so much as we're working on a project together. Michael works as Assistant to the Prefect of the Secret Archives. He introduced me to a tremendously helpful scholar named Simon Ginzberg, a professor at Teller University, who knows a great deal about the substance of my work on the matter of Jewish gold during the war.

"Oh!" she added, beaming, "and remember I asked you about 'Achille' a few days ago? *Cardinal Petrini is—or was—Achille!* I cannot tell you how excited I was to have found him. He spoke for hours with such evocative stories I felt as if I were actually there, during the war."

Saint-Clair was not only taken aback by Hana's disclosure, but stunned by Petrini's surprising admission to her that he was the enigmatic Maquis group leader. He took a sip of his cocktail with an unsteady hand.

"Come to think of it…" Hana paused, a shadow of doubt crossing her face. "Did you know Petrini was Achille all along?"

Facing a moment of truth, Saint-Clair got up to refresh his cocktail. "My dear, this is not something I am prepared to go into at present," he said hesitantly. "For the moment, I will acknowledge that, yes, I did know that Enrico was Achille. But that is all I am able to tell you now. Perhaps later I can divulge more. Can you respect that?"

Feeling rebuffed and confused, Hana looked into her grandfather's eyes, sensing a secret behind them. "Of course, Grand-père. Whenever you're ready," she said compliantly. "But I do want to know the truth."

Saint-Clair sat back down, setting his cocktail on the side table.

"Hana, I don't mean to be brusque. The truth, as you call it, is complicated. And it is not my own story to tell, for that matter. I must confer with others, especially Enrico, but you shall have an answer in time.

"Meanwhile, tell me more about your project," he said.

Hana filled in the details of her research in Paris, of her meetings with Ginzberg and more about what Petrini had told her over dinner, and of Dominic's assistance—excluding only the matter of the Magdalene papyrus.

Saint-Clair listened attentively, impressed

with his granddaughter's drive and intelligence. Then he said, "I was asked by Cardinal Dante as to whether the Church will come in under harsh light in your published work."

Startled by what she just heard, Hana asked, "Did *you* mention my work to him?"

"No," Saint-Clair replied. "He's the one who brought it up, actually."

Hana was stunned. How could Dante possibly know what she was doing at all? Unless… he was responsible for them being followed, and probably intercepting their email!

"Grand-père, what do you know of Cardinal Dante?"

"I know I don't much care for him, as a start. He's willful, pompous, and arrogant, and runs the Vatican as his personal fiefdom, as if there were no higher authority at all. Even the pope lives in fear of him."

Without having even met the man, Hana shared her grandfather's attitude on Dante. She didn't care for him either.

"I'm afraid I don't have an answer for you, Grand-père, or him—nor, as a journalist, would I even be inclined to give one, frankly. His Eminence will simply have to wait to see what comes out."

* * *

After breakfast the next morning, Hana opened her laptop to research the name given to her by Cardinal Petrini—Miroslav Gović.

First, she began with ARHiNET, the Central National Register of Archival Fonds and Collections of the Republic of Croatia. While it was a good resource, it was incomplete and still in the process of digitizing vital state registers from previous years. She found nothing there.

Then, logging on using her special access to Gallica, the digital library of the French Bibliothèque, her search turned up two instances of her quarry:

> *— Subject: Gović, Miroslav (1910-1980) – Portrait*
>
> *— Subject: Gović, Miroslav – Membre d'Oustachi Croate*

She clicked on the *Portrait* link, finding the photograph of a rough-looking man staring back at her; a man who had obviously seen a lifetime of struggle.

Tapping on the second link—"Member of the Croatian Ustasha"—brought her to a short bio page describing Gović's reputation as the "Butcher of Zagreb" and his role with the fascist group, with side links to two brief newspaper clippings in the Croatian language. Hana sent these to the printer, along with the portrait, for later translation and review.

Thinking a genealogical search might also be beneficial, she logged into the Croatian Church Records database for researching recorded baptisms. Croatia was a largely Roman Catholic country, and Catholic baptismal records were efficiently maintained, rarely left undone by parishes even in remote villages worldwide.

After some twenty minutes figuring out the system—all in the Croatian language but significantly more useful with Google's Page Translation service—Hana finally found an entry for *Miroslav Gović*. Though there was nothing more on the man himself, it did reveal his wife's name to be Ludmila, and the baptized son, christened in 1967, was named Petrov.

Petrov Gović. He would be middle-aged now. Figuring he might be helpful to her research, Hana wondered if she would be able to locate him.

She googled his name and was surprised to find numerous search results returned, mainly in relationship with Interpol. Checking his brief biography page on that agency's website, Hana discovered he was Croatia's Special Liaison to Interpol. Certain she had her man, she clicked on the Contact form and, filling in her own contact details for *Le Monde*, included a message requesting an interview, either in Lyon or Rome at his convenience.

This should be interesting, she thought. She tapped on SEND and waited.

40

Pierre Valois had personally set up the private conference call on a secure line from his office in the Elysee Palace, preferring not to involve a secretary. Patching in both Armand de Saint-Clair and Enrico Petrini in Rome, the three began their meeting.

"Gentlemen, I feel I must first apologize for my granddaughter," Saint-Clair said. "She seems to have stumbled onto the name 'Achille' in her research, unaware of its past connection to us and possible implications to our future."

"That's all well and fine, Armand, but what are we to do now?" Valois asked, agitated by the disclosure, unintended or not.

"My friends," Cardinal Petrini spoke up, "we knew this day might come. My chief concern is that we not be politically damaged. Even now there is too much at stake for each of us.

"But, of course, what we did wasn't illegal, per se," he continued. "We weren't petty thieves. There were few laws enforced after the Nazis invaded Italy anyway. And the Vatican was none the wiser after the fact; they lost nothing they legitimately owned. I'm quite proud of what we did, actually, although it's not something we necessarily want the press to learn."

"I have no problem with letting your granddaughter know the top line details of that one operation, Armand," Valois affirmed. "But she must leave our names out of it."

"I fully agree," said Petrini. "It would serve no purpose now except to inspire the passions of those who already pose as our respective enemies. Best not go down that path."

"Indeed, Pierre," Saint-Clair added, "your part in Operation Jedburgh helped you in no small way to become president of France. Because of your efforts you emerged a hero—although, of course, certain details had to be omitted from your campaign due to claimed 'national security' issues."

"Then we're agreed," said Valois. "Make sure my godchild understands what is at stake here, Armand. I'm confident she'll see her way through this.

"Thank you for your time, gentlemen. *Au revoir*," he concluded, and terminated the call.

Hana was working on her laptop in the dining room when her grandfather emerged from his office, having just ended his conference call.

"Alright, my dear. It's time for us to talk," he

said to her.

Hana closed her laptop and moved to the sitting room. Taking a seat, she crossed her legs and folded her arms across her chest, an expectant look in her eyes.

"I just got off a call with Pierre and Enrico, and we all agreed to bring you into the story, on two conditions. First, you must never use our names, or even our code names. The second condition will come after I tell you the details."

Saint-Clair began telling Hana about the group's particular history together, explaining that when the Nazis invaded Italy on September 8, 1943, the Italian government had suddenly been neutralized, and virtually overnight the Vatican became the de facto authority in Rome. Pope Pius XII was fully aware of the impending deportation of Jews from Italy. Moreover, the Vatican learned through one of the Nazi's own SS lieutenants of the terrible fate awaiting deportees at Auschwitz—a fate over which the Pope had done nothing to intervene.

Within days after the invasion, the Nazis, in a brazen act of hubris, demanded fifty kilos of gold from Roman Jews or else three hundred of their kind would be taken hostage from the city's Jewish Ghetto. The Vatican offered half that amount as collateral, a deal brokered by Operation Jedburgh's special operations team "Hugo"—the elite team comprising Enrico Petrini ('Achille') as its commander; Armand de Saint-Clair as its executive officer; and Pierre Valois as the team's radio operator.

Vatican officials were unaware that the Jews had bought more time to come up with the full amount themselves, a fact which Team Hugo intentionally failed to pass back to the Vatican—for Petrini, Saint-Clair, and Valois had found new opportunity in the transaction.

Aware that the Vatican Bank had a massive reserve of gold bullion—much of it stolen by the Nazis and the Ustasha, but protectively "safeguarded" by the Vatican Bank in their names—the team made the decision to redirect the looted gold for use by the French Resistance. The Vatican was now out fifty kilos of gold which they didn't own in the first place—though they would be the first to deny they had ever held such pilfered reserves at all—and the Resistance gained vital resources with which to help defeat Hitler's army in France—there being no way to determine who the gold belonged to in the first place.

"There is a sad postscript to this tale, Hana," Saint-Clair added. "Despite the Jews having conceded to their demands, a month after the invasion, the Nazis arrested over a thousand Roman Jews anyway, mostly women and children, and sent them to Auschwitz, where nearly half of them were promptly gassed. The rest died during their time in the camp. Ultimately, only 16 survived. And still, the pope said nothing.

"So, you now see why we chose not to make public our activities. The second condition we require is that you must not mention the discreet 'migration' of the Vatican gold—which of course was the primary focus of our operation.

"I tell you all of this in confidence, Hana" Saint-Clair finished, "mainly because you happened across Achille's name and were so determined to find the truth. But the truth, in our case, could have dire consequences, despite our belief that, all things considered, we had done nothing wrong."

Having listened intently, Hana was moved by her grandfather's history, and conscious of the possible repercussions should she write about it. "I completely understand, Grand-père," she said. "I would do nothing to bring harm to you or my godfather, or even Cardinal Petrini, who must be especially vulnerable now, given his rank in the Church and as a Vatican official. I will honor your conditions and appreciate your sharing the truth."

Saint-Clair smiled at his granddaughter, thankful he did not have to reveal anything more than what she would accept as the most satisfying answer. His colleagues would be grateful, too, for that was the least of their exploits.

41

An email notification alert pinged on Petrov Govic's computer while he was biting into a *jambon-beurre,* the traditional French baguette layered with paper-thin slices of ham and thick slabs of butter, which he favored when eating alone at his desk. He hated being interrupted while he was having lunch—food being the one thing that gave him sheer pleasure, and his lunch hour the peace to enjoy it.

He had intended to ignore the incoming message until he was finished eating, but then, glancing up at the computer, the name of the Sender caught his eye—*Hana Sinclair!* Nearly choking in surprise, he finished chewing the mouthful he'd been working on and set down the sandwich. A quick flush of guilt came over him, as if he'd been caught in the act of doing something he shouldn't be.

He opened the message and read it. Remarkable timing, he mused. Fortunately, she has no idea who I am, other than the son of my father and an Interpol liaison. She certainly does her homework. But, I sense an opportunity here....

Given the new information he'd come across

while intercepting Dominic's email, Gović had been working on a plan to get leverage on Dante. But for that plan to truly succeed, he needed the original Magdalene manuscript. But Dominic would likely never give it up, for any reason—with the possible exception of protecting someone he cared for. And from his surveillance of the priest and his companion, it was evident Dominic had a closer connection to Hana than he might like to admit. Gović had done enough surveilling to know the signs of a blossoming *affaire de cœur* when he saw one, vows or no vows. He'd also known there was no shortage of fallen priests.

Picking up the phone, Gović made a call. "Roko," he said when Sirola answered, "I want you to prepare our safe house in Rome for a guest, whom I expect should be arriving this Thursday evening. Stay there until I contact you again."

Disconnecting the call, Gović wrote back to Hana, graciously accepting her request for an interview, telling her he would, as it happens, be in Rome this coming week. He gave her an address in the southwestern part of the city, in the Tor Bella Monaca suburb, indicating that, despite the disreputable location, it was a warehouse Interpol used for special operations and would be quite safe for her. He asked her to meet him there at 9:00 p.m. on Thursday.

Earlier that morning Hana had contacted Marina Karpov, the Balkans editor at *Le Monde*'s Paris headquarters, requesting a translation of the two Croatian newspaper clippings on Miroslav Gović, the ones Hana had found in the Bibliothèque's Gallica database. Karpov had assigned the task to an assistant, promising a translated version that afternoon.

In the meantime, Hana had received Petrov Gović's confirmation for an interview, with instructions on their meeting time and place in Rome. *Well, that makes it more convenient*, she thought. *But Tor Bella Monaca? It's one of the seediest parts of Rome. What kinds of operations do they conduct there?*

A chime on her phone notified Hana of a new incoming message. It contained the translated news clippings, along with a brief cover note from Marina Karpov in Paris. Opening the attachments, she read them.

Both clippings contained general reporting on Miroslav Gović's activities in the old Ustasha, revealing a variety of malefactions but nothing much that would contribute to her own project. However, there was one paragraph that stood out, from *Večernjak*, the daily Zagreb newspaper:

> *DATELINE: Zagreb – June 4, 1980*
>
> *… Unnamed sources in Croatia's General Police Directorate say former Ustasha leader Miroslav Gović was suspected of rebuilding the neo-fascist organization before his death earlier this year. Informed sources have long speculated that agents close to Gović, possibly including family members, may have taken leadership roles in reviving the group's illegal operation. Interpol's National Central Bureau in Zagreb has denied these allegations, dismissing them as rumors….*

Hana found this somewhat disturbing. She wondered if Miroslav's son Petrov might be one of those "agents." He was certainly a family member. *But as an Interpol officer, he couldn't possibly be involved!* she considered. *Surely the agency would have done extensive background checks….*

Still, she was unsettled.

42

Walking through the papal gardens following his morning run, Michael Dominic found himself in a serious quandary. He was sitting on one of the most turbulent documents Christianity would ever know, and its release could wreak havoc on religions in every country—not to mention the very Church that formed the backbone of his own beliefs, and the administration that defined ecclesiastical dogma for a billion Catholic souls worldwide.

But to conceal or suppress such a historical treasure would on its own be a betrayal to history, to truth—to the very foundations of everything Dominic believed was right and honorable. This would not be an easy decision, and he needed further guidance. Not the kind of guidance he might expect through prayer, either, for that rarely seemed productive. *Doubts… Always doubts!*

Needing to reflect on the issue more deeply, Dominic headed for Saint Peter's Basilica, where he could deliberate on what to do next. Should he tell Petrini? Would that be his way out of this? Might Ginzberg have a solution? Or should he just go to Dante and confess everything—someone who had the power to move mountains? But at what risk?

Entering the Sistine Chapel from Via delle Fondamenta off the gardens, Dominic passed through the great hall to the back passage leading to the northern nave of Saint Peter's. His footsteps echoed off the wide marble floors and arched ceilings as he walked over the red porphyry stone on which Emperor Charlemagne was crowned on Christmas in the year 800.

The grandeur of Saint Peter's always overwhelmed Dominic, moving him so deeply he was often rendered in awe of his surroundings. Not today. The burden on him was so pressing that he was disinclined toward architectural adulation at the moment. Even the 96-foot tall baldacchino, the massive bronze canopy over the great altar, failed to captivate him as it always did.

Glancing up and down the wide transept to find a seat where he could think quietly, he was surprised to find Cardinal Petrini kneeling in a pew just a few aisles from where Dominic stood.

If this isn't divine intervention, I don't know what is, he thought, pleased at the serendipity.

He joined the cardinal, silently taking a seat next to him.

Turning to see who his new companion was, Petrini smiled in recognition. Still kneeling, he made the sign of the cross, then sat back next to Dominic.

"By the look on your face, should I assume you've come for confession?" the cardinal asked quietly.

Dominic looked down at his hands, folded across his lap, trying to find the right words.

"Rico, part of me says this isn't the right time or place. On the other hand, I can't think of a more perfect setting for what I'm about to tell you. May I speak candidly here?"

"Of course, Michael," Petrini whispered gently. "Right here and now couldn't be better."

"Remember that Saunière letter I shared with you?"

Petrini nodded.

"Well, so much has happened since then, and now I find myself out of my depth, needing your advice.

"While doing some research Brother Mendoza asked me to do for Cardinal Dante, I happened upon an 1896 report prepared by a Monsignor Moretti, a papal legate for Pope Leo XIII. Moretti had traveled to Rennes-le-Château in France to interview Abbé Bérenger Saunière regarding a papyrus Saunière had discovered in his chapel…."

Petrini sat back, listening in astonishment as Dominic related the rest of the story—how Saunière had been blackmailing the Vatican; how he and Hana obtained the manuscript from Madame Dénarnaud; his translation of its shocking content, and Ginzberg's analysis of it; of Dante's presumed interception of his emails, and of he and Hana being followed to France; of the theft of the folioed copy from Hana's hotel suite.... All of it poured forth in whispered urgency as Dominic laid out the events of the past week.

"Where is the original manuscript now?" Petrini asked intently.

"In a safe deposit box in the Vatican Bank."

"Good. I would like to see it, of course, but leave it there for now. Are you *certain* your translation was accurate?"

"Absolutely," Dominic said with determination. "I'd stake my reputation on it. And Simon Ginzberg verified it as well."

Clearly unnerved by everything he had just learned, Petrini sat there, the weight of history bearing down on him in the very heart of the Church whose future lay in the decision now expected of him.

"Michael, I need more time to consider everything you've told me. That Dante must know what you have is an unsettling detail. But this is something about which the pope must be informed. I believe this has to be his decision, not yours or mine, and certainly not Dante's alone. I'll handle him if it comes to that.

"In the meantime," he continued, placing his arm around Dominic's shoulders, "I'm very proud of you, Michael. Though I might question your methodologies at gathering all this information, it appears you've made one of the most profound discoveries in world history, and you've conducted yourself well, given the circumstances."

Overwhelmed with relief, Dominic savored the comforting embrace and desperately needed support of his mentor, despite the repeated admonition. He felt the pressure of the past week's activities ease up, but not fully release. He would like to think that soon this would all be over, yet he knew in his heart that he would never be able to go back to his previous spiritual beliefs and that his life's work would be taking on a new perspective—one that he could not even imagine at this point.

43

Petrov Gović's meeting with Cardinal Dante was set for two o'clock in the Vatican's Government Palace. Though he had had dealings with the Vatican for some time, Gović had never been on the grounds. As his car approached Saint Anne's Gate, he felt a touch of excitement entering the walled city, tempered by the nervousness of his audacious mission.

A Swiss Guard in a blue and black uniform emerged from the guard shack and approached the driver's window.

"*Buona sera, signore*. Corporal Dengler at your service. How may I assist you?"

"I have an appointment with Cardinal Dante at two o'clock." Gović handed Dengler his Interpol credentials for inspection.

Dengler went back inside the guard shack, checked a clipboard for the day's authorized visitors, then returned to Gović's vehicle.

"Thank you, sir. Here are your passes; please place one face up on your dashboard and keep the other with you at all times. Go to the end of this road and park anywhere in the lot to your right, near the pharmacy and post office." He handed

Gović a map of the grounds, pointing to an outlined route. "You can reach the Government Palace along the path I've drawn for you here. Please proceed there directly and you will be escorted to Cardinal Dante's office." Then he smartly saluted and signaled for the boom barrier to be opened.

Passing through the arched portal, Gović drove onto Via di Belvedere, past the Swiss Guard barracks and the Vatican Bank, then turned right at the end, parking in front of the central post office. Exiting the car, he walked through the Belvedere Courtyard into the gardens, beyond the fountains and monuments and along the path Dengler had drawn for him, until he reached the Government Palace in the shadow of Saint Peter's dome.

At the reception desk an efficient nun brusquely reviewed Gović's credentials and his pass, asking that he follow her. They took the elevator to the fourth floor, where his escort introduced him to Dante's secretary, who asked him to be seated until the cardinal called for him.

"What do you mean you don't have the manuscript yet?!" Dante hissed at Gović. "My instructions were quite clear. I presumed that was our reason for meeting today, to take possession of the

damned thing."

"Your Eminence," Gović said, mustering a confidence he didn't quite feel, "I expect to have it in my hands within the next two days. I know exactly where it is and how to get it." This last part was a partial fabrication, intended only to set the tone for what Gović was about to propose.

"Petrov, I'm not playing games here. That document is vitally important to me. Its very existence is devastating to the Church," Dante said, revealing his hand. Gović knew then he could show his own.

"Eminence, that is what I came here to discuss—the actual value of the document to you and the Holy Mother Church. I agree with you, disclosure of the Magdalene's message would shake the very ground on which the Church stands; indeed, that of all Christianity. So, it is our job to make sure it remains completely secure and confidential. Wouldn't you agree?"

Dante stood up from his chair and began slowly pacing the room. As a seasoned negotiator, he knew when cards were being laid on the table. "What exactly are you driving at, Petrov?"

"In exchange for providing you with the original manuscript, I want one hundred million dollars in gold bullion, paid in advance."

Dante turned to Gović, a mix of fury and disbelief on his face. *"One hundred mil…You're mad!* You can't possibly believe I would accede to such an outrageous demand! Do you know who you're dealing with?"

"I know precisely who I'm dealing with—a man who has everything to lose. That gold now sits in the vaults of the Vatican Bank, but it is not among the Church's assets. It rightly belongs to the former Independent State of Croatia, to the Ustasha, and has been held there in its name since 1944, when my father and your predecessor at the time, Cardinal Luigi Maglione, reached an agreement for its provisional deposit. I am now making a formal demand for its withdrawal, something the Vatican has been quite unwilling to do for decades, given the questionable nature of its transfer in the waning days of the war.

"But now," Gović said, with a more confident demeanor, "there will be no further reluctance. Having copies of all pertinent documents, for my purposes the revelations alone would be damaging enough without having the original manuscript. But that you shall have."

Dante sat back down, realizing he had little choice in the matter, a position in which he rarely found himself. But after all, he reasoned, it *wasn't* the Church's gold. He knew of its history, of course, along with other assets dubiously acquired by the Vatican during and after the war. In light of everything, it seemed an acceptable solution even under duress.

"I will give you the gold once I have the document," Dante said as firmly as he could.

"I'm afraid that won't be acceptable, Eminence. I must have a show of good faith on your part—today. You know I'm good for my word."

"You can guarantee that I will receive the original manuscript in two days' time, then?" Dante asked.

"Unquestionably," answered Gović. "My team is making arrangements as we speak." Another fallacy, but as he was driving the negotiation now, it seemed appropriate. "Meanwhile, I will have an armored truck make the pickup from the Vatican Bank this afternoon."

"Very well," Dante said in surrender. "I will clear the way with Klaus Wolaschka now. Ask for him when your transportation is ready."

44

Hana Sinclair could hear the pealing of the distant bells of Saint Peter's strike nine o'clock as she drove into Tor Bella Monaca on Thursday evening, running a few minutes late for her meeting with Petrov Gović.

The address he had given her was just a few blocks away now, at the end of Via dell'Archeologia. She was still troubled as to why Gović had chosen Tor Bella Monaca, or TBM as locals called it, for the interview. Known as the Black Hole of Rome, TBM was the underbelly of the city's multigenerational drug culture. Driving slowly up the street, Hana saw that all the street lights were unlit, though not due to any power issue—they had all been shot out by drug dealers who prefer conducting business in the shadows.

Drab, monolithic apartment buildings looked down on her from both sides of the street, the car's headlights the only illumination up the long vacant road lined with piles of garbage. On one sidewalk she noticed a man sitting in a folding chair in the dark holding a cell phone, the only apparent sign of life she'd seen. As she passed him, he raised the phone to his ear, probably alerting a dealer somewhere ahead of her impending encroachment on their territory.

Hana's intuition cautioned that this wasn't a good idea. But she'd covered war zones before, as an embed in Kandahar during a major Taliban insurgency. *If I could handle that,* she thought, *I could handle anything.* And after all, Gović himself was an Interpol agent and assured her of her safety.

The rental car's GPS unit announced her arrival at the given address, which turned out to be a long dark warehouse, except for one bare light bulb hanging over a side door, swinging in the light evening breeze. She pulled up to the building and shut off the engine, parking next to another vehicle near the door.

As she emerged from the car, a man came out of the side door. At first glance she thought there was something familiar about him, but she couldn't place it.

"Miss Sinclair? Good evening, I'm Agent Roko Sirola, I work with Agent Gović. Did you have any trouble finding the place?"

Hana breathed a light sigh of relief, feeling more confident now. "Good to meet you, Agent Sirola. No, no trouble at all. It's just one of the more unusual places I've conducted an interview."

"I understand," Roko replied with a short

laugh. "TBM is a little sketchy at night, and not much better during the day, but we keep this place as a sort of out-of-the-way safe house for special operations."

"Of course, that's what I imagined," Hana said. "Is Agent Gović here yet?"

"Yes, he is waiting for you inside. Please, do come in."

Stepping into the dimly lit warehouse, Hana noticed dozens of old boxes and crates stacked on high metal shelving, extending as far as she could see in the cold, gloomy building. There were also a number of large machines: forklifts, pallet jacks, industrial trucks, and a wall packed with tools. The most surprising thing she noticed was a shiny steel Garda armored security van parked just inside one of the corrugated rolling warehouse doors, its engine block and exhaust manifold still snapping and hissing from recent use.

Roko motioned Hana down an aisle toward the far end of the warehouse as he followed behind her. Looking ahead she could see a man sitting in a chair in a small circle of light, his face buried in a newspaper. As she and her escort finally arrived to join the man, he lowered the newspaper and looked up into Hana's eyes.

"You!" she said in surprise. "You're the man on the train, and in the Bibliothèque!"

"Good evening, Miss Sinclair," Gović said

matter-of-factly. "I'm so glad you could join us."

"What's going on here?" Hana exclaimed, unnerved by the situation. "And why have you been following us?"

"All in good time, Hana. May I call you Hana?" said Gović, clearly intending to regardless of her answer. "This was the best way I could think of for obtaining something I very much need. Please, have a seat. Can we get you some coffee?"

Hana looked back at Roko, who was now holding a Glock 22 in his right hand, aimed menacingly in her direction. She took a seat in one of the folding chairs opposite Gović. Her mind raced. *What have I gotten myself into?*

"What is it you want desperately enough to kidnap a journalist?" she asked harshly.

"So, no coffee then. Alright, I'll get to the point. You and Father Dominic have kept us very busy this past week."

Surprised to hear Michael's name, she now suspected the object of their intentions. Looking at Roko again, she finally recognized him. "It was *you* who burgled my hotel suite, wasn't it?"

Roko didn't bother responding, letting his silence answer the question. He casually bobbed the gun up and down in his hand.

Gović turned her attention back to him. "By now it should be apparent what it is I want—the

Magdalene manuscript. And the original this time, if you please. The copy doesn't serve our particular needs at the moment."

"I don't know what it is you're talking about," she said nonchalantly, trying to engage a confidence she was having trouble mustering.

"You can dispense with the games, Hana. You're just wasting our time. And until we get what we need, you'll remain here as our guest.

"Obviously you wouldn't have the document with you," Gović added. "No doubt Father Dominic has taken precautions securing it, probably in the Vatican, I imagine, since we did not find the original in your safe."

"If he did have it, what makes you think he'd give it to you?" Hana asked.

"From our surveillance, it seems you two have developed quite a fondness for one another. I'm fairly certain he wouldn't want to see anything happen to you. And apart from Roko's charming nature, he has much experience making bad things happen to good people."

Roko lifted the Glock, aimed it at Hana's head, and pretended to pull the trigger, mouthing the word *"BOOM!"* as he jerked the gun up in mock recoil.

Unfazed, she turned back to Gović. "As a Croatian you must have some sense of your Catholic faith. Do you truly understand the importance of that document to your religion? Or the dire consequences worldwide should it fall into the wrong hands? Or is it just money you're after? Either way, how can you live with yourself?"

"*That* is what the confessional is for, Miss Sinclair!" Gović said with a chuffing laugh. "All sins are forgiven those who repent, isn't that right? Besides, you can't even imagine what my plans are for that document.

"Now, let's make a call to your friend the priest. First, Roko, would you mind making our guest a little less comfortable?"

Roko pulled out two plastic cuff restraints from his pocket, securing Hana's hands behind her and binding her ankles. He held up a black roll of Gorilla Tape in front of her. "Don't tempt me to use this over your mouth," he warned. "It's a bitch to remove."

Gović peered into Hana's purse and pulled out her cell phone. He held it up to her eyes to enable Face ID, unlocking the device, then scrolled through her address book until the name *Michael Dominic* appeared on the display.

"Are you ready?" he asked. "Make this easy for everyone and you'll be out of here in no time."

Gović touched the green Call button. The phone at the other end rang twice before Dominic answered.

"Hey, I was just thinking about you!" he said cheerfully.

"Oh, I doubt that, Father Dominic," Gović said. "Now I want you to listen very carefully. We have your friend Miss Sinclair here, and she's asking you for a favor—one that could, well, save her life."

"Who is this?" Dominic demanded. "Let me speak to Hana!"

"Never mind who I am." He then held the phone up to Hana's ear.

"Michael, it's Gović, the man on the train! Don't do what they ask!" she shouted.

Snapping back the phone, Gović stated his demands. "It's very simple, Father Dominic: I want the original Magdalene papyrus in exchange for your friend here, that's all. I want you to deliver it to me in one hour at the address I am about to give you, near enough to the Vatican that you can walk."

"But I can't get to the document! It's in a safety deposit box in the Vatican Bank, which is closed now."

Gović hadn't anticipated a bank. "Alright," he said, "Tomorrow at noon. We'll take good care of your friend in the meantime—or should I say, until then. What happens after that is your responsibility. And don't try calling back or tracking her phone, as it will be destroyed after we hang up."

Gović gave Dominic an address not far from the Vatican, then terminated the call. Dropping the iPhone on the cement floor, he walked over to the wall to retrieve a hammer hanging there, and, true to his word, smashed the phone to pieces.

"We'll prepare a room for your overnight stay, Hana, and though it won't be nearly as grand as the Rome Cavalieri, it will have to suffice."

Roko cut the restraint binding Hana's ankles, then grabbed her by the arm, lifted her out of the chair, and took her to a small room with an army cot and a thin, dirty blanket on it. Pushing her inside, he locked the door.

"Don't bother screaming," he said. "Nobody pays attention to such things anyway here in Tor Bella Monaca. And we'll be just outside the door. Get some sleep."

45

Frenzied by the call he'd just received Dominic considered his options. Instead of the Magdalene manuscript itself, he could bring a comparable document in Koine Greek, one that closely matched the real manuscript in appearance, and try to pass that off to Hana's captor. Would Gović really know the difference?

Then he remembered something Hana said during the brief call—"*...the man on the train*"—which meant it could be the same person who intercepted their email. So, this Gović character probably already has the copy he'd sent to Hana. It might take a seasoned eye, but it would be a fairly simple matter of comparing both documents and discovering the lookalike replacement.

He could notify the *Carabinieri*, the Italian national police, but Dominic had no idea where they were holding Hana. Besides, and more crucially, it would be too risky explaining the Magdalene manuscript's role in all this. That is not how he wanted things to go.

Wait! Hana could still have the AirTag tracker in her wallet!

Dominic said a quick prayer as he called up

the Find My app on his iPhone. When the display refreshed, there it was—an icon labeled "*Hana's wallet*" appeared live on the map, sending its signal from a mapped area in Rome called Tor Bella Monaca.

Now what? He knew he needed help, but whose? Who could he turn to? *Ginzberg was too old, and I don't want to put him in danger as well,* he thought. *Petrini? Dante?* His mind raced for options. And then it came to him.

Karl Dengler! Who better than a trained military mind and body to be at his side in such a high-risk situation? And as Hana's cousin, he's already invested.

Looking at his watch he saw it was ten o'clock. Hoping Dengler was still awake, Dominic took out his phone and sent him a text: **Karl, it's an emergency. Please call me.**

A few seconds later Dominic's phone rang.

"*Karl?*" he answered desperately.

"What is it, Michael?"

"Hana's in danger! I must see you now, it's urgent."

"You bet, I'll be right over." Dengler hung up.

The Swiss Guard barracks were on the other side of Saint Peter's. Dengler ran the short distance to Dominic's apartment in the Santa Marta guesthouse. Since the pope also lived in Domus

Santa Marta, the building was well-guarded day and night by Dengler's fellow soldiers who, after recognizing him, let him pass.

Entering the building, he found Dominic's apartment and knocked on the door. Dominic opened it and let him in.

"Hana's being held hostage!" he blurted out. He went on to briefly explain her captors' ransom demands for a particularly valuable manuscript they wanted in exchange for her release.

"Who are these people?" Dengler asked.

"I have no idea. Hana shouted the name *Gović,* but who knows if that's even real."

"Gović?!" Dengler exclaimed. "I know that name..." He thought for a moment. "An Interpol agent named Gović came through the gate yesterday to meet with Cardinal Dante! It's got to be the same one."

"Holy shit!" Dominic whispered. "Dante's fingerprints have been all over this from the beginning. He's had our email intercepted so he definitely knows about the manuscript. I imagine Interpol could easily arrange for such intrusions. It wouldn't even surprise me if Dante's involved with Hana's capture."

"Where is the document now?" Dengler asked.

"In a safe deposit box," Dominic said. "The plan is to withdraw it tomorrow and take it to the kidnappers by noon. We must free her, Karl."

"Do you know where they're keeping her?" Dengler said, his anger mounting.

"I do." Dominic described the AirTag tracker he had dropped in Hana's wallet, showing Dengler the Find My app and its mapped location.

"Brilliant. Why don't we just go get her now?" Dengler said stoically, as if rescue missions were something he pulled off every day. "That bastard has my cousin, and he has no right to hold her hostage for any reason. I say we take him out tonight, along with whoever's with him. They won't be expecting an ambush. Are you up for it?"

Unaccustomed to such bold action, Dominic looked at his friend apprehensively, agitated by the situation, but impressed with Karl's take-charge attitude, grateful he had called him.

"We won't be alone, either," Dengler said. "I'll ask a couple of my buddies to join us, they'll be game for some action. Meet us at Saint Anne's Gate in thirty minutes."

Dengler returned to the Swiss Guard barracks where most of his off-duty colleagues were working out or playing video games or still sleeping for their approaching midnight shift. One of the soldiers, a strapping, dark-haired lad named Lukas Bischoff, had just finished his workout and was about to take a shower when Dengler approached him.

Speaking in a low voice, Dengler said, "Lukas, I need your help, but right up front I have to tell you it may be dangerous. My cousin Hana has been kidnapped and I need a team to rescue her—*now!* Are you in?"

Lukas wasted no time in responding. "Whatever you need, Karl. Full gear with weapons?"

Dengler nodded affirmatively. "This is off the duty log, obviously. And we'll need one more man...."

"I'll get Finn Bachman. He'll be up for some action." Seeing him across the room, Lukas motioned for Finn to join them, then filled him in.

Dengler turned to his laptop and brought up Google Earth in satellite mode, entering the address Dominic had given him. He zoomed in closer to inspect their destination. "Our target is a warehouse in TBM. We'll take my rig."

There was a slight pause as both men looked into the others' eyes. Dengler looked at them. "What?"

Finn shrugged. "It's a pretty tough area."

"I know," Dengler acknowledged. "Are you two up for it?"

"Yes," both said at once. With Finn now on board, the three geared up for their hasty mission.

Changing into street clothes, Dominic ran to Saint Anne's Gate twenty minutes after Dengler left his apartment. Hovering nervously near the guard shack, he began pacing in the dim shadows, waiting for Dengler and his crew. A few minutes later they appeared, approaching Dominic as quietly as cats in the night.

Dengler made introductions. "Michael, this is Lukas and Finn, the best of the Guards. I've given them basic details, and we've already checked out a satellite view of Tor Bella Monaca. The address shown in your app is a warehouse. Depending on how many we're up against, we'll be as prepared as we can be."

Dominic saw that each of the young men, steely-eyed and dressed in commando gear, were also wearing shoulder holsters and Kevlar tactical vests. Finn handed a vest to Dominic.

"Put this on, Michael," Dengler emphasized. "Just in case."

Heading to the parking lot, they all loaded up into Dengler's black Jeep Wrangler and headed out the gate, their Swiss colleagues waving them through with a salute.

It was closing in on eleven o'clock when the Jeep

rolled into Tor Bella Monaca. Turning up the Via dell'Archeologia, Dengler doused the headlights as he slowed the vehicle. The only other cars on the street were all parked, theirs being the only one in motion. It was a moonless night, and the entire area was pitch-black. The only light visible came from scattered windows of the imposing apartment buildings on either side of the street. Even at this hour, a kid on a bicycle was watching them, using his cell phone to alert associates of incoming traffic.

"The warehouse is at the end of this road," Dengler said quietly. "We'll park a block away and walk in from there. Michael, you should wait in the car."

"No way!" he countered. "I got everyone into this mess. I'm going in, too."

"Then stay behind me at all times," Dengler insisted, placing a firm hand on Dominic's shoulder.

With the Jeep parked on a dark side street a block from the warehouse, the four men emerged from the vehicle, each of the Guards checking their weapons one last time. Forming up single file, they walked silently toward their target, three Sig P220 pistols drawn and ready.

46

Lying on her side on the dingy cot, Hana felt humiliated. She should have heeded her earlier instincts and cleared out of Tor Bella Monaca when she sensed the threat this part of the city posed. She couldn't believe she'd been so reckless, so easily taken in.

Poor Michael, she worried. What have I done to him? I've not only jeopardized the manuscript, now I'm exposing him to God knows what. There's no way these men will let me go—I've seen their faces. I know who one of them is….

She sat up on the cot and tried to loosen the restraint cuff binding her wrists. The snug plastic bit into her skin roughly as she struggled; there was no way she could remove it.

Standing up, she moved to the door and put her ear against it. She could hear muffled voices and the sound of music echoing in the large warehouse. Searching the dark room, she found nothing useful to aid in her escape. She could only wait it out, listening to her captors for clues to what would become of her.

A few feet outside Hana's door, Petrov Gović

and Roko Sirola sat in folding chairs, each with a *jambon-buerre* sandwich in hand while drinking Peroni beer. On a radio in the distant background Luciano Pavarotti was singing Puccini's "Nessun Dorma," the tenor's voice echoing softly throughout the warehouse as the two men talked.

Guardedly approaching the warehouse, Dengler, Dominic, Lukas and Finn kept in the shadows surrounding the building. As they came upon the side door, a single light threatened to expose them. Dengler quickly slipped up to it, wrapped a rag around the bare light bulb hanging over the doorway, then used his pistol to quietly shatter the glass bulb, extinguishing the light. He gently tried the door handle. It was unlocked.

Opening the door cautiously, they entered the warehouse, hearing the faint sound of music in the distance. Though this part of the building was dark, there was a light at the end of the long main aisle, in the direction of where voices were heard. Two men were talking.

"Getting that gold was a brilliant tactic, Petrov," Roko said. "I'm a little surprised Dante turned it over to you without more of a struggle."

Gović smiled self-assuredly. "Dante has too much to lose to chance that document ever being made public. Even without having the original, he knows that exposure of what we do have—the Saunière letter, the Moretti report, and a copy of the Magdalene manuscript—will show the world that the Resurrection was a myth. Even if it plants a tiny seed of growing doubt, I expect the Church would do just about anything to avoid its disclosure.

"And the gold wasn't even theirs to begin with!" he emphasized. "It belonged to my father and the other patriots who helped him establish the roots of the Ustasha. This bullion will be of supreme help in furthering our cause, Roko. No longer will the Jews and Serbs and those aligned with them stand in our way. *Za dom–spremni!*"

"Za dom–spremni!" responded Roko loyally, his arm held high in salute.

"Za dom–spremni, my ass," said a voice in the dark just beyond the circle of light.

Roko jolted upright, his sandwich falling to the floor as he reached for his gun. Karl Dengler stepped out of the shadows, his Sig Sauer held out with both arms extended, and fired off two quick shots, hitting Sirola dead center in the chest. He went down.

Lukas, Finn, and Dominic now showed themselves, the two Swiss Guards holding their weapons aimed at Petrov Gović.

Gović stood with his arms raised, looking down in surprise at his fallen comrade. He looked back up at Dengler, then at each of the faces surrounding him.

"Is anyone else here with you?" Dengler demanded angrily. "Where is Hana?"

"Do you have any idea who I am?" Gović said loudly, lowering his arms. "This is an official operation of Interpol, you imbeciles! You have no cause nor right to be here. But you *will* be charged with murder!"

"Keep your hands up!" Dengler barked. "I'll ask you one more time—where is Hana Sinclair?"

"I'm in here!" Hana shouted from behind a nearby door, pounding it with her foot.

Dominic rushed to open the door, but it was locked. *"Where's the key?"* he asked hurriedly, looking at Gović.

"In his pocket," Gović said as he gestured to Roko's body.

Dominic didn't wait. "Stand back, Hana." From a few feet away, he dashed toward the door, giving it a solid slam with his right shoulder. The flimsy door gave way.

"Michael! Thank God!" she said, tears filling her eyes. With her hands still bound, Dominic hugged her tightly.

"Anyone have something to cut through this cuff?" he asked the others.

Lukas stepped forward, whipping out a Swiss Army knife. "Standard issue. We never go anywhere without it," he said, grinning as he severed Hana's restraint.

Now freed, she launched herself at Dominic, hugging him fiercely. They held each other for a few moments, breathing heavily, until Hana saw her cousin standing with a gun pointed at Gović.

Pulling away from Dominic, she rushed toward Dengler, embracing him as Finn covered the Ustasha leader. "Karl, thank you so much."

She paused for a moment, then said, "Wait, how did you *find* me?"

Dominic reminded her about the AirTag tracker in her wallet.

"But they destroyed my phone!" she countered. "How did you get the signal?"

"The tracker chip's signal is relayed on *any* nearby iPhone using iCloud," Dominic said, grinning. "We got lucky. While he was completely unaware of it, Gović was sending us your location through his own iPhone. Yours wasn't needed at all."

Hana absorbed this with admiration. Gović, on the other hand, was chagrined at having been so easily complicit in the disruption of his own plan. He cursed them all under his breath.

Then Hana recalled something Gović and Roko had said as she listened from behind the door.

"Michael, I heard them talking about Dante

giving them some gold, apparently a lot. Come to think of it, I saw an armored van when I came in."

"Dante? *Gold?!* That would answer so many questions," Dominic said angrily. "He's obviously been behind this the whole time."

With Hana leading the way, and Lukas and Finn shoving Gović behind her, Dominic and Dengler followed the group to the other end of the warehouse, where they had first entered the building. There in the shadows sat the Garda armored van, its keys still in the ignition. While Dominic flipped on the overhead lights, Dengler unlocked the back doors and swung them open.

"Holy Mother of God," Dengler said, then whistled. Stacked neatly inside the van, glowing brilliantly, was a fortune in gold bullion. On each bar the embossed golden edges of the Imperial Eagle above a Nazi swastika glinted in the light.

Hana was in awe. "To think that this has been sitting in the Vatican Bank for seventy years. If that isn't a textbook case of complicity…."

Hana stepped back as the others moved forward for a better view, spellbound by their discovery. Gović stepped to the side and furtively moved his hand down to his belt. In an instant he threw his left arm around Hana, his right hand clutching a KA-BAR tactical knife he had concealed there and pressed it against her throat. Hana shrieked.

"Make one move and she dies!" Gović shouted. Instinctively, Dengler raised his pistol level with Gović's head. Lukas and Finn did the same but stood back cautiously, angered by their distracted attention and failure to check him for weapons.

Without thinking, Dominic, standing next to Gović, thrust his right arm beneath the crook of his opponent's elbow, pulling the knife away from Hana's throat as he pushed Gović's right shoulder back. Surprised by the sudden action, Gović began flailing the knife to find purchase, struggling to overcome the younger and stronger man. The blade found its mark, slicing across Dominic's right forearm. He grunted in pain, while at the same moment bringing his knee up with a mighty force, plunging it furiously into Gović's groin.

As Gović doubled over in agony, Dominic wrenched the knife out of his opponent's hand. The blade was already close to Gović's throat. In a desperate motion Dominic pulled up with all his might, hoping it would land anywhere it would count. In a lethal arc, the wicked blade ripped through Gović's carotid artery, spewing blood over both men. The Interpol agent slowly dropped to the warehouse floor, falling backward with sufficient force that his head cracked loudly on the cold concrete, echoing throughout the warehouse.

Dominic was bleeding badly. He fell to his

knees next to Gović's body. Dengler rushed to his friend's side, shouting to the others to find a first aid kit. While Finn ran off to locate one, Dengler took a closer look.

"You'll be fine, my friend," he said, inspecting the gash. "It could have been worse."

"It hurts like it's worse!" Dominic croaked, attempting a smile while grimacing in pain. The smile faded when he looked over at Gović's body, realizing he had just killed a man. *In God's name, what have I done?*

Hana knelt down next to him, placing her hand gently on his shoulder. "Don't blame yourself, Michael. Everything happened so fast."

Dominic looked desperately into her green eyes, eyes lined with concern. Though still in shock at the horrible act he had just committed, he deeply wanted to embrace her right now. And by the look on her face, she wanted the same thing. Neither of them acted on it, the shared moment mutually acknowledged, the carnage around them too sobering.

Finn had found a first aid kit in the armored van and quickly brought it over to Dengler, who first disinfected Dominic's wound, then bound it with bandages and tape. "You need to get to the dispensary when we return to the Vatican. They'll take it from there."

"I don't know how to thank you all," Dominic

said, looking at each of the Swiss Guards. "Especially you, Karl, for bringing these two brave men along."

"Are you kidding?" said Lukas gravely. "We train for this kind of action every day, but never get a chance to use it. I'm just happy no one else got hurt. This could have gone down very badly, Michael. That was a big risk you took. But as it turned out, you were the real hero."

"What do we do now?" Hana asked.

"Well," Dengler said, "this *is* TBM. Bad things happen here every day. I say we just take the gold and leave the bodies and let the *Carabinieri* deal with it. They'll assume Interpol had some kind of rogue operation here gone bad."

"I agree," said Dominic. "That would be the best plan. Hana, are you okay to drive your car back to the hotel? The guys will follow you."

"Of course," she said, as she retrieved her purse. "Michael, are you going to be alright?" Her eyes conveyed more than her simple words.

"Sure," he said, meeting her gaze. "I'll be good to go as soon as I have this cut looked after. I'll give you a call in the morning."

Dengler and his comrades rolled up each of the two bodies on old tarpaulins they found in a corner of the warehouse. Standing there watching them, Dominic said a silent prayer for the life he had just taken.

Sanitizing the scene, Dengler made sure there had been no sign of their presence in the warehouse.

Satisfied with his inspection, he and Dominic got into the armored van and headed for the Vatican, while Finn and Lukas drove Dengler's Jeep as they followed Hana safely to the Rome Cavalieri, then returned to their barracks.

It was after midnight when Karl Dengler, driving the armored van, was waved through Saint Anne's Gate by his fellow Swiss Guards. He parked the truck near the Vatican Bank's main entrance.

"There's no safer place for millions of dollars in gold than right here," he said with satisfaction.

"The rest is up to Cardinal Petrini," Dominic said. "He'll know what to do with this."

Dengler locked the doors of the van, then put his arm around Dominic tenderly as he escorted him to the 24-hour dispensary for treatment of his wound.

"You know, Karl, you're the best kind of friend," Dominic acknowledged as they walked across the parking lot. "You bravely put your life on the line for us tonight. When you do find the right man, he would be incredibly lucky to have you. You need to know that."

Dengler blushed in the dark, pulling Dominic a little closer to him briefly, protectively. "I may have already found him," he whispered, smiling. "I have a feeling Lukas is 'on my team'…."

47

Dominic skipped his morning run the next day. Despite the necessity of his actions the night before, he had killed a man, and the terrible act itself weighed heavily on his conscience. He had called Cardinal Petrini and asked if he could stop by his apartment, where he gave him a full account of the night's events.

Petrini was stunned by Dominic's tale, not only by the retrieval of a fortune in Nazi gold, but by the onerous fact of having taken a man's life in the process, regardless of circumstances. The strain in his protégé's countenance was obvious, and Petrini offered to hear the young man's confession to help ease his burden.

With some relief, Dominic began the ritual, only to break down in tears when he spoke of killing Gović, never expecting to confess such a thing in his life.

"Michael," Petrini said comfortingly, "this was not a malicious act on your part. There was no premeditation, you were only behaving in self-defense, in protection of yourself and your friends. This was a courageous and selfless deed, and God will see it for what it is. You are absolved with His mercy."

His head in his hands, Dominic took a deep recovering breath to revive himself. "Thank you, Eminence. Thank you so much."

After Petrini dispensed his penance, Dominic said an Act of Contrition, then felt a strong need to celebrate Mass to help get distance from the darkness engulfing him.

He made arrangements to preside over the noon Mass that day in the Church of Santa Maria della Pietà, one of the nine churches and chapels on the Vatican grounds, and the one he always felt most contented in, its humble altar encircled by an intimate apse reminiscent of the one he served in as an altar boy in Queens. The rituals of the Mass—the solemn intonation of prayer, its quiet dignity, even the heady perfume of incense—gave him the kind of comfort he could find nowhere else.

After the procession and altar preparation, Father Dominic began the liturgy. Just after the halfway point in the service, he intoned the several elements of the Eucharistic Prayer. It was only when he neared the end, reciting the anamnesis, did he stumble.

> "Wherefore, O Lord, we thy servants, as also thy holy people, calling to mind the blessed Passion of the same Christ thy

> Son our Lord, and also his Resurrection from the dead and his glorious Ascension into heaven…"

Dominic looked down at his golden chasuble, symbolizing the royal robe thrown over Jesus as Roman soldiers mocked him and set upon his head a crown of thorns, recalling Christ's scourging and Crucifixion. He just stood there, suddenly silent, as the two altar boys and other congregants present in the church looked up, wondering if something was wrong.

Suddenly overcome with emotion, his eyes began to sting. Tears coursed down his cheeks. Knowing what he knew now, the sacred words rang hollow. Once again, he felt like an impostor. Everything he had gone through over the past few weeks played over and over in his mind as he stood alone at the altar.

He looked up and out over the congregation, the eyes of every person watching him, waiting for the summation of prayers before the Rite of Communion. Gathering every bit of strength he had, Dominic took a deep breath and concluded the ritual. Sighs of relief echoed throughout the chapel.

By the time he celebrated Communion, a sense of spiritual tranquility had returned. As the people came forward and knelt before him, Dominic looked into the face of each supplicant. Placing the sacred host on their tongues, he was reminded of the spiritual balm the act provided, realizing there is a greater truth to the teachings of Jesus Christ, and that removing one of the mysteries of Christianity—the Resurrection—would undermine those truths, destroying the spirit of those who needed God for so many reasons. It was then he understood what had to be done.

Following Mass, Dominic went back to his apartment to call Hana. She answered after the first ring.

"How are you, Michael," she said with concern. "Tell me everything."

"Not surprisingly, I didn't sleep very well," he admitted. "The dispensary patched me up and gave me some pain pills. I told them I fell against one of the steel shelves in the Archives and they didn't press me for details. I just tossed and turned the rest of the night. And while I realize Gović deserved what he got, I just wish it didn't have to be me that dispensed justice like that. I can't shake it."

"Consider the alternatives, what *could* have happened. You acted on instinct, doing what had to be done. I'll be forever grateful to you and the others for rescuing me. It was very brave.

"I also think you know that both Karl and I care for you very much, each in our own way," she added knowingly. "He told me about his feelings for you, and how compassionately you handled his coming out."

"I'm a lucky guy to have both of you in my life," Dominic replied. Then, hesitantly, "And I'll tell you what I told him, that if things were different… well," he stumbled, "things… might be different… I hope that makes sense."

Hana let out a quiet laugh. "I understand, Michael. All too well."

An hour later Dominic returned to Cardinal Petrini's apartment. There was still much work to be done.

"This is only conjecture on my part," Dominic began, "but I'm pretty sure Dante had been working with Gović all along—having Hana and me followed in France, intercepting our email, possibly tapping our phone calls… As an Interpol agent Gović would have had access to all such capabilities. We know he had copies of the Saunière letter, the Moretti report, and the Magdalene manuscript—all of which I'd emailed to Hana and Simon—so we can presume those have already found their way to Dante.

"We can also assume," Dominic continued,

"that Gović decided to blackmail Dante with exposure of the Magdalene document, which is how Gović ended up with millions of dollars in Nazi gold in that armored van."

Petrini followed Dominic's logic, concurring with his assessment.

"I don't think it would be helpful," the cardinal said, "for us to reveal last night's events to Dante. In this case, the less he knows, the better. We don't want him holding a man's death over you, at the very least, which would be consistent with his diabolical nature. And with Gović out of the way, he'll have to conclude the gold went with him.

"As for that gold," Petrini added thoughtfully, "I think this is a job for Team Hugo. We'll transfer the bullion to where it can be properly returned to Holocaust survivors and their families. And we'll do it anonymously, requesting there be no media involvement. It's the only way."

"Now," Dominic said gravely. "What about the most important element in all this, the Magdalene manuscript?" He reached into the backpack he'd brought with him and pulled out the folio containing the original papyrus. He handed it to Petrini, whose rheumy eyes glistened in reverence as he held one of history's most sublime yet incendiary documents.

"I really have mixed feelings about this, Rico,"

Dominic said, "the consequences of which are too sweeping to imagine. The document itself is a profound historical truth, a first-of-its-kind discovery about which the world deserves to know. On the other hand, its release could unleash truly damaging chaos among the faithful. No one would be spared its influence."

Petrini's solemn face told Dominic they were in agreement, these points having already been considered by the esteemed prince of the Church.

"Michael, I have given this much prayer and deliberation myself in recent days. I cannot in good conscience bear responsibility for the disintegration of Holy Mother Church, or of other religious institutions, regardless of the fact that truth is being suppressed. It even pains me to say so. But this is not my decision alone. The Holy Father must make the final determination, perhaps in consultation with his advisors. In the end, the burden will be his, and his alone, as Christ's vicar on Earth.

"In the meantime," Petrini concluded, "we must soon pay a visit to Cardinal Dante. He has much to answer for."

48

As the early evening cast long shadows through the windows of his office, Cardinal Dante pressed the buzzer beneath the edge of his desk, signaling to his assistant that he was ready to receive his visitors.

Father Vannucci knocked gently, then opened the tall doors. Cardinal Petrini and Father Dominic entered the expansive room.

"Good afternoon, Your Eminence," they said simultaneously, taking their seats in front of the cardinal's desk.

"Good day, gentlemen," Dante said curtly. "What is it I can do for you?"

"It's not so much what you can do for us, Fabrizio" Petrini said matter-of-factly, "but what we will all do moving forward."

Dante was nonplussed but curious. "Go on," he said, lighting a cigarette.

"As you are no doubt aware," Petrini began, "Father Dominic has come into possession of an item of singular historical importance. Without belaboring the mechanics of *how* you'd become aware, suffice to say we know of your less than moral methods."

Dante choked slightly as he exhaled a plume of blue smoke.

Petrini continued. "If it was only this document alone, there might be cause for misinterpretation by some. But as we are all also aware that Bérenger Saunière had been blackmailing the Vatican for some time, and of Monsignor Moretti's report attesting to his own investigation, there's sufficient evidence of longstanding credibility."

Petrini paused to let this sink in before continuing.

"Obviously, public revelation of this document would have profound repercussions among the faithful, not to mention the Church itself. So, we have decided to—"

Dante angrily interrupted him. "'*You*' have decided? Who are *you* to make such decisions, Enrico? I insist you hand over that manuscript to me at once, and *I* shall decide what will be done with it."

"I'm afraid you have no say at all in the matter, Fabrizio. We have already spoken with the Holy Father about this matter," Petrini said firmly. "Its fate is sealed. The pope, with my support, feels your intercession will only complicate things unnecessarily."

"Now you listen to me— " Dante began angrily, tapping an ash in the amber bowl but missing it.

"No, you'll listen to me, Dante" Petrini countered, "because I also speak on behalf of His Holiness, with whom we just met. Your actions of the past several weeks have been deplorable. Having Father Dominic and Miss Sinclair followed, having their email intercepted, your loathsome dealings with the Novi Ustasha and their repulsive agents, and probably countless other exploits of which only you are aware. These are the repugnant acts of a man who has lost all notions of civility and leadership."

"And how do you account for turning over all that *gold* to Gović?" Dominic demanded.

"How... how do you know about any of this?!" Dante muttered in confused outrage, as the litany of misconduct stacked up against him.

"You are relieved of your duties, Cardinal Dante," Petrini concluded. "His Holiness has asked that I take over as Vatican Secretary of State, effective immediately. You will be reassigned as archbishop of Buenos Aires. Good day, Eminence."

Petrini and Dominic left the room. Angrily crushing out his cigarette in the amber bowl, Dante lit another and stood up, pacing the room as he considered this new situation. He had worked hard to get where he was, and he wasn't about to go down quietly.

Or should I, he thought. Perhaps a humble

acceptance of this contrived punishment might suit his purposes after all. He could maintain the strong and loyal constituency he had established here in the Vatican—discreet as it has been over the years—and he was not without influence or serviceable connections in Argentina, a dynamic Catholic outpost growing stronger with each passing day—and home to the largest population of German World War II emigres driven out of their homeland, many with Ustasha affiliations. Petrov Gović had introduced him to that deep-seated community over the past two decades, and their political ties could be instrumental, not to mention their financial resources, about which he knew a great deal.

Petrov Gović had a son who was the Ustasha cell leader in Buenos Aires, didn't he? Dante considered. I believe his name was Ivan….

49

French President Pierre Valois had flown in from Paris for the event. Baron Armand de Saint-Clair, already in Rome with Cardinal Enrico Petrini, had invited top representatives of the World Jewish Restitution Organization who had flown in from Jerusalem for the private ceremony.

The small group had assembled in secret, with the legendary heroes of Team Hugo presiding over the transfer of the largest Holocaust survivor settlement of Nazi plunder since the end of World War II—one hundred million U.S. dollars in gold bullion. The conditions of the meeting were simple: no questions would be asked as to its provenance, no media involvement would be permitted, and no receipt would be issued. This was to be, as President Valois termed it, *une affaire d'honneur*.

Simon Ginzberg, fully aware of the implications of the Magdalene manuscript, had pledged his silence on the matter to both Dominic and Petrini. The newly public release of millions of Pope Pius XII's ecclesiastical documents would keep him occupied with research for his remaining years.

Cardinal Fabrizio Dante had relocated to Buenos Aires, taking the palatial residence of the archdiocese as his new home. He was now in control of nearly three million Catholic souls in the Argentine capitol. The elaborate invitation-only installation ceremony was attended by thousands in the grand Metropolitan Cathedral. In the front row sat numerous dignitaries known to the new archbishop, including one particular VIP whose personal backing he would come to rely on appreciably; a prominent Croatian named Ivan Gović.

Still in Rome, Hana Sinclair had filed her story for *Le Monde,* which earned her a front-page byline. Under the banner headline, "Old Complicities, New Atonements," the piece detailed the shady dealings of the flow of Nazi gold involving several prominent European Central Banks over numerous decades, prompting new investigations into their post-war activities. There was much more Hana had wanted to include, but for obvious reasons she omitted many of the more sensitive elements, including the recovery of gold from the Vatican Bank. She would go on to receive the prestigious Albert Londres Prize in Journalism for her efforts.

The ranks of the famed Pontifical Swiss Guard, already a closely-knit group, had quietly learned the most salient points of their comrades' honorable deeds. Based on merits alone, without having to disclose specifics, the Commandant of the Guard had petitioned the Holy Father to award Corporals Karl Dengler, Lukas Bischoff, and Finn Bachman with the esteemed Benemerenti Medal for distinguished services. Michael Dominic and Hana Sinclair stood by proudly among the assembled troops, brilliantly clad in their dress gala uniforms with red-plumed helmets, as each man received their commendation.

Karl Dengler, widely praised for leadership among his colleagues, was promoted to Sergeant of the Guard. His best friend, Lukas, stood next to him, eyes glistening with an intimate pride as he saluted, then hugged, his brother in arms.

After the ceremony, Hana took Dominic aside. As he led her arm in arm beneath the shady trees of the Vatican gardens, Hana spoke first.

"My grandfather and I leave for Paris tonight, Michael, but I wanted this time alone with you, to thank you for everything—especially the honor of your company during our adventures. You are the rarest of men, and as you say, if things were different… we might have gone on to more escapades."

"Who's to say we won't?!" Dominic replied, a mischievous grin on his face. "We don't know what the future holds, Hana. I'm sure our paths will cross again. We may have many more adventures yet to come."

They stopped in front of a large replica of the Grotto of Our Lady of Lourdes, stepping inside the cool, tall arched expanse of ivy protecting a white marble statue of the Blessed Virgin Mary.

Hana put her arms on Michael's shoulders, then reached up, kissed his cheek, and looked longingly into his dark brown eyes.

"Another time, then," she murmured.

"Another time," he whispered.

* * *

Father Michael Dominic walked alone through the vast underground Miscellanea, the amber pools of light preceding him as he headed toward the enigmatic room known as the Riserva. Brother Mendoza had finally given him his own key, so now there was no need for an escort by the prefect.

He unlocked the heavy door, flipped on the overhead light, and entered the room, closing the door behind him.

With one last look at the ancient papyrus of

Mary Magdalene, he closed the folio and opened the *armadio* containing the most sacred written relics of Christianity the Church possessed, a fitting repository for a manuscript whose contents were simply too challenging to the status quo. Still burdened with mixed feelings but acceding to the pope's decision, Dominic shoved the folio toward the back of the great cabinet, slipping it into a narrow niche where only he would know its place.

Closing and locking the wooden door, Dominic headed back toward the elevator. As he walked among the Gallery of the Metallic Shelves, his eyes danced across the millions of other unseen documents sitting on miles of shelving, wondering what else lay in store for him in the months and years to come.

Only God knew.

Epilogue

Countless stalactites hung like icicles from the ceiling of the *Grotte Trou la Caune* cave near Périllos, a small town in southern France near the Mediterranean Sea. Tapering columns of stalagmites, formed by eons of calcified water dripping from above, rose intermittently from the floor bed, surrounded by shimmering crystals and other minerals which formed in nooks and crannies.

A vast pool of stagnant, emerald green water, brilliantly illuminated by shafts of daylight streaming in through open light wells in the roof of the chamber, formed a verdant natatorium for the pale salamanders and Iberian frogs native to the area.

At nearly one meter in length with a black zigzag pattern down its back, a *Vipera berus*, or common European adder, had just finished its last meal of frog before settling in for its winter hibernation. Seeking a dark, cool place, the snake slithered deeper into the cave, away from the light, crawling up several small boulders until it found a suitably flat limestone slab.

A small rift behind the smooth rock provided

just the right protection from potential predators during its long winter stay, so the adder made itself comfortable atop an ancient wooden reliquary hidden beneath the slab.

Coiling itself for warmth, its head resting atop the object's iron ornamentation, the snake settled in for the season.

Author's Note

Thank you for reading ***The Magdalene Deception***. I really hope you enjoyed it and suggest you pick up the story in the second and third books in this series, ***The Magdalene Reliquary*** and ***The Magdalene Veil***, and look forward to coming books featuring the same and new characters.

Dealing with issues of theology, religious beliefs, and the fictional treatment of historical biblical events can be a daunting affair.

I would ask all readers to view this story for what it is—a work of pure fiction, adapted from the seeds of many oral traditions and the historical record, at least as we know it today.

Apart from telling an engaging story, I have no agenda here, and respect those of all beliefs, from Agnosticism to Zoroastrianism and everything in between.

Many readers of The Magdalene Chronicles series have asked me to distinguish fact from fiction in my books. Generally, I like to take factual events and historical figures and build on them in creative ways—but much of what I do write is historically accurate. Here, I'll review some of the chapters where questions may arise, with hopes that it may help those wondering.

PROLOGUE

The Cathar fortress on the peak of Montségur, France, is an actual historical monument. The entire Languedoc region was central to Pope Innocent III's Albigensian Crusade and is depicted historically here in nearly exact detail.

Though Abbé Marty was in fact an authentic Cathar cleric at Montségur, the activities given him in this book are purely fictional.

CHAPTER 6

The Riserva is an actual room in the Vatican Secret Archives where the Church's most sensitive documents and artifacts are kept. As there are no known photographs or other descriptions available, I have conceived my own interpretation of what that room might be like for conservation purposes.

CHAPTER 8

Bérenger Saunière was in fact the vicar of Rennes-le-Château in the Languedoc region of southern France in the late 19th century. Numerous legends surround him and his assistant, Marie Dénarnaud, who was also a real person.

Abbé Saunière did find several scrolls in a Visigothic altar in his church, though I have taken creative liberties with what he found for this story.

CHAPTER 13

Again, descriptions of Bérenger Saunière and Marie Dénarnaud and their activities are all historically accurate.

As for Hitler and the Allied powers' use of tarot cards and astrologers—also accurate, among the more bizarre historical nuggets I was able to dig up.

Otto Rahn was also a historic figure, as were his expeditions seeking the Holy Grail. His book, *Crusade Against the Grail,* is real and still in print.

While Nostradamus was obviously a historical figure, the quatrains I proposed here are fictional. Saint Malachy was also real, as was his curious prophesy of the popes.

CHAPTER 17

The Nazis' SS-Ehrenring, also called the Death's Head Ring, was an actual symbolic ring personally given out by Heinrich Himmler. There were an estimated 11,000 such rings distributed, each of which had to be returned to Himmler on the death of its wearer.

One of the more enlightening facts for me to

have discovered was the Ustasha, a fascist organization—and ultimately de facto government—of the Independent State of Croatia during World War II. In the Balkans, the Ustasha did rival the Nazis for fearsome treatment of Jews, Serbs, and Roma gypsies in their own concentration camps, in order to enforce a more racially pure Croatia under forced Catholicism. The Vatican did have full diplomatic relations with this heinous group, and participated in the Franciscan ratline for Nazis escaping prosecution.

CHAPTER 19

Wolfram von Eschenbach's epic poem *Parzival* was, of course, genuine, and it is believed by many Grail scholars that "Monsalvat" mentioned in the work actually referred to "Montsegur."

The Last Will & Testament of Bérenger Saunière is in fact genuine. I can't believe I actually found it, as hard as it was to locate.

The French Resistance Maquis fighter known as "Achille" was, in fact, an actual historical figure. Little is known about him, though, so what you find here is purely fictional.

CHAPTER 23

Marie Dénarnaud's niece, Élise, does not exist (as far as I know, she had no family).

CHAPTER 27

While there is a Gnostic text called the *Gospel of Mary*, which scholars do attribute to Mary Magdalene's life, it should be clear that the manuscript I attribute to her is entirely fictional.

CHAPTER 28

While Cardinal Lucido Parocchi was an actual Church figure in the late 1800s, the papal legate I describe here, Monsignor Franco Moretti, and his letter are of my own imagination.

CHAPTER 29

ECHELON is an authentic surveillance program operated by the United States with the aid of four other signatory states to the UKUSA Security Agreement: Australia, Canada, New Zealand, and the United Kingdom, also known as the Five Eyes. My description of its processes, however, is almost entirely my own creation…but given my technology background my guess is I came pretty close.

CHAPTER 31

While there are many who believe Jesus Christ and Mary Magdalene may have been married, and may have had children, I have no evidence of that; consequently, the assertions here (as well as her papyrus) are depicted fictionally.

CHAPTER 35

The safe cracking tools used by Roko Sirola—including the hotel keycard emulator—are all real products anyone can buy. As for the default codes used in hotel in-room safes, all that is entirely real. Try it next time you stay in a hotel room…

CHAPTER 37

Operation Jedburgh was a true event, a mission coordinated between US and British intelligence agencies.

The description of Ustasha treasure, including the Mafia's help in melting gold bullion for deposit in the Vatican Bank, is all factual.

Archbishop of Croatia Aloysius Stepinac was also a real figure and his activities documented here are all authentically recorded.

CHAPTER 40

Sadly, the story about the Nazis demanding fifty kilos of gold from Roman Jews or face dire consequences was true.

FINAL NOTES:

I have been to the Vatican myself in past years and give an account of—to the best of my memory (and extensive research)—descriptions of actual rooms, buildings, gardens, and official protocols used by Vatican employees and the Swiss Guard.

Descriptions of all actual buildings and roads throughout the book are accurate, thanks to the marvels of Google Earth and other resources. Hotels, restaurants (even menus), airports, airlines and flight times are all real.

When you have a moment, may I ask that you leave a review on Amazon and elsewhere? Reviews are crucial to a book's success, and I hope for the *Magdalene Chronicles* to have a long and entertaining life.

You can easily leave your review by going to my Amazon book page.

If you would like to reach out for any reason, you can email me at gary@garymcavoy.com. If you'd like to learn more about me and my other books, visit my website at www.garymcavoy.com.

With kind regards,

Gary McAvoy

Acknowledgments

I wish to thank several friends for their invaluable help along the way: Yale Lewis, Gregory McDonald, John Burgess, Michelle Harden, Dr. Kurt Billett, and Cyndee Irvine for their perceptive minds in helping bring this book to life; my editor Sandra Haven, whose expertise literally reshaped the book; Fran Libra Koenigsdorf, who I wasn't lucky enough to have as an English teacher until my 60s; and Ron Weekes, for his deep and helpful connections inside the Vatican.

CREDITS

"Bérenger Saunière." Wikipedia: The Free Encyclopedia, Wikimedia Foundation Inc., 14 September 2019, at 02:32 (UTC), https://en.wikipedia.org/wiki/Bérenger_Saunière. Accessed 13 October 2019.